"YOU'RE SO MUCH LIKE STAN," SHE MURMURED

His arm suddenly abandoned Corrine. The man beside her leaned forward and his large hands with the strangely graceful fingers clasped each other until the knuckles showed white. She could feel his frustration, his anger as he pulled away from her.

"I'm Derek!" The resonant voice was tight with tension as he stared into the fire.

"I'm sorry, Derek. Please forgive me," she whispered. Now she missed the feel of his hard, muscular thigh and the slim contour of his leg. She ran her hand through her long hair. "It's just ... Stan seems to live on in you, somehow. You're so much like him—"

"No!" He jumped up from the leather sofa and placed both hands on the mantel. "I'm not like anybody, dammit! I'm me! Derek Moar ..."

ABOUT THE AUTHOR

Karen Field informs us that her husband and three adult kids are as excited as she is about the publication of *Time Will Tell*. Fiction writing represents a midlife career change for Karen, who worked as an office manager and a legal secretary before trying her hand at writing. Nicknamed the Storyteller in the sixth grade, Karen has finally realized a lifelong dream. We hope this talented new author will provide us with many, many more fascinating stories!

Karen Field

TIME WILL TELL

Harlequin Books

TORONTO • NEW YORK • LONDON
AMSTERDAM • PARIS • SYDNEY • HAMBURG
STOCKHOLM • ATHENS • TOKYO • MILAN

Published January 1987

First printing November 1986

ISBN 0-373-70244-2

Printed in Canada

For Tom
with love

PROLOGUE

Circle City, Indiana
Halloween, thirty-four years ago

THE NIGHT BORE the chill of an Indiana autumn succumbing to winter. Black asphalt glistened, slick with rain, and streetlights wrapped in a foggy haze shone eerily on the road's gleaming surface. Fall Creek Parkway, a thoroughfare running in an east-west direction through the north side of Circle City—population 427,173—stretched into the distance. Up ahead, occasional pairs of headlights shone, moon-white and hazy in the mist.

At a curb near the intersection of Fall Creek Parkway and Delaware Street, a lone woman hesitated. She pulled the lapels of a lightweight maroon raincoat closer around her neck. The coat gaped open over a distended abdomen and the navy-blue maternity skirt beneath it was damp.

At a sudden clap of thunder, the young woman jumped in fright. Eyes the color of sapphires opened wide and round. Beneath her soaked head scarf, her sandy hair lay matted and dripping. She shivered and coughed.

With a halting gait, the woman crossed Fall Creek Parkway and made her way slowly over the bridge that spanned White River. A yawning maw of blackness dropped from the bridge's concrete parapet; the falling drops of cold rain could not be seen disappearing into the flowing river. For five blocks she continued south on Delaware Street, walking slowly, halting at times to press her hand in fright upon her swollen abdomen whenever a contraction hit.

A large brick apartment building loomed three-stories high on the southwest corner of Delaware and Twenty-second streets. The young woman raised her eyes to a lighted bay window on the second floor. She halted to stare at the number on the brick apartment building.

Her chilled fingers crept into her raincoat pocket. They emerged with a small slip of paper. By the light of a street lamp, she squinted at the crude handwriting. The name, Katherine Brandt, R.N., and the address of the brick building had been written on the paper by the heavyset cook at the restaurant where she had worked in the kitchen for the past six months. No questions had been asked.

She climbed the steps and went inside. In the foyer of the building, she paused, grateful for the dry warmth. A spasm of coughing seized her, shaking her violently.

Slowly she climbed a set of stairs bathed in bleak yellow-white light. When she stood before the apartment door marked 2-C, an uncontrollable trembling seized her, and a chill reached into the depths of her bones as the viselike pain of another labor contraction washed over her.

Gentle strains of radio music drifted through the closed door. She lifted a cold hand to knock.

A pleasant voice sounded. "Who is it?"

"Help me, Miss Brandt! Please!" It was a desperate voice filled with fatigue.

The door swung open. The woman standing in the doorway was petite, with short shiny hair. Her face was kind. "Yes?" she asked, frowning as her eyes scanned the woman. "What can I do for you?"

"Are you Katherine Brandt?"

"Yes."

The pregnant woman leaned a shoulder against the doorway, strength ebbing from her. A cold hand dipped into her pocket and emerged with the damp slip of paper. "Louise Bales...gave me this," she gasped. "You helped her deliver in the hospital. She said . . . you were so kind to her. She said you could help me. I think . . . I'm ready to deliver."

"Come in," said the nurse, pulling tightly on the belt of her flannel bathrobe. As the woman obeyed, swaying, the nurse's strong arms went around her to give support. "My God, you're chilled to the bone! Give me the name of your physician and I'll call him."

"I don't . . . have a doctor." The woman's voice gave way to a racking cough.

"Then I'll take you to Presbyterian Hospital. It's less than two miles away from here," said Kate Brandt, leading the rain-soaked figure to an armless chair in a warm tidy living room.

"No, I can't go to a hospital!" the woman protested weakly. "I don't have the money. Sixty dollars is all I've been able to save. It's yours if you'll help me deliver and...make arrangements for the baby. I can't keep it." She opened a change purse, pulled out some worn folded bills and held out the money.

"I work on the obstetrics floor of Presbyterian. I'm not a midwife. Have your pains started yet?" asked Katherine Brandt sternly, refusing to look at the money.

The pregnant woman nodded her head, replaced her money, then pulled off her rain-soaked scarf. "About three, four minutes apart." She glanced at the drug-

store watch she wore. "My water...hasn't broken yet."
Louise had told her what to expect. The prospect filled
her with terror. "I can't have this get into the newspaper. It'll kill my mother if she finds out. She lives here
in Circle City. Don't you understand?" Tears broke free
and rolled slowly down the damp, ashen face.

Kate Brandt's glance fell to the woman's left hand.
There was no wedding band on the third finger. Nor was
there an engagement ring. Though World War II had
been over for eight years, an unwed mother in Indiana
was still an object of disgrace, often ostracized by the
rest of the community.

"She doesn't know?" Kate asked, uneasy.

"I left home before...I started showing. I told Mom
I had a job out of state." The woman's every breath was
a struggle. "Every Sunday...I phone her. I pre-
tend...I'm calling from Pennsylvania. I send her...
money—what I can—regularly. She lives on my step-
dad's railroad pension. He's been dead almost six
years."

Another fit of coughing seized the woman. She
leaned back in the chair, closed her eyes and fought for
breath. The suffering in the pale face silenced the
nurse's unspoken objections.

"How do you feel?" she asked when the woman's
body relaxed.

"Is this what it's like when you're dying?" asked the
young woman weakly.

The nurse in Kate Brandt took charge then. She
helped the stranger out of her wet clothes, toweled her
chilled skin dry and wrapped a clean, warm blanket
snugly around her.

"What's your name?" she asked briskly as she
wrapped a towel around the wet hair.

"Helen Hersh," the woman replied faintly.

"How old are you, Helen?"

"Nineteen."

"Your first pregnancy?"

"Yes."

"Come in here." She led her visitor into a tidy bedroom, supporting her with a strong arm. Once there, Kate turned down the covers and helped the woman lie down, supporting her head and shoulders with both pillows.

"What about the father? Can't he help?" asked Kate, popping a thermometer into her patient's mouth and positioning it under her tongue.

Helen shook her head. Blue eyes of striking clarity and depth fastened on Kate. The anguish in them haunted the nurse as they pleaded for her understanding. Helen took the thermometer out of her mouth. "He doesn't know I'm pregnant. He's a student at IU. He's twenty. His family...would disown him if he married me. He'd probably end up...hating me...for robbing him of everything he's entitled to." The woman's faraway look changed to one of defiance. "I won't tell you his name. You can't make me."

Kate inserted the thermometer again and gave Helen a reassuring pat on the shoulder. She went to the tiny kitchen to place a kettle of water on the stove to heat. Perhaps a few sips of hot tea would help her patient warm up and calm down. While the water heated, Kate checked the temperature reading. One hundred and three degrees, just as she suspected. She did a brief examination of Helen with a sterile surgical glove. Yes, the young woman was almost fully dilated, also as Kate had suspected. She applied a stethoscope to the distended abdomen and listened for a fetal heartbeat. It

came through strong and clear. And then she realized
there were two heartbeats. She listened intently, then
straightened, alarm on her face.

After leaving the cup of hot tea in the hands of the
shivering patient propped up in the bed, Kate went to
the telephone in the living room. She dialed the number of Presbyterian's switchboard. Her hands were unsteady.

"I've got to get hold of Dr. Christopher Albert, res-
ident physician. Obstetrics. He should still be on the OB
floor. It's an emergency. Tell him Kate Brandt is calling. I'll hold." The nurse kept her voice low, glancing
back at the bedroom doorway.

Moments stretched into eternity for the twenty-five-
year-old nurse. She heard a loud groan from the bedroom and heard the teaspoon clatter to the floor.

"Hello, Kate. I just finished duty. I'm bushed!"
groaned a husky male voice on the telephone.

"Chris, I need you! Can you come over to my place?
Make it fast!" Fear was making her shake.

"What's up?" The husky voice was instantly alert.

"A woman just walked into my apartment off the
street. She's dilating rapidly. First pregnancy. No pre-
natal care, no physician, no money, no husband. No
emotional support from her family. And she's got a
respiratory infection, with a one-hundred-and-three-
degree fever, severe coughing and weakness. I detect
rales. Could be pneumonia."

The man gave a deep groan.

"Worse than that, Chris." Her voice dropped to a
whisper. "There are two fetal heartbeats. What if one
of the infants is in the breech position?"

"You're up a creek without a paddle, lady, that's what," Chris boomed. "Hold her off as long as you can. I'll be right there." With that, the line went dead.

From the bedroom came a frightened cry for help.

CHAPTER ONE

A SILKEN REPOSE had settled over the third floor of Presbyterian Hospital. Luncheon trays had been removed from all the rooms, and colorful striped drapes had been drawn against the bright July sunlight. A private room at the middle of the east end of the floor, number 3218, lay steeped in a languorous, dim light.

Corinne Daye, just brought up from the recovery room, lay motionless in the warm bed, too drowsy to move, her slim body pleasantly heavy. Eyelids with long, curving lashes opened slightly. A wall painted pale yellow converged into misty focus.

She saw her husband, Stan, standing at the foot of the bed, his six-foot-two frame towering over her. His blue eyes gazed at her lovingly, and a piece of his wavy, sandy-colored hair fell lightly upon his broad forehead as always, softening the angular, smooth-shaven face. His lips lifted in a tender smile.

She smiled, too, in drowsy contentment. "Stan?" she mumbled, her lips almost too thick to move. "Why don't you come to bed?" She fought to keep her eyelids open, but she lost the battle. There was no answer from the foot of the bed.

She struggled up through the unnatural drowsiness and forced her eyelids open again. To her surprise the space at the foot of the bed was empty. She felt a dull ache that stretched from her chest to her left arm—an ache from which she was somehow detached. As her glance traveled around the room sluggishly, she became aware of two armchairs, one in green vinyl and one in blue, and striped drapes of orange, green, beige and black. A TV was mounted on the wall close to the ceiling.

Suddenly she knew she was not in her bedroom at home.

Where am I? Is this a hospital? she thought confusedly. And then images emerged in her mind slowly and with frightening clarity.

She had been in her Buick Regal, driving home from her law office in the heart of downtown Circle City. As she had approached the intersection of Meridian and Eighty-sixth streets, she'd acknowledged that the light ahead was amber and would soon be changing to red. She had released her foot from the accelerator and had hit the brake pedal. But although she had pushed the pedal to the floor, the car had not stopped. It had sped on without slowing and had hurtled into the intersection, straight toward another car, which had entered the intersection on a green light.

Corinne's throat had closed in panic and her hands had frozen to the steering wheel. She'd heard the crunch of metal and glass as the two automobiles collided and had flung up her hands to protect her face. A pain had exploded in her left arm as she was flung against the door on the driver's side.

The car had spun out of control on the crowded street, slick with rain. The dull sound of another crash had reverberated in her ears as the Buick had slammed with a jerk into an unyielding utility pole. She'd received a blow to her chest and had lurched forward against the steering wheel....

A pain in her head.

A merciful blackness...

"Stan? Where are you?" Corinne whispered, drowsy and content in room 3218, her eyelids drooping closed again. She was so relaxed, lost in a drugged, floating state.

Poised on the velvet edge of sleep, Corinne heard the murmur of women's voices in the hall beyond the opened doorway and felt reassured. She was not alone in Stan's absence. She concentrated on listening to what the women were saying. Her ears were her only link to the outside world.

"Your patient in 3218 was written up in this morning's paper. Front page, no less! She probably rates because she's an attorney. If I had wrapped my car around a telephone pole, you'd have found a notice an inch long buried in the food section beside an ad for antacids." The woman chuckled good-naturedly.

"That's better than in the obits. You know, I never dreamed I'd be taking care of Stanford Daye's widow." The second voice was pitched slightly lower, an alto to the other woman's soprano, and it possessed an air of authority the first voice lacked. "What a magnificent hunk of man *that* man was. He was on staff here before you came, wasn't he?"

"Yes. I came here about a year ago. The other shift nurses told me about him and Dr. Perlman. Wasn't that a tragedy? By the way, I bought the morning paper. I thought maybe others on the desk might want to see the write-up on 3218."

"Thanks. I haven't seen it yet. My alarm didn't go off this morning. I almost didn't make it in by seven," said the alto voice. "Does the *Star* article mention the hospital?"

The other woman began to read out loud. "Corinne Daye, thirty-two, Circle City attorney, was injured in an accident involving three automobiles at the intersection of Meridian and Eighty-sixth streets yesterday at five-thirty p.m." The woman spoke so softly that Corinne had to strain to hear what she was saying.

"Her Buick Regal failed to stop at a traffic signal and collided with an Oldsmobile driven by Tamara Horner of this city. Miss Horner's vehicle had entered the intersection, heading east, and was struck broadside and pushed into the path of a Ford Thunderbird heading west and driven by Henry Remes of South Bend. Miss Daye's vehicle, out of control, crashed into a utility pole.

"Mr. Remes was treated at Presbyterian Hospital for abrasions and contusions and released. Miss Horner is in satisfactory condition at Presbyterian, with head and face injuries. Mrs. Daye's condition is more serious. She suffered multiple fractures of an arm and ribs, and a concussion, according to a hospital spokesperson.

"At the time of the accident, Mrs. Daye did not have her seat belt fastened. A blood test confirmed that Mrs. Daye had no trace of alcohol in her bloodstream, and there was no evidence of drugs. The cause of the accident may be related to brake failure and is now under investigation by the CCPD. No charges were filed." Corinne heard the faint rustling of newsprint, then the voice again. "What's Mrs. Daye like?"

"Attractive enough. Dr. Blackwell's orders are to keep her sedated today. He set the bone and applied the cast to her arm this morning."

"When did Dr. Perlman's plane crash?" asked the first voice in a curious tone.

"Over two years ago. In December. A storm hit out East that petered out before it reached us."

"Why were they flying to Boston, anyway?"

"Harvard Med School was holding a surgical seminar. A surgeon from Europe was demonstrating a new technique in thyroidectomies. Perlman was a graduate of Harvard, and he let everybody know it, too!" the alto voice said dryly.

"You'd think Dr. Daye would have gone into a cushy practice with his father," the other woman mused. "I wonder why he didn't."

"William Daye is the cardiologist for all the socialites in town. I guess Stan Daye didn't want to specialize in cardiology. Or socialites. He became a damned good surgeon. I have a friend who works in OR who used to assist him."

"Maybe he couldn't stand his father," said the first voice dryly. "I avoid William Daye whenever I can, especially when his overbearing wife is around. God, that woman!"

"You know, Stan Daye didn't even resemble his parents physically. That's the puzzler. He was six foot two. William Daye is five foot ten . . . with a paunch."

The two voices giggled.

"Maybe the milkman was six foot two," said the first voice conspiratorially.

"With any other woman you might suspect that, but not Eileen Daye. A man would have to produce pedigree papers before she'd go to bed with him. Stan Daye was their only child. They waited long enough after marrying—ten years."

"Hmmm." The other voice contemplated this for a moment, then asked, "What happened to Dr. Perlman's plane?"

"Blown off course by the storm. I heard a rumor the wings had iced up. It came down in a farmer's field near Syracuse, New York. Caught fire."

Corinne made an effort to sit up, her mouth painfully dry. She yearned for a sip of water—no, a cup of coffee to restore her senses to their usual sharpness. Only when she tried to reach for the call button did she become aware that her left arm was immobilized in a heavy cast. Her right arm was strapped lightly to a board. An intravenous needle was in her vein, and the plastic intravenous tube leading from the needle was taped to her arm. Something constricted her chest. She fell back on the pillow, exhausted from the effort of lifting her head.

"How's your famous patient doing?" asked the first voice in the hall. It sounded as if the women were standing next to the doorway.

"Very well. All her signs are stable. Her ribs are taped and the cast will be on for six weeks. Dr. Blackwell may keep her here during that time to keep an eye on the concussion. It's mild, they think. Dr. Albert says Mrs. Daye needs a good rest. He calls her a workaholic, says she lives on coffee and cigarettes. Most attorneys I've taken care of do."

"Ah, huh! If she stays in here, Dr. Blackwell will take her off the cigarettes, right?" asked the first voice. The alto voice sounded a relaxed chuckle.

Corinne heard a faint voice call the name "Leslie."

"I'm coming, Mae." The alto voice drifted down the hall.

Silence settled over room 3218 once again. Corinne quit resisting the bed and let her body go limp between the cool sheets. The clean room, with its soothing pale yellow walls, a framed print of wild geese in flight

against a sanguine sunset, and a telephone on the bedside table, slowly came into clearer focus.

"Stan?" she whispered, her chin quivering as her
mind began to clear. The conversation of the two nurses
had brought her back to reality.

Almost unwillingly, she remembered the last time she
had heard her husband's voice. It had been over the
telephone, two weeks after their return from a second
honeymoon in Jamaica—the celebration of their fifth
wedding anniversary. The December day had been gray
and overcast. Stan's deep, resonant voice had vibrated
in the receiver, tickling her ear deliciously.

"Honey, I'm leaving for Boston in an hour with
Henry Perlman. Dr. Lingemann of Bonn is giving a
demonstration of a new technique. Henry and I will be
back the day after tomorrow. I promise!"

"That's what you said the last time you flew to Boston with Henry, and you stayed three days," Corinne
had protested. "We have a date with Chris and Kate
Albert at the Columbia Club on Friday night. You
wouldn't stand up your own godparents, would you?"

"I'll be back Friday morning. I swear it. Your sexy
new dress will not go to waste. If Henry gets nostalgic
with former classmates and insists on remaining longer
like last time, I'll catch a flight out of Boston and call
you from the airport to come pick me up. That's a
promise! Okay?"

You never came back, damn you. You lied to me.

The hand at the end of the arm taped to the board
clenched into a fist while waves of repressed anger broke
free in Corinne—anger toward Henry Perlman for ne-
glecting to perform his preflight check with the airport
before taking off on that fateful trip home, and anger

toward Christopher Albert for refusing her a last glimpse of Stan.

Chris had stood in front of the fireplace in the den of the brick trilevel home Corinne had inherited from her parents—the home she had shared with Stan after their marriage. The silver-haired, lean man with the lined face had stood with his back to her, arms crossed over his chest, and stared into dancing yellow-and-blue flames as he spoke.

"A search party found the plane, Cory. Near Syracuse." His head had been bent, and his voice had betrayed no emotion.

"Thank God! Where is he, Chris? I want to go to Stan." She had started toward the doorway intending to run upstairs to pack her suitcase.

"You can't be with him, Cory." His husky voice had trembled as he'd turned to face Corinne. She'd been astonished to see tears in the steel-gray eyes. "The plane caught fire. The searchers found two charred bodies inside. I left word with the coroner to call me as soon as they arrived."

"Stan . . . dead?" Corinne had whispered, her knees giving way. She'd sunk onto the den's leather sofa. "He's here? In Circle City?"

"It isn't necessary for you to go down there. I already identified the body."

"*You* identified Stan? Without me? How could you? I'm his wife!"

"It would do you more harm than good, young lady. I'm trained in medicine—" his voice had broken and his gray eyes had shimmered "—and it was almost more than *I* could handle. Remember Stan the way he was. That's best."

"Are you certain, Chris? Maybe it wasn't Stan." Corinne had reached for the only ray of hope she could find. "He was upset with Henry because of the time before. Remember? Henry had prolonged their trip for three days. Stan threatened to get a seat on a commercial jet out of Boston if Henry behaved that way again. Maybe they had an argument and Stan took that commercial flight after all. That could have been someone else riding home with Henry." Her eyes pleaded with him to accept the possibility, to allow her one slim thread of hope.

"No, Cory. The dental records checked out. It's Stan all right. Dental records don't lie." Chris had shaken his head slowly, wiping his eyes with the back of his hand.

Flames had leaped and danced merrily in the fireplace, crackling, while shadows flickered over the textured ceiling of the den.

Corinne lay motionless in the hospital bed, her eyes still closed. Had her mind been playing tricks on her when she had seen Stan standing at the foot of her bed? He had looked so hale and hearty, of solid flesh, not like an apparition. Had she been hallucinating? Or was he really in hiding somewhere? Had he read about her accident in the *Star* and stolen up the fire-exit stairway to catch a glimpse of her, assuming she would be dosed with medication?

Questions tormented her, invading her dreamlike state. A tear rolled slowly down Corinne's cheek. She heard the soft sound of a nurse's oxfords and sensed someone entering the room and halting beside the bed.

"Mrs. Daye, are you awake yet?" The alto voice spoke loudly. "Katherine Albert is here to see you."

Corinne felt a familiar hand slip into hers in a reassuring grip.

"Hi, Cory. I just wanted to tell you I'm going to stop by your house to pick up Penny. I'll need your door key. I'll take Penny home with me to stay until you go home."

Corinne's head rolled on the pillow. Her eyelids lifted sleepily. A face came almost into focus. "Chris? He won't mind?"

"Mind having that sweet little dog around? Of course not. He's delivering a baby now. He'll be down to visit you soon. I see Jim Blackwell did a good job on your cast."

"It feels like a hunk of cement," Corinne mumbled, licking her dry lips.

"I know just what it needs," mused Kate. "Decoration. Did I tell you I'm taking a watercolor class now?" She didn't wait for an answer. "I'm going to make you a piece of wearable art. It's the big thing in fashion now. Tomorrow I'll bring colored markers, and we'll pretty up the cast. Red tulips might look nice and pink carnations. Oh, how about fruit, too?" Kate rattled on. "A big orange and a pink peach smack on the elbow."

Corinne felt a twitching at the corners of her lips, a tug that resulted in a weak smile. She liked the thought of the shock that would be on Jim Blackwell's somber face when he found a fat pink peach painted on his plaster handiwork.

THREE WEEKS LATER, the end of the second week in August, baskets of flowers lined the floor and the window ledge of room 3218, creating a rainbow. Pale blue irises and bold spears of white gladiolus, sent by William and Eileen Daye, rose tall from a vase resting on the polished tile floor. A vase of red carnations, a gift from Kate and Chris Albert, a pot of yellow mums from

Meg Krens and pots of pink azaleas from other friends were perched on the window ledge, dazzling in the yellow-white sunlight that poured over them. Each floral gift bore a stiff card identifying the sender and giving wishes for Corinne's speedy recovery.

It was the heavy, musky, scent of the dark red roses, however, that dominated Corinne's senses. On the table beside the bed stood a green floral vase filled with thirteen perfect blossoms that were velvety to the touch. The bouquet had been left at the nurses' station the day before with only Corinne's name and room number on the card. There was no signature. No one at the desk had noticed who had left the flowers.

Corinne felt she was smothering in the roses' scent. Her heart hammered whenever she summoned the courage to look at them. Only Stan had ever given her roses, but never thirteen. The unlucky number made her uneasy.

"You're not getting the rest that Dr. Blackwell was hoping you'd get, Corinne," sighed Leslie Kramer, the nurse with the alto voice, as she checked the tape covering Corinne's ribs. She pulled Corinne's satin gown back down, then pulled up the sheet and smoothed it. "Your secretary is much too efficient. She brings the office to you." The nurse was frowning, as if she disapproved.

Corinne leaned back against the pillows of the upraised bed. A small dictating machine rested on the mattress beside her. A microphone was in her right hand. Her practice couldn't come to a grinding halt just because her car had run into a telephone pole.

Leslie Kramer returned the pile of letters to be answered to her patient's lap. "Work is all you people think about," Leslie said dryly. "And you always think it can't wait." She sighed. "There's a man waiting in the hall to see you. A police officer."

Corinne suddenly yearned for a cigarette. "Tell him to come in," she told Leslie, trying to sound unconcerned.

The nurse hurried out of the room, her white uniform rustling, the soles of her white oxfords softly slapping the polished tile floor. Then Leslie's pleasant voice drifted through the open doorway. "Mrs. Daye can see you now."

The man who entered the room wore a blue-and-gold uniform, with a gun and holster strapped to his hip. The sight of the gun made Corinne nervous. All guns made her nervous. They had but one purpose. To kill.

"I'm Sergeant Masters." He extended his hand. His clasp was warm and firm, although his manner was restrained. He was tall like Stan, and his face had a western-style ruggedness. When he noticed the colorful images on her cast, including a fat peach painted on the elbow, he broke into a wide grin. The hazel eyes that flickered over her face sparkled with merriment, then sobered.

"You wouldn't happen to have a cigarette on you, would you?" asked Corinne hopefully, looking around the room for an ashtray. Leslie had removed them all on the physician's orders.

He shook his head. "Sorry, ma'am. I quit five years ago. Doctor got you off cigarettes? How long has it been?"

"Three weeks. I've survived this long. Maybe I'll make it." She sighed.

"May I sit down, ma'am?" he asked. At her nod, he lowered himself onto the green vinyl armchair. "Nice flowers," he said, looking around the room. "My wife likes flowers, too."

"I presume you're here about my car?" she asked, prodding him. Meg was due to arrive any minute. Corinne had two more replies to dictate and wanted Meg to take the tape back to the office with her and type the letters.

He sat up straight and seemed grateful that she had brought up the subject first. "Your car was checked over very carefully, Mrs. Daye...."

"And...?"

"You were completely out of brake fluid at the time of the accident."

"That's impossible," protested Corinne. "I have the car maintained regularly at the dealership where I bought it. The brakes were fine that morning when I drove to work. They just suddenly failed as I was driving home. I explained all this to the insurance adjuster who came to see me."

"Where do you park your car during the day while you're at the office?" he asked, taking out a notebook from his jacket pocket.

Puzzled, Corinne gave him the name and address of the indoor parking garage where she leased space by the month. "Does anyone else have a key to the car?" he asked.

"Only my husband. We bought the car three months before he... was killed in a small plane accident," Corinne answered weakly. She tried to remember if Stan's keys had been in the small box of personal effects that Chris Albert had handed her after he'd broken the news to her.

"There was a break—a very fine slit—in the brake-fluid line," Sergeant Masters continued.

"From the accident, of course," Corinne interrupted.

"I don't think so, ma'am," the policeman said stiffly. "Our expert thinks someone put it there with a very sharp instrument. The slit was in just the right place to allow the fluid to drip out slowly."

Corinne stared at the man. What he was suggesting was ridiculous. "But who would do such a thing? And why?"

"I hoped maybe you could tell me, Mrs. Daye. Any ideas?" He leaned forward in the chair, his hazel eyes appraising her reaction.

"None at all. I'm on good terms with everyone...I think."

Sergeant Masters rose slowly, frowning. He wrote his name and telephone number on the top sheet of the pad he held in his hand and gave the sheet to her. "If you get any ideas, call me. And you'd better keep your seat belt fastened while driving from now on. It's the law in Indiana, you know. Next time you might not get off so lucky."

"There won't be a next time, officer," she mumbled, still craving a cigarette. She was out of the mood now to dictate the remaining letters. Someone trying to kill her? The prospect was too ridiculous to take seriously. She watched the figure in blue move to the foot of the bed.

"If I were you, ma'am, I'd have dead-bolt locks put on all my outside doors at home. And don't hang around late at your office alone until we get to the bottom of this."

His hazel eyes held hers steadily for a moment. Then he looked away and gave a slight nod in curt farewell. He headed for the open doorway, almost colliding with a tall, shapely woman coming into the room. The woman held a briefcase in one hand and pulled a small shopping cart loaded with law books with the other.

"Excuse me, miss. I'm sorry," said Sergeant Masters.

Margaret Krens froze for a moment and didn't answer. She pushed the cart back into the hall. Masters passed her, beaming an appreciative smile. Then he paused in the hallway and faced her.

The corners of Meg's lips lifted slowly in a practiced smile.

"You're Mrs. Daye's secretary, aren't you? I'm Glenn Masters."

"Meg Krens. I'm Mrs. Daye's *assistant*. This is a professional call, I presume? You're not serving a warrant, are you?"

"No. I'd like to question you sometime about your boss. Can we arrange a meeting?" he asked.

"Let's talk right here. I have nothing to say to you that I can't say in front of Mrs. Daye. I've been working for her for five years."

Masters glanced uncomfortably into the room. Corinne was sitting up in the bed, watching them. "Does she have any enemies that you know of? Anyone trying to get even?" he asked, dropping his voice.

"Oh, there might be an irate husband whose wife got a bigger divorce settlement than he would have liked or a spouse who wants custody of a child. Mrs. Daye has a civil practice. Her clients are all solid-citizen types. Accident liability, divorce, probate—things like that. Why do you ask, anyway? Is this about the Buick?"

"It's totaled," Sergeant Masters answered grimly. "It's a miracle she came out so well."

"She's a positive thinker," said Meg, shrugging.

"No enemies?"

"Does *she* know of any enemies?"

"No."

"Well, I don't, either. You're barking up the wrong tree, mister."

The man's affable manner hardened as a result of the attractive woman's brusque levity. He cast his eyes to the tiled floor of the hallway floor and hurried away.

"Meg, you shouldn't answer that way," Corinne chided as Meg pulled the cart into the room.

"A uniform doesn't scare me. These guys watch too many cop shows on TV. Makes them think they have to live up to their TV image. A simple car accident and he wants to make an FBI case out of it. Of course, you are a Banbury," she said, referring to Corinne's maiden name.

"What does that have to do with anything?" asked Corinne, suddenly tired. The heavy odor of roses was making her ill.

"Your father. Banbury Manufacturing. Why else do you think your silly wreck made the front page of the morning paper?"

"My father and mother died when I was in college. Their bankrupt company was sold. There is no glory in that. I'm still trying to live it down. What's the weather doing out there?" asked Corinne irritably.

"What's the middle of August always like around here? Ninety-two and incredibly humid. The air in my Datsun 280 ZX just went out," Meg complained, unloading the cart. Fine beads of perspiration dotted her upper lip. Damp auburn tendrils curled on her neck. Her hair was a pixie cap of lush, thick reddish-brown curls, but the pixie appearance ended there. Her face was composed, almost haughty, with glittering emerald-green eyes, a slim, pert nose and cupid's-bow lips; her body was all woman. The expensive tailored gray business suit she wore did little to hide the generous swell of bosom, nor did the slim suit skirt disguise her perfectly proportioned thighs and calves.

"Do you think there's anything to his cock-and-bull suspicions?" Meg asked. Her manner was almost challenging and puzzled Corinne. She tightened inside with caution. As an employee, Margaret Krens was a jewel of jewels—a self-starter who never needed to be told what to do twice, a woman who could pacify any distraught client before he or she reached Corinne. Meg was also a whiz at keeping the books. Corinne had turned over complete control of the financial records to her secretary with a free mind and trusted her to write the necessary checks. Meg was a take-charge type of woman who attended college classes at night with the dream of attending law school one day, and Corinne wanted to help her to realize her goal.

Yet Meg was a bit on the unpredictable side and needed kid-glove treatment. She did not always react as Corinne expected her to react. This was one of those times. Meg seemed totally focused on the policeman's visit.

"No, I don't," Corinne answered carefully. "As a policeman he's trained to perceive events in a certain way, just as I'm trained to interpret events from the legal standpoint or as a physician's trained to look for medical aspects."

Meg's attractive face relaxed unexpectedly, and she gave a gentle smile. "I was afraid that he had upset you for nothing, Cory. You've been through enough what with that lump of cement round your arm, your ribs taped and the work that keeps pouring in."

"I'm glad I have you to rely on."

"Maybe you're pushing yourself too hard. Maybe you ought to let up some," said Meg with a look of concern on her face.

"You can't write the brief on the Hawkins case for me. The trial is coming up soon," said Corinne.

"No, I can't."

"Someday, though. When you've got your B.A. and are admitted to IU's law school, I'll let you take over some of the legal research."

"I'd like that," said Meg. "Just don't push the panic button because of the boy in blue's visit. You're too sensible a woman to let yourself become scared of shadows on the wall."

"Why don't you take Monday off and take your car in to have the air conditioner checked out? Pay yourself your salary for the day when you make out your paycheck," said Corinne. She was tired, even though she had lain in bed much of the day. She could use a day off, too.

"You mean it?" asked Meg.

"Do I ever say anything I don't mean?"

"No, Cory, you're straight as an arrow," Meg answered softly, a tender smile playing over her lips. "Today's mail," she said. She laid the worn leather briefcase that bore the gold initials C.B. on top of the clean white bedspread.

"You look thirsty. Help yourself to the ice water." Corinne nodded toward the plastic pitcher next to the vase of roses on the bedside table. She smiled affectionately at the young woman who had proven herself such a capable girl Friday and had helped keep her practice functioning.

Meg helped herself to a clean glass and filled it with cold water and ice. The ice tinkled as it bounced against the walls of the glass. She raised the glass to her lips, drank greedily and eyed Kate's handiwork on the cast. Corinne knew Meg didn't see the humor in it. To her, the colored flowers and fruit would seem silly, lacking in dignity.

"Who sent the roses?" Meg asked as she put the glass down.

Corinne's heart skipped a beat. "The florist failed to enclose a card."

"It has to be a man, then. You know, if Stan were alive, he would probably send roses after seeing the article in the paper." Meg was staring into the empty glass she held in her hand.

Stan alive and well and failing to contact me? Corinne thought, all strength draining from her. Yes, the presence of another woman in Stan's life would explain that. *Some men find their way out by running,* Meg had once said. Her own father had run out on her mother when Meg was only three.

Does Meg have a boyfriend? Corinne wondered. Most women talked about their boyfriends but Meg never did.

"There are two dictation tapes in the table drawer. That takes care of all the correspondence except for two letters. But there's no rush on those," said Corinne dully. Her head was starting to throb from just thinking of Stan. She wished Meg would not mention his name so often.

"I'll take tomorrow off. Oh, James Gaterow called."

"He's offering a settlement in the Debra Hawkins case," Corinne guessed. The accident liability trial was in four and a half weeks. That gave her just ten days after her release from the hospital. It was too little time for such an important case.

"His client is willing to offer ten thousand," said Meg.

"To hell with that!" Corinne's body warmed with instant anger.

"I told him you wouldn't go for it," answered Meg, shrugging.

"Eight-year-old Debra Hawkins is in a wheelchair for the rest of her life due to the negligence of his client," Corinne snapped. "Three medical experts are willing to testify Debra will never walk again. Only ten thousand? I figure two hundred thousand based on loss of future income." There was an angry pause. "Who's going to support Debra for the rest of her life?" she demanded. "Her parents are barely scraping by. It's a matter of justice."

"I told him you wouldn't go for it," Meg repeated, her voice lacking in expression. The emerald eyes stared at the floor.

"Go on home now, Meg, and take tomorrow off with pay. Thanks for coming today," Corinne said tiredly.

"The jury will decide the Hawkins matter. You can't play God. Remember that," warned Meg. "See you on Monday." She left without a backward glance, the empty pullcart rolling behind her.

With her one good hand, Corinne struggled with the buckles of the worn briefcase that had once belonged to her father. A large and flat object was in the briefcase, covered by some opened mail. The contents of the envelopes had already been checked by Meg. Corinne grasped the edge of the package and pulled it out.

She gasped. It was Stan's colored photograph from the credenza in her private office. As clear sapphire eyes

gazed back at her from the slim metal frame, the heavy
scent of roses smothered her and she wanted to scream.

The old ache deepened as her eyes traced the line of
her husband's angular face. They paused on the reso-
lute jaw that could harden in stubborn determination
when he was sure he was right. They touched on the slim
well-shaped nose with the slightly flared nostrils and
settled on his sensuous lips. She recalled how they could
be warm with the soft breath of passion yet astonish-
ingly hard when passion seized him. She noted the firm
chin bearing a hint of a cleft.

With the tip of her finger, Corinne sadly outlined the
soft waves of sandy hair that graced his wide forehead.
Although her fingertip met only the smooth cool glass,
her mind remembered and her nerves experienced the
soft, sleek, hair.

Corinne blinked back sudden tears. Her eyes wandered slowly over the soft snowy-white collar of his
sports shirt and the Shetland wool crew neck sweater she
had given him one Christmas. The sweater's blue, gray
and wine hues complemented the tanned complexion of
the striking man who wore it. He had acquired the tan
on the Jamaican vacation from which he and Corinne
had just returned. Soon after the studio photo had been
taken, he and Henry Perlman had flown to Boston.

Corinne slowed her breathing and tried to calm herself. She lay back against the pillows and closed her
eyes. All thoughts of the brief for the Hawkins trial fled
her mind.

"DR. BLACKWELL SAYS the cast comes off tomorrow
morning before lunch." Chris Albert's energetic voice
filled room 3218. September sunshine streamed through
the window, less concentrated, less ardent in its warmth

than it had been six weeks earlier. Corinne was grateful her sentence was over. She contemplated the size of the bill her insurance company would pay—she hoped.

"I'll be here at eleven tomorrow to take you home," said Kate quietly, standing next to her obstetrician-gynecologist husband.

Corinne looked affectionately at the husband-wife team. "That's kind of you, Kate. I'll never forget how you've given Penny a home these past six weeks. Has she been any trouble?" asked Corinne anxiously.

"No, dear, she's a sweet little dog—"

"No, she isn't. She bit me!" Chris interrupted his wife. His lined face looked stern. He held up a thumb that had a definite cut on it. Kate threw her husband a reproving look.

"Oh, no. What happened?" asked Corinne, dismayed.

"She zipped under our bed—all fourteen inches of that pint-sized body—while we were changing clothes for the night, and the damned pooch refused to come out!"

"I told you not to reach under the bed to grab her. Why don't you ever listen to me?" said Kate.

"Then the dog snored the whole damned night! That mutt's snore would do a drunken sailor justice. She's louder than Kate."

"I do not snore. I talk in my sleep," Kate said with dignity, ignoring her husband and addressing Corinne. "What bothers him is that he can't understand what I'm saying. Or to whom." She smiled sweetly, turning to her husband.

"I'm sorry Penny bit you, Chris," said Corinne unhappily.

"I'm not. Chris deserved it. He came home from the hospital in a foul mood," declared Kate. "He was on call for two other doctors."

"Don't worry, Chris. Penny's had her rabies shots," Corinne said, hoping to appease him.

"The trouble is, he hasn't," quipped Kate, throwing an amused glance toward her husband. "It's the dog I'm worried about."

"Oh, come on!" Chris grumbled, his famous bluster settling to rest. He reached down and took Kate's hand in his.

"You've done so well here, Cory. For a while Chris and I were really worried about you. Jim says you're healing well, ribs included. The X rays look good. You've shown real stamina in staying off the cigarettes the past six weeks. We're proud of you! But this accident..." Kate's eyebrows drew together in a worried frown. Chris released her hand and suddenly walked around the bed to the window. He stood, staring out.

"Don't apply Freudian theories to my accident," Corinne warned, tension in her voice. "A police expert checked my car after it was impounded. All the power brake fluid had leaked out. He wasn't sure why," she said vaguely, not wanting to cause them concern. "So you see, no subconscious death wish after all, Kate. Just a lack of brake fluid."

"Oh, Cory, I am relieved." Kate took Corinne's hand and squeezed it affectionately.

"Stan's parents were here to see me yesterday. Eileen told me you and Chris have plans to attend a concert with them next week."

Kate sighed. "The last two years have been very hard on Eileen. Her whole life was wrapped up in Stan. She needs to get out more. Chris and I are trying to see to that," said Kate.

Corinne's gaze dropped carefully to the sheet and bedspread folded neatly over her chest. She had never felt comfortable with her mother-in-law. She had never felt Eileen Daye had fully accepted her as her beloved son's wife.

"I'm glad you've gotten over your obsession, Cory." Kate smiled as a mother would smile at a favored child, placing her hand affectionately on the painted cast of which she was proud.

"What obsession?" asked Corinne.

"You know...." Kate faltered, glancing at Chris, who stood looking out the window, his back to them, listening to every word. "That irrational belief that Stan may still be...alive." She smiled too brightly.

"I...still...have the feeling that he is," Corinne confessed. "I even saw him the first day I was in this room. He was standing at the foot of the bed."

Kate's dignified face went pale. Chris slowly turned, his face drawn. "Call Warren Trevis, Cory," advised Chris.

"Why do I need a psychiatrist?"

"He was Stan's friend from medical school. He's your friend, too. Tell Warren about this delusion," Kate pleaded. "Accept his help." Her eyes, usually serene, were shadowed with worry. She sat on the side of the bed and embraced Corinne, cradling the younger woman's head on her shoulder.

"All right, Kate," sighed Corinne, knowing this was the only way to silence Stan's godparents and rid herself of their well-meaning but oppressive concern. At

least, she would be going home tomorrow and the
damned cast, the humorous piece of "wearable art,"
would be off.

CHAPTER TWO

"I'M GLAD YOU CALLED my office yesterday, Cory. When were you released from the hospital?" The voice of the man sitting opposite Corinne in the small booth was hypnotically lulling. Warren Trevis's dark eyes held Corinne's with a masterful intensity. The short, carefully trimmed beard and well-tailored suit gave Stan's friend an older, sophisticated appearance.

"A week ago. Kate Albert drove me home," answered Corinne, tilting her wineglass and staring into the dark claret. "She thinks you're the best."

The man seated opposite her at the tiny table in the cocktail lounge of Circle City International Airport gave a flattered laugh. His eyes took inventory of her long-sleeved dusky rose silk dress, and he studied her face for the slightest change of expression, the faintest tremor in her voice.

The hand that rested on the tabletop moved slowly to cover hers. "I'm so glad you called me, Cory."

"Kate Albert insisted," Corinne said stiffly, not daring to glance at his hand. "She refused to leave my house until I did. Kate thinks I'm...headed for trouble."

"The accident? Were you trying to harm yourself, Cory?"

The question was the one Corinne had expected—and had dreaded. With her free hand she grasped the stem of her wineglass and took a long sip. The dry wine left a warm trail inside her chest as it slid downward to her stomach.

"The brakes failed. It was a freak malfunction."

An indulgent smile crept across his bearded face. "Don't think of me as a psychiatrist, Cory. I'm your friend. I was Stan's friend. That's why I suggested we meet here at the airport before my flight to San Francisco leaves. I'll be in Oahu for two weeks, giving a paper on schizophrenia at the Association's conference." He paused. "Nine days of that time are my own—to swim, walk the beach, indulge myself in luaus and watch the moon rise over the palm trees."

"Alone? Isn't Lisle going with you?" Corinne asked, thinking of Warren's sophisticated wife, who owned several highly successful dress shops.

"Lisle and I are undergoing a trial separation right now. She's on a buying trip in Paris." He raised his glass of sauterne by the stem and slowly rotated the glass beneath his nose, inhaling the aroma. His face was inscrutable.

Corinne took note of the trace of silver at the man's temples, the aloofness in the patrician face and the perfect posture. It had been over three years since she had seen Warren Trevis. She had felt little rapport with him then and felt even less now. Corinne eased her hand from beneath his and let it sink safely into her lap.

"You're living like a nun, I see." His voice was coolly disapproving. He raised the glass, opened his lips sensually and drank. "You're repressing your libido, my dear. You're damming it up, and one day, retribution will come...." He let his voice fade dramatically.

"I'm damming up nothing. I'm attracted to men," she confessed. "I... just can't give in to the feeling, that's all. Stan was the only man for me from the moment I met him when I was in law school and he was at IU Med School. In five years of marriage, Warren, I never allowed another man to..." She took a deep swallow of wine.

He nodded his head of dark well-groomed hair. An insinuating smile played over his lips.

"Stan is dead, Cory. You failed to work through the successive stages of grief. Chris Albert deserves a reprimand for refusing to allow you to see your husband's body, but of course, his field is obstetrics, not psychology. You're stuck in the stage of denial. Let me help," said Warren Trevis softly, his brown eyes brimming with compassion.

"I cope with a heavy work load and I'm functioning quite well, thank you," Corinne said stiffly. "I called your office yesterday to make an appointment only because of Kate Albert's insistence that I do so." She wondered why she had agreed to meet the man at the airport before his plane left.

"Hasn't any man shown interest in you recently, Cory?" he asked, his eyes riveted to her face.

Corinne's eyebrows rose in surprise at the directness of the question. It was true that since Henry Perlman's plane had crashed, she had dated only a few times. She was tempted to tell Warren of the Bar Association Christmas party she had attended last December. James Gaterow had invited her to accompany him, and she had agreed, not really knowing why. Gaterow had a reputation for being tough in the courtroom—she'd seen his toughness firsthand, having lost to him twice—and he had won a grudging respect from her for being hard to beat. Gaterow, a former high school quarterback, still had a sturdy physique. He was divorced and those who knew him thought he was ruthless. The rumors about him, she discovered, were true.

Corinne gave an involuntary shudder as she remembered that evening. Gaterow had drunk too much and had pawed her roughly when he took her home, obviously expecting her to give her all in return for dinner and two cocktails. She had slapped him in anger and drove the stiletto heel of her evening shoe hard into his instep. Then she'd threatened to call the police and press charges unless he left her house immediately.

Gaterow had left. But he'd exacted his revenge. A month later a gleeful male colleague made reference to the new nickname for Corinne that was traveling the halls of the municipal building. The nickname was Ms Mackerel. Translation: Cold fish.

"I've been too busy to date," she told Warren.

The bearded face opposite her was impassive, but the dark eyes burned. "Join me in Honolulu when the conference is over," he said suddenly. "We'll have nine glorious days together, walking the beach, baring our bodies to the sun. I'll make you glad to be alive, Cory. Nights under that huge bright moon... I don't regard you as a patient—we're friends. I'll release you from your inhibitions, I'll set your libido free—"

"Warren, for God's sake!" muttered Corinne in exasperation, lapsing into the phrase she heard Meg utter so often.

A waitress with a trim figure approached the small booth in which Corinne and Warren Trevis sat.

"Are you Dr. Trevis?" asked the waitress. "The girl on the phone told me to look for a bearded, good-looking gentleman." The woman spoke almost shyly.

Warren Trevis gave a satisfied smile. "Yes, I'm Dr. Trevis."

"Your secretary is on the line, sir. She says it's important."

"I'll come to the telephone right away." He stood, excused himself to Corinne and went toward the bar, where a telephone sat, the receiver off the cradle.

Corinne breathed a sigh of relief, then sank back into the booth and closed her eyes. Warren's unwelcomed invitation to Hawaii had brought back other images behind her closed eyelids. She recalled the tranquil view of the Stony Hill Hotel in Jamaica and the fifth wedding anniversary trip she and Stan had taken shortly before he had flown to Boston.

Every morning they had taken a dip in the pool before breakfast. They had laughed at lot and had kept to themselves as all lovers do. They had dined on glistening china and had taken long walks, arms around each other, yielding to impulsive kisses every now and then. The setting had been perfect: tropical greens and brilliant flowers set against shimmering seascapes where the Caribbean crashed against rocky coasts and the tide undulated on palm-fringed beaches of fine white sand.

And the nights . . . the nights had been heavy with the perfume of flowers kissed by silver moonlight. She remembered how, back in their room at night, her light-hearted chuckles had been stilled by Stan's passionate kisses. He had left no part of her unexplored; had left her burning and filled with hope. . . .

Warren thinks I'm frigid, thought Corinne. The exotic mental images faded.

"Cory, are you asleep?"

She opened her eyes, glanced at her watch and managed a polite smile. "Your flight will take off in twenty minutes. Hadn't we better find the gate? You don't want to miss your plane."

They finished their wine and he paid the waitress. Then, they walked down a long blue-carpeted corridor and passed through the metal-detection arch. At the reception area, a sign announced the flight departing for San Francisco. Before she could stop him, he seized her around the waist. His kiss came down hard upon her lips before she could avert her head. She stood frozen, immobilized by the warmth of his lips, drawn into the kiss almost against her will.

A blaring voice announced a flight number, saving her. Warren released her, looking toward the gate. "I'll expect you. I'll call you to find out when your flight is due to arrive, and I'll meet you at the airport." He sounded like a father commanding an obedient child.

"Fine. You do that, Warren," she said, pushing against his chest. He left her with an air of confidence that she would soon be his.

Corinne started back. She felt guilty, knowing she had led the man on. She had no intention of meeting Warren Trevis in Hawaii. He was still a married man; he and Lisle both had big egos, that was all. In time, their injuries would heal, whatever they were. Corinne remembered the two of them from cocktail parties in the past. Lisle was tall, slim and always dressed in a classic style. Her dark hair was long and elegant. She and Warren were well suited to each other, in Corinne's opinion. "Ms Mackerel, indeed!" she muttered aloud to herself. She passed her fingertips lightly over her lips. The impression of Warren's kiss still lingered there.

Crossing the lobby, Corinne passed the sprawling ticket counter and headed toward the escalator. She descended slowly to the lower level from which the parking lot could be reached. Her mind was on the afternoon's appointments. She had to hurry to the office or she would be late for her three o'clock one.

Upon emerging from the escalator, she was seized by the odor of coffee wafting from one of the restaurants. She gazed out over the crowd of deplaned passengers waiting to reclaim their luggage from a conveyor belt that at the moment stood motionless without a single suitcase on it.

"What's the delay?" she overheard one woman complain.

Corinne ducked into the restaurant, yielding to the craving for hot, energizing brew and wishing fervently that she had a cigarette to accompany it. That craving was diminishing slowly, though, day by day.

A tiny table with two chairs just outside the entrance of the restaurant provided a safe place in the growing crowd of baggage claimers. Corinne glanced around her, enjoying a new sense of freedom. How wonderful it was to be out of that hospital room. How wonderful to have the use of her left arm. One hand gently probed her ribs beneath the silken surface of her bodice. The skin was free of the binding tape, and all soreness was gone.

While sipping the hot coffee, Corinne took a closer look at her surroundings. The conveyor belt had sprung to life and was now filled with suitcases of every color, size and shape. She lapsed into travel reveries of sandy beaches and waving palm trees. Warren had painted an enticing picture of Hawaii. Now Corinne longed to feel hot sand between her bare toes and warm sun on bare back and legs. She could almost hear the rhythmic pounding of the Pacific as frothy waves lapped the beach in her imagination.

Her daydreams were abruptly halted by the sound of a baritone voice. Controlled but firm, it soared in resonance over the noisy confusion.

"You've got the wrong bag! That one is mine! Look at the tag on the handle. That's my name. Hand it over!"

Corinne froze at the sound, wondering if Warren's dire prediction had come true. It felt as though her heart had stopped beating. Was she going crazy? The timbre, the inflection, even the attitude of authority were familiar to her. Only one man in the world she ever knew had a voice so distinctive. She lowered the hand holding the coffee cup as she stood to survey the milling crowd.

"No, I'm not mistaken. That one over there on the conveyor must be yours. It looks like mine. See over there?" The voice carried like wind over the crowd, propelled by an impatience marked by fatigue.

The Styrofoam cup went down on the table. Hot black coffee spilled in all directions, staining the long sleeve of the rose-colored silk dress Corinne wore. Meanwhile, passengers, triumphant in the luggage safari, were heading out metal-framed glass doors. Beyond the doors, a long row of taxis waited at the curb.

In desperation, wondering if her sanity really was in question, Corinne stepped away from the table. Her anguished glance ricocheted from the crowded, moving conveyor belt to the doorway to the escalator and back to the mob assembled along the conveyor.

"That's *all right*. No, I'm *not* angry!" The volume of the voice and the emphasis on certain words revealed that he was. *Just the way Stan used to react when wrongly challenged by his parents,* Corinne thought wildly. She zoomed in on the voice coming from the center of the throng with a radar borne of desperation.

She spotted a tall man plowing his way through the crowd. He held a worn leather suitcase before him like the blade of an icebreaker. Corinne's heart skipped a beat. She recognized Stan's familiar profile. It was marred only by a well-trimmed mustache. It was the same sandy hair but he wore it straight now; no wave softened his high forehead. And instead of the casual clothes Stan usually wore for travel, he was wearing a conservative gray pinstriped suit. A tan-colored trench coat was draped over his arm. The long purposeful stride animated by nervous energy was the same, however. He walked with the same agile grace, possessed the same lean, virile figure.

Stan!

Inside herself, Corinne screamed his name. Her lips were too numb to respond. The man was heading for the glass doors. Mesmerized, Corinne stared at the solid back, the same wide shoulders that had first attracted her the day she had met him in the cafeteria line on campus.

The glass doors closed behind him. He approached a taxi. The driver took the suitcase and leather briefcase from him and threw them into the trunk of the cab. She saw Stan fold his six-foot-two-inch frame into the rear seat of the cab and pull the cab door shut.

All of Corinne's energy was mobilized. She broke into a run and headed toward the glass doors, her heart thudding against tender ribs. The yellow cab was already pulling away from the curb as she pushed the door open, panting. She silently repeated to herself the number of the departing taxi.

"Follow that cab!" she said, gasping, as she jerked open the rear door of another taxi waiting in line.

"You a cop?" asked the driver, staring at Corinne's reflection in the rearview mirror.

"I . . . work in the court, yes," replied his passenger, her mind racing as she watched the rear of Stan's cab disappear around the bend of the narrow airport lane. She had no police badge to show. How long would this idiot wait before he pulled away from the curb? "That man ahead has . . . violated parole," she stammered, making up the first excuse that popped into her head.

Where was Stan going? Was he on his way home?

The taxi's engine burst into a roar. The cab leaped forward. "I'll stick close to his tail. Don't you worry," said the heavyset driver.

Corinne's nerves were coiled tight. She leaned back stiffly against the rear of the seat and tried to relax. Both taxis turned onto the Airport Expressway and gained speed to merge with the heavy traffic flow.

Questions poured through Corinne's agitated mind as they turned onto the exit ramp to head toward the downtown area on the interstate. Who was the poor soul who accompanied Henry Perlman on that fateful ride in December over two years ago? Where had Stan been hiding all this time? Why had he failed to get in touch with her?

Who is the other woman?

All other thought ceased for Corinne. Her mind went perfectly still at the cavernous ache that question brought. Yes, there had to be another woman as Meg had implied. It was the only explanation for Stan's absence, his monstrous silence for over two years. Her joy turned to despair; her gratitude to anger.

"Do you have a cigarette on you?" she leaned forward to ask the driver. "I'll pay you for it."

"Sorry. I gave them up. Didn't want trouble with my ticker," answered the driver, taking a hand off the wheel to point toward his chest. His full, round face was reflected in the rearview mirror.

Everything around her seemed unreal: the overcast sky of early September, the sound of trucks pounding along the interstate. Corinne let out a controlled sigh. She reached for a red-and-white candy mint in her coat pocket. Her hands trembled as she fought the snug plastic wrapper, trying to get at the mint inside.

The taxi ahead darted into another lane and sped up. Traffic was heavy and formed a barrier between the two cabs. "You're losing him!" Corinne cried in frustration. The cab in which she was riding surged ahead.

Seconds stretched into minutes as moving waves of metal and glass on wheels rushed toward the downtown skyline en masse. The jutting silhouette of the Marotte Bank Tower, where her office was located, loomed into full view. *Perhaps he's on his way to my office,* thought Corinne, becoming more tense. *To talk about a divorce, maybe?*

The cab ahead veered to the right and onto the exit ramp. Corinne's driver followed in hot pursuit. They were soon caught in the choking stream of traffic on the main east-west street downtown. The cab ahead swung abruptly to the left and parked in front of the door to the Empire Suites Hotel.

Just the sort of place Stan would select, thought Corinne, simmering with agitation. Stan's driver hopped out briskly to open the trunk and unload Stan's worn suitcase, a piece of luggage Corinne had never seen before. Neither was the briefcase he carried in his hand familiar. He mounted the six red brick steps briskly and disappeared behind the glass door.

Dismayed and confused, Corinne paid her driver, stepped out of the cab quickly and slammed the door, her raincoat slung over her arm. With her heart ticking wildly in her throat, she ran up the red brick steps, wanting to keep Stan in sight.

Water cascaded soothingly down the limestone ledges of the huge fountain in the center of the lobby. Fig trees rose green and leafy from wooden planters. Above her towered eighteen floors while below her, not visible from where she stood in the lobby, lay a subterranean level of retail shops. Corinne moved closer to the marble registration desk, keeping out of sight behind one of the huge wooden pillars.

"I'm Douglas Johnson. I was due to arrive yesterday but I missed my plane," she heard Stan tell a desk clerk.

There was a short pause, and then the clerk responded, "Yes, Mr. Johnson. We received your reservation from the Spurgon Corporation in San Francisco. You've been assigned suite 1802 on the eighteenth floor, sir. We hope your stay with us will be enjoyable. If you need anything, please contact the concierge on your floor. She will be glad to help you." The well-groomed reservation clerk was handing Stan a key. His suitcase had disappeared, probably into the hands of a luggage attendant, Corinne thought. She noted that Stan refused to relinquish custody of his briefcase.

Stan walked toward the elevator. How well Corinne knew that confident stride. The ache was unbearable as she watched him step into the elevator. He remained visible through the glass walls as it went up.

Corinne leaned against the large pillar, out of sight of the desk. She felt betrayed. "Douglas Johnson, indeed!" she muttered. What was his game? Indignation became her fuel and energized her.

With a measured stride, trying to appear nonchalant, Corinne finally strolled to an elevator and went inside. The door closed. It began its ascent to the eighteenth floor.

What will I say to him? thought Corinne, steeling herself against tears. It hurt to no longer be wanted. And she had no plan of action, no opening remarks prepared as she would have in court.

The elevator doors parted and Corinne stepped into a carpeted hallway. Immediately an attractive woman in a dark two-piece dress came forward to greet her.

"Eighteen oh two, please. I have an appointment with Mr....Johnson," said Corinne, almost choking on the name.

The concierge led Corinne to a doorway and gave a pleasant smile.

"Thank you," murmured Corinne formally. She waited to knock on the door until the concierge returned to her desk. *Get his side of the story first,* thought Corinne, straining to remain objective.

The door swung open without warning. "Briggs, I'm sorry I'm late—" The resonant voice halted abruptly. Sapphire eyes stared down at her with no sign of recognition. "Yes?" he asked.

The game was more than Corinne could bear. "Let me in," she murmured in a low voice, and he complied, stepping back. Quickly she closed the door behind her, glancing down at his stockinged feet, then lifting her eyes. Stan was without suit jacket or tie, and the first three buttons of his crisp white shirt were unfastened. Darker tufts of thick hair peeked out from the deep V of his shirt. She dragged her gaze upward, all resolve to be tough deserting her. Her gaze hovered on the hint of a cleft in his chin. Her knees began to weaken.

She desperately wanted him—wanted to feel the warm strength of his arms hard around her, wanted to feel his hungry kiss. For a moment, she felt dizzy and feared she would faint.

He reached out and cupped her elbows to steady her. Her heartbeat sped up at the warm pressure of his touch.

"Is something wrong? Are you ill?" he asked.

In the sapphire eyes there was still no sign of recognition. Corinne felt the urge to scream. All sorts of conjectures streamed through her anguished mind. Had he suffered amnesia? Was he on drugs? Had he joined up with the CIA for an overseas assignment, as he used to joke about doing, and been mentally injured by some enemy?

One resolve dominated Corinne now. She would rip asunder the veil of mystery that had separated Stan from her for over two years. Truth would prevail.

"Where have you been all this time?" Her voice was husky with emotion as her dark eyes devoured his face. "I've waited so long for you." She reached out unsteadily to touch his chest, and her fingertips crept into the mass of coarse hair. How wonderfully warm his skin felt.

He frowned, looking puzzled, and retreated several steps into the room, backing away from her. "I missed my plane out of Los Angeles. I had to take a later one. I'm sorry I couldn't keep my appointment with Mr.

Briggs here last night. I tried to call him at home and got no answer. Are you his store manager?''

He's sick, thought Corinne, dazed, as she moved into the room and closed the door behind her. Yes, Stan's mind had been affected. An accident perhaps, not related to the plane mishap. Or maybe he had fallen into the hands of someone unscrupulous, become the victim of a mind-altering drug. Such things did happen in espionage circles, according to books. *Go slowly,* Corinne cautioned herself. *Humor him. Don't drive him away.*

"I can't believe you don't know who I am. I've been waiting for you ... all this time." Her voice had gone husky with sexual tension and with emotion so intense that she feared she might burst.

A call girl? he thought, puzzled. Would Don Jennings of Spurgon go so far as to have one on hand to meet him, knowing about his breakup with Mitzi? The prospect seemed a bit farfetched although Jennings's corporate influence was powerful, spanning the continent. The woman knew where he was staying. It had to be Jennings's influence at work. The idea of a call girl for his convenience was not to his liking. He knew he should send her away. Yet, she was so appealing, so intense ... even beautiful.

His eyes kindled as they locked with hers. His sensuous lips curved into the magnetic smile that was so familiar to Corinne. He seemed uncertain as to what was expected of him. Almost against his will, his eyes flicked downward to her soft pink lips, then traveled upward to the luminous, dark orbs devouring him. His voice was suddenly husky, filled with longing. "You're too lovely a woman for any man to keep waiting. I'm sorry ... truly sorry...."

The apology, although inadequate for two years of hell, mollified Corinne somewhat. If Stan's brain had been affected in some way, through no fault of his own, he deserved her understanding, not her anger. He needed to be touched, reassured that all would be well soon. Corinne moved toward him and encircled his waist with her arm. She placed her head in the comforting bend of his neck where it met his shoulder. It was a gesture she hoped her husband would recognize; it was the silent signal she had used in the past to show she was ready to share affection and love.

"Tell me what you can . . . about this past year," she murmured. Her thigh met his hard, muscled one and her breast beneath the silk dress pressed against his firm chest. A wave of remembered sensation began to sweep over her, immersing her in a heady warmth.

Despite his reservations, his body seemed to be reacting with a mind of its own. His stubborn jaw tightened. "Are you high on something?" he asked, his breath coming faster as she drew even nearer.

"High on you, darling," Corinne whispered. "I watched you in the lobby. You're still the most magnificent man I've ever seen."

"You mean—you saw me in the lobby? And you want me? Just like that?" he said gasping. She felt the muscles in his body harden and his abdomen tighten. He was becoming a coiled spring ready for action. She had been a faithful wife for five years, and now her reluctance to forgive all without due process melted in the heat that was emanating from his body.

"I want you very much!" she whispered, and her eyes misted with tears as she made the confession.

His eyes widened and he blinked in disbelief. Mitzie had never come on to him this way. She usually had to be coaxed.

The silence in the elegant room with the high ceiling wrapped around them. The door to the terrace was ajar. *He was out there when I knocked,* thought Corinne. A cooling breeze swept her face.

She was barely aware of it as strong arms went confidently around her. He took her eager lips in a searing kiss, finding the lingering taste of mint on her tongue and sipping it greedily. His mustache brushed her upper lip, tickling it. The warmth of his body encompassed her, igniting the heat with her. Her hips moved involuntarily, pressing against him in slow motion. Their mouths parted as each took a gasping breath. He was changing his mind about sending her away.

He gave a ragged sigh, forgetting all about the person named Briggs. Corinne raised her head and rained fervent kisses on his soft neck, tasting his skin with nibbling licks and gentle nips. He tasted salty, and the distinctive masculine scent of him was filling her nostrils, urging her on. He imprisoned her in his arms, and an eagerness to shed her clothes took control of Corinne.

"Touch me, darling!" she whispered, and driven by a force rising up from deep within her, she sought his mouth.

The words, the kiss proved electrifying. A strangled sigh came from deep inside his throat as she pressed her breasts against his chest and locked her arms around his neck. He moved his hand up her back with gentle pressure, bringing a wave of delicious tingles up her spine in its wake. Then he cupped the base of her neck, supporting her head firmly.

Her lips parted. His tongue penetrated her mouth as if it belonged there, thrusting deeply. Yet Corinne sensed that a small part of him was still trying to resist what he was feeling. The palm of his large, strong hand was roaming her back, producing delicious sensations.

"That perfume...God, I love that perfume!" he said, moaning, pressing his slightly roughened cheek against hers. She felt the last of his resistance melt away. He wrapped his arms around her possessively.

Joy filled Corinne. Stan remembered the scent of the French perfume he had given her as a gift during their trip to Jamaica. She remembered a medical article she had read with him long ago about how recognition of odors remained even when memory of events were lost due to brain damage. Slowly Stan would remember her, no matter what he was blocking out. The healing was beginning now. She burned to hasten the process.

"Let me see you, darling. You're a sight for sore eyes," Corinne whispered huskily. He was fully aroused; that was obvious to her. He made no further protest, but stood motionless.

She tugged his shirt off and gazed at the profusion of curled hair on his broad chest, not stopping to consider that Stanford Daye had never donned a dress shirt without putting on an undershirt first. She was being swept along in the whirling rapids of almost three years of sexual repression. Her fingertips made lazy circles over his tightening pectoral muscles, and coarse hair tickled her palms. The lazy circles drifted downward over his smooth abdominal skin until her fingertips invaded the sanctity of his leather belt.

"I've needed you, darling, can't you see that?" Her whisper was fervid as she pressed her lips against the warm chest and gently sucked. His chest was damp with perspiration, and Corinne was glad, knowing this was another sign of his arousal. Despite the mystery of the lost years, she was sure of one thing at least: Stan still wanted her.

The last bit of stubborn resistance flowed out of him, and a surge of strength so great swept through him that it was frightening. Strong arms picked her up. She kicked off her shoes. He carried her to the bedroom and set her down gently on her nylon-clad feet. He folded down the blue-green bedspread to the foot of the king-size bed.

She waited, trembling. Midafternoon sunlight filtered down through the skylight. With his sapphire eyes misted with desire, he released the buttons at the front of her rose silk dress. He slipped the dress from her shoulders, letting it fall from her arms in silken whispers to the carpeted floor. He pulled the satin, lace-bordered slip over her head. It, too, dropped to the floor and nestled on the gossamer pile of red.

She helped, sitting on the edge of the bed and pulling down the sheer panty hose that clung to her legs. His eyes devoured her as he watched the silky nylon peel away. Her pulse pounded in her temples, banishing all thoughts of her usual tidiness.

A small animal sound echoed from the depths of his throat, and the sound quickened her own excitement. Stan had changed in subtle ways. He seemed more direct now, more earthy in his response, and she assumed she had her rival to thank. She rose from the side of the bed and kissed his shoulder, pressing herself against him in her need.

He responded by stepping back and quickly divesting himself of the rest of his clothing, not giving her the opportunity to undress him leisurely. His clothing, too, fell pell-mell on the floor. "These will only get in the way," he murmured, stripping off her satin bikini pants. They slid enticingly down her legs, forming a gold puddle around her slim ankles. She stepped out of them and kicked them away.

To Corinne's astonishment, he grasped the fullness of her buttocks with his large warm hands, lifted her onto the bed and placed her in a kneeling position. He followed suit. Warm excitement flowed through her as he lowered his head and moved his arm around behind her, supporting her at the waist. Thrilling lips were pressing fervid kisses on her shoulder, moving slowly to the hollow between her breasts. His hand roamed her thigh, slipping around to the innermost part and moving upward. As his mouth found the ripened peak of her breast, his searching fingertips gently touched the most sensitive part of her, her feminine citadel.

She gave a joyful cry. Fine beads of perspiration blossomed on her, dotting the hollow between her breasts.

His mouth worked its magic, his tongue pulling her nipple erect, his teeth teasing it ever so gently. Her hands roamed his back, urging him on. It was then that she noticed the small strawberry birthmark over his shoulder blade. Joy exploded within her when she recognized the feature that Stan had so often made demeaning jokes about. It was the final proof that he was Stan. Because of the birthmark, she had once dubbed him the Strawberry Kid. He'd always grinned whenever she'd said it.

Her other breast ached for the same blessing of sensation. It did not have long to wait. She uttered a soft moan of delight at the insistent tug deep in her pelvis. Her entire body tingled, she was summer-warm to the soles of her bare feet as she knelt on the smooth, cool sheet. Filtered fragments of golden sunlight from the skylight stretched across the huge bed.

"Don't stop," she whispered as the palms of her hands delighted in the smoothness of his back and his narrow hips and buttocks. She drew provocative circles around the strawberry birthmark, then trailed her fingertip upward to the sensitive nape of his neck while her lips drew into a languid smile.

Stan was hers again. At last. She could feel it.

The joy of triumph poured through Corinne, an exhilaration unlike anything she had ever known before. She felt fully alive, filled with hope for the first time since Jamaica.

"Are you ready?" His voice was heavy, thick. He was breathing harder. Passion lent a haze to his magnetic eyes. She was too breathless to speak. She could only nod, a smile imbuing her face with radiance.

Corinne felt the surge of raw desire tear through him. Her throbbing breasts were pressed up against his chest, and his ardor caught and further inflamed hers as he lowered her to the bed. The sheet was cool beneath her back as she parted her legs in joyous surrender. She reached up for him in total acceptance.

The lean, muscular length of him covered her, and his strong hands slipped under the soft curve of her buttocks, fitting her to him. He filled her easily; their bodies conformed to each other's as a hand to a glove. Like a benevolent victor, he entered the hidden haven of her, delighted by her moist, velvety warmth. She was seized by a delicious weakness, overwhelmed by her urgent need.

She wrapped her legs around his waist, became one with the maelstrom tempo that animated him. All thinking ceased in Corinne as she merged into one flesh with him, rising higher and higher as the tempo increased. She held nothing back, her one goal to make her husband happy.

He made her happy in return.

They parted and lay side by side, their bodies spent. She experienced a floating sensation in the cool, peaceful room.

"You'll get cold," he mumbled, pulling the sheet and blanket gently over her and settling close beside her under the protective warmth. They lay together, contentedly drowsy, bodies touching lightly beneath the comfort of the silken sheet and cozy blanket.

Midafternoon sunlight faded into dusk. The dinner hour passed them unawares, and then the dusk yielded to moonlight, but as the silver light coming through the skylight bathed them, they awoke, refreshed, and made love again. Once Corinne teased him by referring to him as the Strawberry Kid, expecting his usual laugh. To her surprise, no laugh came.

The pale light of morning woke them with a blue haze that gradually changed to gold. Corinne stretched lazily, content with the hard, lean length of him close beside her in the wide bed. Filled with happiness, she slipped naked from the warm bed and went to the bathroom. Returning, she decided to organize the clothing spread out on the carpeted floor.

Corinne picked up each item, draping his apparel over the metal valet form in the corner. She pulled open the folding door of the closet to find a hanger on which to place her dress.

The light of the closet came on automatically when the doors were pulled open. A shock wave rippled through her. A revolver in a holster was hanging over the hanger that held Stan's gray suit jacket.

She turned, wide-eyed, toward the bed. Stan was sitting up in the bed, rubbing his eyes sleepily. His expression changed instantly when he realized she had seen the gun.

"Don't touch that!" he said quietly, leaving the bed and walking toward her, his movements lithe but cautious. He took his clothes from the metal valet and proceeded to drape them on hangers himself. He stood naked with his back to her. Her eyes drifted over the lean, muscular body she had loved for so many years. Suddenly she wondered if she had ever really known him at all.

"Stan, why do you carry a gun?" she asked, mystified.

Her eyes then came swiftly upward to the strawberry birth mark. Shock pierced Corinne like a sharp knife. The mark was over this man's right shoulder blade, an observation that had escaped her in the heat of passion because the mark was identical in color, size and shape to that of her husband's.

On Stan, the mark had been over the left shoulder blade.

A feeling of humiliation crept through Corinne as the man turned to face her. The sapphire eyes were coolly appraising; all tenderness was gone.

"Who in hell is Stan?" asked the naked stranger.

CHAPTER THREE

THE BRIGHT, CLEAR LIGHT of early morning illuminated suite 1802. Derek Moar stood in the sunlight on the balcony, which faced east to overlook Monument Circle, the curving brick one-way street that formed a circular frame for the commemorative spire that stretched three hundred feet in the air.

His troubled glance kept returning to the woman who sat on a chair, clad only in her raincoat. *Why doesn't she move? Why doesn't she talk?* he asked himself. Looking at her now, he felt strangely guilty without knowing why. The velvety-brown eyes were dull and lifeless as they stared, unseeing, at a futuristic steel-and-blue glass monolithic skyscraper that rose over thirty stories high.

He was afraid to leave her alone even for a second, fearful that she might throw herself over the railing. He had to crash that invisible wall she had drawn about herself and bring it tumbling down. Now he gave it a try.

"What is that building?" he asked, gesturing toward the building with which the woman seemed so absorbed. His stare was so intense, his expectation she would answer so strong that Corinne finally made a response.

"The Marotte Bank Tower."

"And that?" He continued to point.

"The United Life Building. Next to it is the Metro Health Plan building." The dam was finally breaking. She'd had to acknowledge his presence at last.

"The church there?" He pointed toward a spire that tapered toward a light blue heaven.

"Christ Church Cathedral." She sighed, weary with the interrogation.

"And that?" A squat, solid structure that hinted of crowds and bleachers had caught his eye.

"The new sports arena. And that's a department store over there, okay?" She pointed to a nearby building.

"Touché," he said, laughing. He couldn't help staring at her, couldn't help but notice that her white raincoat reflected the sunlight. Barefooted, the clean, fresh breeze playing with her tousled shoulder-length brunette hair, she seemed a beautiful waif in need of protection.

They were shrouded in silence, eighteen stories above the ground. To a man who lived in Chicago and was accustomed to the rumble of elevated trains and the dissonance of traffic, this place, with its absence of street noise and smog, was a wonderland. He knew traffic jams existed here—he had been in the middle of one when the cab had brought him in from the airport—but where were the impatient horns, the angry engines?

He gazed without embarrassment at the woman who sat as still as a sculpture. He felt as if they shared a small island high in the sky. It was a feeling he liked.

"What's your name?" he asked. *Tell me your sorrow,* he wanted to say, but didn't dare.

She gazed at him with eyes filled with sadness, as though it were difficult for her to speak. "Corinne," she answered. "Corinne Daye. That's D-A-Y-E. No one spells it correctly the first time." She gave a faint smile.

Her response filled Derek Moar with hope. He was neither a psychologist nor a social worker; just a former FBI agent, now a private investigator. Was she ill? Manic-depressive? She'd sure been turned on high when she'd come into the room yesterday afternoon. He had seen drug users, and he would swear she was not one. Her pupils had looked normal, and there had been no needle marks on her arms. How those arms could embrace. What warmth they contained—not for him, it seemed, but for someone named Stan.

He lifted his hands to the lapels of his suit coat. "Look, I'm sorry I'm not the man you mistook me for. Is there anything I can do to help? Do you need money, Corinne? If so, it's not the end of the world. I'll be glad to make you a loan."

She closed her eyes, and her face looked weary. Her head began to sink. Then she straightened, ramrod erect with pride. She looked straight at him. "No, thank you. What did you say your name was? I don't think we've been introduced."

Her remark was so incredible, considering their strenuous lovemaking, that words failed him. His hand went to the back of his neck, and he massaged it—something he did whenever he was troubled.

"Don't do that!" she cried, staring at him.

"What? What am I doing?"

"Rub your neck that way."

"Why not, for crissake?"

"Stan did that, too. Whenever he was concerned about a patient and he didn't think the patient would make it through surgery."

"Stan is a physician?"

"He was. He's...dead." The silence was strained.
"Stanford Daye was my husband."

He brought his hand slowly down to his side. He
didn't want to alarm her. Despite her natural beauty, her
dignity, the lady had to be crazy.

"You can't tell me from your husband?" He wondered which hospital he should call. There were five
telephones in the suite, including one in each of the two
bathrooms. He would be able to sneak a moment to
himself to get her help.

"You don't believe me," she said sadly.

"Oh, no it's not that. I haven't had my coffee yet,
that's all...."

"Please don't patronize me. I still don't know who in
the hell you are."

He hesitated for just a split second. "Douglas Johnson, vice president in charge of Development for Spurgon Corporation, San Francisco, California."

Her eyes rose to stare at him. They were calm and
appraising, not the eyes of a crazed woman out of touch
with reality, who couldn't distinguish between her own
husband and a total stranger. "You seem very proud of
that title."

His face grew warm with embarrassment. "Well—"
he shrugged "—I guess I am."

"I'd like some coffee, too, Mr. Johnson." She rose
from her chair. He tensed, watching her warily in case
she made a dash for the railing. "I have no intention of
jumping, Mr. Johnson. I'm not mentally disturbed."

He blinked several times and tried to figure out what
to say next. "I was informed that they serve breakfast
from a bar out in the hallway. Would you like some?"
His eyes appealed for cooperation.

"Thank you. I'd like something to eat very much. I'm hungry," she confessed.

"Room service is available at eleven. I'll order a nice lunch for us both then. Give us time to talk."

"Look, Mr. Johnson, you owe me nothing. I owe you nothing. Everything's squared. After a cup of coffee, I'll be happy to go. You won't be bothered with me again."

"We talk, okay?" He took her arm and led her from the balcony into the living room, closing the door to the balcony tightly behind him. "Just sit down at the table." He gestured toward a small round table topped with green marble, surrounded by four art deco upholstered dining chairs.

She obeyed. Seemingly aware of her bare feet for the first time, she stared down at them.

Derek hurried into the hallway, where an attendant filled two china cups with black coffee from a silver server and handed him a plate piled with fragrant, flaky breakfast rolls and pats of butter.

"Continental breakfast," he told Corinne when he placed the repast on the marble table.

"I know that," she said flatly, giving him a scathing look. His glance flickered to her left hand. The wedding band was either silver, white gold or platinum. The engagement diamond was the size of a headlight.

"Sorry."

"May I use your bathroom first?" she asked.

"Of course."

Since there were no windows from which to jump in the bathroom, Derek relaxed and enjoyed his coffee, saving the rolls until she could join him.

In only a minute or two, she was back, fully dressed but with her hair still uncombed. She looked perturbed.

"I see you're wearing the revolver."

"I feel undressed without it." He attempted a smile.

"I think I need that coffee!" She sat in a chair and drank the coffee in one long swallow, without taking a breath. Next she started on a roll, buttering it, and he felt much better. They ate together in companionable silence.

"I'll get us refills on everything," Derek offered, and he did.

When he came back the color had returned to her face. "Do you have a cigarette?" she asked.

"Nope."

"That's what I was afraid of." She frowned and leaned back in her chair. "If your name is Douglas Johnson, why is the name Derek Moar on the tag on your luggage?" she asked. The suitcase was next to the closet in the bedroom, but she had been too occupied to notice it last night. Only while dressing a few minutes ago had she noticed the tag.

He adopted a fixed stare. *Damn, how do I get out of this?* he wondered, stalling for time. Of all the crazy things, to forget to replace the name tag on his luggage with his alias. *Moar, you're slipping!* he berated himself silently. "I borrowed the suitcase from a friend," he said, trying to sound calm.

"Mr. Moar, I don't believe you." The look she gave him was unemotional. "I am not concerned with the nature of your little game. I am not a part of it." She rose to leave. "Thank you for your hospitality. I'll be leaving. What did you do with my purse?" Her gaze was sweeping the living room.

So that's the angle! he thought, stunned. The mind of the law enforcement officer began turning. Now it all made sense. He had been set up. She would accuse him of stealing her purse with all the family jewels in it. She would threaten to call the police and press charges unless he gave a huge amount of money, of course. Calling the police in would blow his cover for sure. *What an ass you are, Moar!*

"You didn't have a purse with you when you knocked at my door," Derek declared firmly. A muscle in his jaw throbbed. He no longer trusted Corinne. He'd never make the mistake Morey, his partner, had made on the raid in Chicago when bank robbers had been holding four bank employees hostage. Morey had trusted the wrong person, just once, and it had cost him his life and had almost cost Derek his leg.

The woman stared at him, a look of disbelief in her eyes. Then she frowned, as if trying to remember. Suddenly, recognition brightened her eyes, making them appear feverish. An expression of dismay took hold.

"Oh, no! The cab!" she whispered, her face ashen. "My credit cards, my driver's license, my keys, checkbook, business cards..." She stared at him, feeling helpless. Then she rushed to the living room telephone and punched a number in haste. Quickly he slipped into the bedroom and lifted the extension. He held his hand over the mouthpiece.

"Meg, thank God you opened up a few minutes early."

"Where the hell are you, Cory?" Meg complained. "You missed your three, four and five o'clock appointments yesterday. Three new clients, and you never showed. They were upset. I made up a story about your arm giving you trouble and you having to go back to the hospital as an outpatient—"

"Did they believe you?"

"Sure, why not?"

"Give yourself a raise in your next paycheck."

"How much?"

"Twenty dollars a week."

"I should have told a bigger lie for that amount. So where are you?"

"I'm at the Empire Suites," said Corinne. Astonished silence hung on the other end. "There's something I need you to do for me. Call the Urban Cab Company and ask if someone turned in my shoulder bag. You know which one I mean."

"The beige one with the black trim?"

"Yes. I took a cab from the airport to the Empire Suites around two. I left my purse in the back seat. Ask the dispatcher to contact the driver right away and send him to my office. Tell the dispatcher there's a nice reward for both of them and take the money out of petty cash. Cancel all my appointments for the rest of the day, lock up the office and bring the purse to me here. Suite 1802."

"You spent the night there? With whom?"

"You have to see for yourself. Just bring me my purse and keys. I left my rental car at the airport. I'll need you to take a cab to the airport and bring the car downtown to the parking garage while I work on the Hawkins brief in my office."

"Give me the telephone number there. I'll check with the Urban Cab Company and get back to you right away."

Corinne recited the number on the face of the telephone. "I'm so glad I can count on you, Meg. You always come through in emergencies. Hurry, please."

Corinne hung up, craving more coffee. She went into the hallway with both empty cups. She smiled at the attendant and asked for refills on the coffee. The white-coated employee was polite but gave her a knowing look.

When she returned, walking slowly with the filled cups, Derek was standing in the middle of the living room. His expression was inscrutable. "You're an attorney," he said in a flat voice.

"For the past eight years. You were listening on the extension. Shame on you." She placed both hot cups on the dinette table.

"It's my phone," he declared, continuing to stand until she had seated herself.

Could Stan have been one of a set of twins? The thought hit Corinne with such force that her hand trembled as she lifted the cup to her lips. *Had* Stan been adopted? But why would the Dayes have kept it such a well-guarded secret? It made no sense.

Except for the birthmark, it would have seemed more likely to Corinne that this man really was Stan and was lying to her. Yet... the way this man made love was somehow different. He held nothing back. He seemed so much more open and direct in his passion than Stan had ever been.

"Did my secretary's voice sound at all familiar to you?"

"Why should her voice sound familiar to me?"

"You might have known her once," said Corinne.

His sigh was one of frustration. "Look, I was born here, yes, but I left Circle City at the age of four. I don't even remember visiting Santa Claus in that department store building over there. How would I remember your secretary?''

"You were born here?" Corinne asked.

"Yes."

"What are the names of your parents?"

"David and Erna Johnson," he replied, giving the correct first names. "What are the names of your parents?"

She had to smile. The interrogation would not be one-sided. "Banbury. Charles and Crystal Banbury. He was in machinery and tools."

"He owned a manufacturing business, you mean?"

"That's what I said."

"Not exactly."

"*You* sound like the lawyer," Corinne said dryly, wondering why his expression changed suddenly. He looked apprehensive. "So you still want me to call you Mr. Johnson?"

"After last night Doug or Douglas would be more appropriate, don't you think?"

"Last night was nothing personal," she said stiffly.

"It wasn't? What could be more personal?"

Her face grew warm and the warmth crept downward to her neck, shoulders and chest.

"You're blushing, Corinne." He was amazed. He couldn't believe a modern woman knew how to blush.

"Do you mind terribly if I borrow your comb? I'd hate for Meg to see me this way."

"Sure." He grinned. "You're welcome to use my toothbrush, too." The look of reproach she gave him silenced him effectively.

He led her into the bathroom and handed her his comb and brush. He stood in the doorway and watched the long, full sleeves of her silk dress sway as her arms moved, watched the bosom of her dress lift and settle back into place over her full, upturned breasts. Her cleavage was subtly revealed at the base of the V neckline. His eyes slid from her lovely, womanly rear, which beckoned like a pear ripe for the plucking, to her lovely curved legs, trim ankles and slim feet, which disappeared into a pair of gray pumps.

He wanted her. Again. Not only her body but *her*. He wanted to embrace that energetic spirit, let that lava flow of passion warm his limbs and spur him to greater faith in his own worth.

Beneath that cool determination he sensed a tender, compassionate woman. *She makes Mitzie seem an inexperienced teenager by comparison,* he thought in surprise.

Corinne's arms were suspended in midair. The lapels of her dress gaped slightly. He glimpsed the lacy wisp of bra that stretched snugly around the full globes of her breasts. He felt a tightness in his groin, and his face betrayed his thoughts.

She was watching him in the bathroom mirror. She turned her head and looked directly at him with those velvet-brown eyes. His hopes soared. She put the comb down.

"No." Her silky voice softly filled the small room.

"No harm in thinking, is there?" Reluctantly his gaze released her. He turned away and returned to the living room. He felt uncomfortable about lying to her about his identity, but what choice did he have?

No one was supposed to know who he was or why he had come to Circle City. One slim lead—no, two leads really, since Matt Briggs was one—pointed to the fact that Circle City might be the base of a national counterfeit videotape operation, a possibility that Sam Shuster, head of the Video Software Marketing Society, had suggested. If that were so, Derek knew the FBI would jump in with both feet, because of the law Congress had passed in 1982 regarding copyright protection.

Derek had been surprised to be called to Hollywood to confer with the head of Metro Mega Studio, which was owned by the conglomerate called Spurgon Corporation. As a former FBI agent, Derek was the logical man to do the preliminary legwork, gathering data that Arnold Zinser, the head of the regional FBI office in Circle City, could use to obtain search warrants for retail video stores and video production houses.

Derek smiled to himself, a wry grin. He wondered if Arnie had put in a good word for him to get the assignment. They had had a good friendship going during the days of academy training.

"No harm in thinking at all," Corinne declared briskly, coming out of the bathroom. She was tempted to put through another call to Meg but decided not to rush her. "Last night was a mistake, that's all. A comedy of errors."

"I would hardly call it that," Derek exclaimed, hurt.

"No reflection on you, Douglas, of course. You were absolutely perfect. I'm just not a person who goes for one-night stands."

"Neither am I. Please call me Doug," he asked. The name Douglas grated on his nerves.

"May I please see your driver's license, Doug?" Corinne held out her hand with a quiet authority. He was taken aback but decided not to argue with her. Now that her shock had passed, she seemed a different person, one he liked even better. He reached into his pocket and drew out his wallet, then handed it over to her.

"You'd make a great cop, you know that?" he asked.

She was surprised by his reaction. She opened the wallet and studied the operator's license issued by the state of California to Douglas Johnson. The physical description matched. She memorized the San Francisco home address given. Then she slowly flipped through a bevy of credit cards, all issued to Douglas Johnson. If this was false ID, it was well done, the result of a great deal of trouble on the part of more than one person. She looked up in regret. He really wasn't Stan. She was both disappointed and relieved at the same time.

His facial expression was aloof. He knew he had her. "I told you. I had to borrow the bag from a friend and I forgot to remove the luggage tag," he said. As soon as she left, he would rip the damned thing off the handle of the suitcase.

"I'm sorry, Doug. Forgive me. I was trying to prove you were someone you're not." She sighed and returned to the balcony. Closing her eyes, she lifted her face to the warming sun. He pocketed the wallet, silently praising Don Jennings for doing such a good job in obtaining the identification. He stood in the opened doorway to the balcony.

"I'm not sorry, Corinne. Stan was a very lucky man." He was convinced she was greatly exaggerating the resemblance, but at the same time, he wondered if it were true that every living person bore a strong resemblance to someone else, someone totally unrelated to him or her. He wanted to know more about the circumstances of her husband's death—he wanted to know everything about her. If only there was more time!

"What do you do with Spurgon Corporation? Why are you here?" asked Corinne. Her voice was gentle, her manner accepting.

"I'm in charge of development. Spurgon is interested in diversifying further, in buying video retail stores, perhaps even a video production house. I'm here to check out such businesses in the Circle City area. Spurgon can pay a good price and is willing to keep present management and personnel, if we find well-run businesses that are good prospects."

"You mean profitable. A good bottom line." She chuckled. He was intrigued by the beauty of Corinne's face when she smiled. It glowed with a freshness, a vigor that had nothing to do with makeup. A longing to know her better began to stir in Derek.

"Of course, what else? Is there any other consideration?" he answered crisply.

"I guess not." She sighed. "Business is not my forte. I have a good law practice, a decent income. Also high overhead. I let my assistant, Meg, handle the books and write checks on the office account to pay bills. I want to be free to do legal research and trial preparation and counseling. That's where I'm strongest. I may have a prospect for you, if he's interested in being bought out."

"Who?"

"I'll have a talk with him and have him contact you here, okay? I'd rather not divulge any names at this point."

All five telephones rang in the suite. It was more a velvet murmuring than a metallic clatter. Corinne reached for the one beside the art deco sofa. "Do you want to get on the extension?" she asked Derek. He declined.

"Corinne Daye here."

"I found the purse," said Meg. "The driver just delivered it. I gave him a hundred dollars from petty cash. That's not too much of a reward, is it?"

"Heavens, no." As usual, Meg had done the right thing, thought Corinne.

"Nothing's missing. I checked the contents."

"Meg, that's great! I'll keep my head on straight from now on. Lock up the office now and bring me the purse. Then I want you to make the trip to the airport by cab to pick up my car and take it to the garage—"

"I insist you both be my guests for lunch. I'll call room service," Derek said, speaking loudly to catch her attention. Their gazes locked and held. His proved the stronger.

"Meg, we have a luncheon invitation. Don't stop for anything to eat on your way over here," said Corinne, subdued.

"Who is the generous man?" asked Meg.

"You'll have to find that out for yourself." As Corinne hung up, she realized she was very interested in getting Meg's reaction. Meg had worked for Corinne for two and a half years before the plane crash. Meg had seen Stan many times when he'd stopped by the office to meet Corinne.

Did I imagine the resemblance to Stan? Is my mind playing tricks on me? Corinne was worried. An objective reaction from Meg would answer the question.

"Meg will be here soon. The Marotte Tower is only a short walk from here," said Corinne. She returned to the balcony and leaned over the railing, basking in the sunlight. As Derek observed her silently through the opened doorway, the suite began to feel like home. Corinne's presence furnished that vital element.

He wanted to see her again as often as possible before he had to return to Chicago, his assignment completed. How he could get her to agree to it was now the question. Perhaps the secretary would prove an ally. He would try over lunch.

A firm knock sounded on the door. "I'll go." Corinne rose instantly from the chair and left the balcony, crossing the living room to open the door herself. Derek positioned himself next to the wall, behind the wet bar that separated the kitchenette from the living room. From there, he could observe Meg Krens before she became aware of him.

A woman slightly taller than Corinne stood in the doorway to the hall. He noted hair that was a cap of tight auburn curls, skin that was as fair as porcelain. Her lips were lightly reddened and shaped in a pouty cupid's bow. The beige suit Meg wore emphasized a well-proportioned figure. She was wearing one shoulder bag and carrying another one, which was lighter in color, with black trim.

Yet, despite Meg's obvious femininity, Derek sensed a toughness about her that puzzled him. His impression of her was that she was a well-sharpened knife encased in a most attractive sheath. The two women seemed an odd pair as he observed them conversing with each other, a study in contrasts. Corinne possessed a true inner strength, but he wouldn't have labeled her tough. She was much too compassionate.

"Everything is in your billfold. I checked. Nothing is missing. The driver was honest." The alto voice was firm, not soft. The emerald eyes were not soft.

"I want you to meet someone, Meg. Our host for lunch. He's waiting to order until we tell him what we want. Come on in," said Corinne. She looked expec-

tantly toward Derek and stepped aside. She held her
breath for Meg's reaction.

The eyes of Meg Krens fixed upon Derek and opened
wide in shock. Her pale complexion went ashen. The
cupid's-bow lips fell slack in astonishment, and she
sucked in a great gulp of air. She looked as if she had
encountered a ghost, and for an interminable length of
time, it seemed she was unable to speak.

"For God's sake! Stan!" she finally gasped. "Why
aren't you dead?"

CHAPTER FOUR

DEREK STOOD with Corinne's business card in his hand, staring down at it. Both women had left suite 1802 an hour ago. The dishes from lunch had been removed. The maid had been in to change the bed linen and clean the bathrooms. No trace of the attractive woman who had made such an impact on Derek remained, not even the scent of her perfume. He had only this card.

Derek turned the card over. On the back, Corinne had written her home address and telephone number. It was an invitation for him to call her at home. He felt encouraged.

The reaction of Margaret Krens when she had first seen him still puzzled Derek. It was naked fear—of seeing a ghost perhaps—but certainly of something else. Derek couldn't define the missing element. He just felt it in his gut, and the feeling bothered him.

Derek wandered out onto the balcony, strangely discontented. The balcony, the lovely rooms with the pastel wallpaper, the tasteful art deco furniture all seemed to be awaiting Corinne's return. He suddenly felt lonely. Standing in the shade that spread over the balcony in midafternoon, he felt the full impact of his solitary life. He felt a yearning—for roots, a place to call home. Most of all, it was a yearning for a lovely, intelligent, passionate woman with whom he could share every day of life.

He leaned on the railing with stiffened arms, feeling the rhythm of the downtown area moving below him. *But what do private investigators have to offer a woman?* he thought dejectedly. *Here today, somewhere else tomorrow.*

Corinne had made no secret of it. She hated guns. He felt the weight of his beneath his armpit, hidden under his jacket.

A subdued knock sounded on the door. Jolted from his reverie, Derek left the balcony and went to open the door. He looked down on a balding man who was about five feet eight or nine.

"Mr. Johnson?" asked the balding man, looking up.

Derek nodded. "Mr. Briggs?" he queried in return.

The shorter man nodded, glancing fearfully over his shoulder toward the closed doors of the elevator and the empty hall. He hurried into the room. Derek closed the door. Only when the little man heard the lock click into place did he visibly relax, extending his hand for the traditional handshake. The grasp was firm, the hand a bit pudgy.

"Doug Johnson," Moar introduced himself. "Do you think you are being followed?"

Briggs nodded, took out a yellowed handkerchief and wiped his damp forehead. He was overweight and had been hurrying.

"Sit down, Mr. Briggs." Derek gestured toward the beige sofa.

"Call me Matt." Briggs settled into a dining chair instead. "My wife didn't want me to come here. She thinks my turning in that SOB down the street to the Video Software Marketing Society will only lead to trouble." His voice was ragged. He was blinking rapidly. "She thinks organized crime might be involved in large-scale duplicating of videocasettes. You know, the big guys. What do you think?"

"Maybe so, maybe not. Organized crime gets blamed for everything these days. There are a lot of independent entrepreneurs engaged in felonies all over the world, Matt. Video piracy is a worldwide problem. Don't jump to conclusions. Come on, relax." Derek gave a winning smile. "I just need you to give me some information. How about a cold beer, Matt?"

The round face brightened. "Don't mind if I do, Mr. Johnson."

"Call me Doug. We're working together now, right?" Derek pulled out two cold cans of beer from the refrigerator under the counter in the kitchenette. After Corinne and Meg had left, he had made a quick trip to the stores on the basement level for a few essentials: beer, a bottle of Scotch, milk, breakfast cereal, bread and luncheon meat. He had also bought two packs of cigarettes and matches for visitors.

"Thanks." Briggs reached out a pudgy hand for the cold beer and opened the top. "Are you with the FBI?" The balding man sounded hopeful. He took a long sip and let out a satisfied sigh.

Derek frowned. "Where did you get that idea?"

"From the head of the VSMS, Sam Shuster. He's the one I talked to on the phone the day I called in my complaint about *Maxi Man* being available under the counter at a retail store down the street from my west-side store. Metro Mega hasn't even premiered it yet." The round-faced man talked in a nervous staccato.

"I'm a vice president at Spurgon Corporation. Sorry, Matt, I'm not with the FBI," said Derek.

"A VP?" Briggs raised his eyebrows. "Never had beer with a VP before."

"First time for everything," said Derek, smiling ghtly.

"Somebody had to steal a print of that film from Metro Mega to make illegal copies, right? Down the street from me, those illegal copies are selling like hotcakes." Briggs was wound up. Derek could tell this was his favorite subject. "They're selling lots of other stuff, too—counterfeit copies sold as authorized studio copies. They're asking only twenty dollars each! I gotta charge forty to eighty dollars for studio-authorized tapes if I make any profit. My customers are all going to the competitor down the street to do their buying. If this keeps up, I'll go bankrupt in a year!" Briggs complained. "And I run my two stores in accordance with the law. Where's the justice in that? I got a wife and two kids to support." Matt Briggs pulled a crushed cigarette package from his jacket pocket and thrust a finger inside. He cursed softly under his breath. Derek felt sorry for him. The man was tied up in knots.

"Here, Matt." Derek rose from the sofa and took two packs of cigarettes, different brands, and a pack of matches from one of the drawers in the kitchenette. He placed the items on the dinette table in front of Briggs. "Help yourself," Derek said. "Take what you want."

"Gee, thanks." Matt stared at both packs on the table. "Neither one is my favorite brand, but right now I don't care. My wife didn't want me to come here. She got all upset when Sam Shuster at VSMS called me back and I promised to talk to you." He snatched up a pack, opened it and pulled out a filter tip. He wet his lips, placed the cigarette in his mouth and turned the tip slowly. Derek stared, fascinated by the ritual. The older man's hands shook slightly as he struck a match and held the flame to the cigarette's tip. "Want one?" Matt asked, holding the pack toward Derek.

"No, thanks. I quit when I graduated from college," said Derek.

The overweight man inhaled slowly and closed his eyes. He seemed to relax. His eyes opened. He appeared absorbed in the abstract design of the pastel wallpaper on the living room wall as he spoke slowly. "I never made it to college. Had to go to work full-time right out of high school. My father was disabled. My mother was always laid up, first with one thing, then with another. You know how it goes." He didn't sound bitter. "Wasn't able to get married until I hit the mid-thirties. Great little woman, my wife. She always puts me first. You know what I mean? We got two girls, ten and twelve. You married, Doug?"

"Not yet," Derek answered with a half smile.

"When you find the right woman, you'll know. Believe me, you'll know," Matt said softly. He gave Derek a wink, then took another swig of beer. Derek was pleased Briggs was beginning to relax. "You got a view of downtown from there?" Briggs looked at the door leading to the balcony.

"Yes."

"Can I take a look?"

"Sure," said Derek, rising from the sofa. He walked to the terrace door and opened it wide.

"Hey, thanks." Matt Briggs almost smiled and rose from the chair, still clutching his burning cigarette and dripping beer can. Derek accompanied his guest onto the balcony and stood with his hands on the railing. The wind was cool now, and the sun was sinking in the west. The balcony was steeped in deepening shadows. The rooftops bore a golden glow and the glass walls of the skyscrapers reflected the blazing gold of the setting sun.

"Man, look at that, will you!" Briggs said in a tone of awe. "I've lived in Circle City all my life. Born and raised here. Wouldn't live anywhere else. The town never stops growing. Has a population of almost eight hundred thousand people now. Keeps getting better, too. Me, I just keep getting older." He looked at Derek and a wistful look passed over his round, full face.

A sudden compassion for the older man whose hands trembled when he lighted up seized Derek. "We all do, Matt. It's the price we pay for life. But, chances are, we get better, too, as we go along." Derek grasped Matt Briggs's shoulder and gave an encouraging squeeze in a gesture of camaraderie.

"I did the right thing when I called VSMS to report the guys selling the phony stuff, didn't I, Doug?" He spoke softly, as he gazed down on the cars moving around the circle, his brows furrowed with worry, his face glistening with perspiration.

"You mean, when you called to report to Shuster that a salesman named Tony had come to call on you? That this Tony had offered to furnish you with illegal copies at fourteen dollars a piece and wouldn't take no for an answer?" asked Derek, remembering the call that came from Don Jennings a few days after Shuster had made his report to the Metro Mega executives. It was that phone call that had involved Derek in this investigation.

"I told that Tony bastard to go fly a kite. 'I run a clean business, I don't break the law,' I told him. That SOB just laughed, like I was a real joker or something."

A steady breeze blew against Brigg's pant legs, making the bottoms strain forward, revealing socks that were not matched in shade. *He has trouble seeing colors,* thought Derek, who was beginning to like the man. "Tony left you a telephone number where you can reach him, didn't he?" he asked.

"Oh, sure. No address, though. He keeps stopping by every Monday morning, regular. He keeps saying 'You'll play ball one of these days, Matt.' 'Matt' he calls me! I never told the bastard to call me by my first name."

Briggs lunged through the doorway opening and went back into the suite. He swooped up the opened pack of cigarettes, and his hand shook when he lit one. *He's afraid of these people,* thought Derek. Maybe he was wise to be afraid. Yet Derek knew he had to ask Matt Briggs to go that one step farther that no law-abiding citizen should be asked to go.

Derek waited until the first cloud of exhaled smoke streamed from Briggs's nostrils before making his suggestion.

"Maybe you should play along with them, Matt. But play their game by *our* rules."

Light-colored eyes were staring at Derek. The flame on the match burned down almost to the end. Matt Briggs dropped the charred inch. It fell to the pastel carpet. Derek bent to pick it up before the carpet was singed.

"You and Shuster want me to tell this Tony 'okay'? You want me to place an order with him?"

"Yes, Matt. And we would like that transaction taped. We'll furnish you with the equipment and show you how to use it. It's easy to do."

"You want me to do... undercover stuff for you?"

"Yes."

Matt Briggs sucked furiously on the burning stick of tobacco. Smoke formed a wreath around his balding head. Derek was reminded of a volcano ready to erupt and had to suppress a smile. "My wife won't like this! Not one bit!" Briggs muttered.

"Then don't tell her. Don't worry her."

"You kidding? Keep something from my wife? You've never been married, that's for sure," Briggs muttered.

"You're the only link we have to them, Matt," said Derek, leaning forward on the marble table. His eyes were imploring the bald-headed man to show the courage Derek instinctively sensed in him. "By 1990, Shuster predicts one of every two American homes will have a VCR. That's fifty million VCRs. Unless we start combatting this abuse now, Matt, it will snowball into an avalanche that will wipe out every honest businessman like yourself and maybe seriously cripple the whole movie industry. This operation right here in Circle City may be a big one—duplicating here and distributing nationally."

Derek had good reason to believe this was the case, but he didn't want to worry Matt more at the moment. He was scared enough. Derek knew these boys could probably play rough.

"You want me to go along with them? And wear some kind of bugging equipment when Tony's around?" The pudgy hand that held the cigarette was trembling slightly.

"All I can do is ask you, Matt." Derek straightened and shoved his hands in his trouser pockets. "You have to volunteer. I won't blame you if you decide not to cooperate with us."

The pale eyes fixed on him. "Us? You mean, the FBI?"

"I personally know the head agent of the Circle City office. I have reason to believe he and his office will become involved."

Briggs was seized by a spasm of coughing. He held on for dear life to the cigarette burning between his fingers. "You...got...another beer? My...throat's dry," he gasped.

Derek opened another can of cold beer and thrust it into the empty pudgy hand resting on the marble table. Briggs took a series of long fortifying swallows. "You want me to call Tony and tell him I see the light, right?" A wry grin split the round face.

"When my missus finds out, I'll be seeing stars, that's what," he said. "I won't lie to her, understand? She deserves the truth. When I tell her I'm doing this for Uncle Sam, she'll go along with the idea. Not too willingly, but she'll go along. She's a great wife and a good mother, but she worries. You know how women are." He gestured with the hand holding the beer. "Or you'll find out, Doug, when you meet the right woman. You'll know she's the right one." Matt winked at Derek. "Go get your tape recorder. I'm ready to tell everything I know about the store down the street."

As Derek walked into the bedroom, he suddenly became aware of the odor of Corinne's perfume. It came from out of thin air. All he had to do was to think of her and there it was.

At the same moment, in her office, Corinne Daye picked up the telephone, ignoring the work sheets for the Hawkins brief spread out on her desk. The Hawkins trial was scheduled in only two days. Although it was an important case and Debra's future depended on the outcome, Corinne was having difficulty keeping her mind on her work. One idea nagged her. She had to give in to it. She phoned Kate and Chris Albert's number. Kate's cheery voice answered.

"Hel-lo."

"I want you and Chris to come to my place for dinner tomorrow night at seven o'clock," said Corinne. "It's very important, Kate! I apologize for the short notice. Please persuade Chris to ask another doctor to take calls for him until about ten." She held her breath. What if they already had another engagement they couldn't break?

"Let me check the calendar, Cory." There was a pause. "Tomorrow evening is clear. I don't know if Chris has something special on that isn't down here. I'll have to check with him. What's up?"

"You'll see for yourself. You both must come," said Corinne, tense. "Call Chris at the hospital right away, check with him and call me back soon as you can."

"What's the rush? Oh, Cory, it's a man?" She sounded pleased. "I'd love to meet him."

"Don't get your hopes up too high, Kate," Corinne said dryly, remembering all the occasions that Kate had encouraged her to begin dating again. "You may be in for a surprise! I'll wait for your call. I'll be here at the office until at least six."

"I'll track Chris down and call you before five. So long."

Corinne replaced the receiver slowly and stared at the sheets of paper spread over her desk and saw not one page of her hasty handwriting. Suspicions mingled with questions raced through her mind. Her thoughts kept returning to the one couple who had known Stan all his life, the one couple who had been good friends with William and Eileen Daye since Stan's birth.

She failed to notice that her office door had been eased open by three or four inches. On the other side of the door sat Meg at her desk in the reception room, typing in another brief on the computer keyboard.

Suddenly Corinne made an expensive decision.

She went to her personal file cabinet in her private office and took out a paperbound book titled Private Investigators, U.S.A. that had been published three years earlier. Her eyes slid down the columns of names. Derek Moar was not listed under San Francisco, Chicago or Los Angeles. She looked up from the thick paperbound book, puzzled. She bent her head again and her lustrous hair fell forward over her face. Her finger traced a line of names under the heading San Francisco. Holding the place with her finger, the book open, she returned to her desk and called a long-distance number.

"Shapiro here," a man's voice answered.

"Corinne Daye here, Mr. Shapiro, I'm an attorney in Circle City, Indiana."

"What can I do for you, Ms Daye?"

"Verify an address for me. Find out what you can about this man." She gave the name Douglas E. Johnson and the address and number she had memorized from his driver's license and had jotted down later.

"That address is out near Fisherman's Wharf, a good residential section—old homes converted to apartment buildings."

"Talk to the neighbors. Talk to the building manager. Talk to anyone you can. Find out what you can about Johnson and make it fast. Will you have time to do it?"

"Sure. You want a written report in the mail?"

"Of course. But give me the results by phone immediately. Call my home tomorrow evening between six and seven." She gave the man her home telephone number. "What do you charge?" She winced when she heard his hourly rate.

"You still want me to do the job?" asked Shapiro.

"Yes. I think this name is an alias. I also want you to check up on a Derek Moar. M-O-A-R. I don't have anything on him. They are the same man, I suspect."

"I'm on my way. Thank you for your business. I'll call you back." The line went dead.

Corinne hung up slowly, feeling an unexplained dread. She looked up, startled to see Meg standing in the doorway. "Yes? Are you done with those wills for Mr. and Mrs. Anderson?"

"Yes. You can call off Shapiro. I already have what you want," said Meg.

"What are you talking about?" Corinne was puzzled.

"I talked to the switchboard operator at Spurgon Corp," said Meg, leaning against the frame of the doorway.

"I didn't ask you to do that," Corinne said in wonder. The idea had not even occurred to her. Since Stan's death, Corinne had given Meg considerable latitude in making her own decisions in regard to digging up new information and pulling loose ends together. She and Corinne worked smoothly together as a business team. Corinne discovered her client load had doubled as a result, and fee revenue had more than doubled.

"I asked to speak to the secretary of Vice President Douglas Johnson. I gave a phony identification. She told me there was no secretary assigned to a man by that

name. He had no office. There is no man by that name
listed on the company's organizational chart. But that
name *is* listed on the monthly telephone list given to her.
She said she was supposed to tell anyone who called for
'Mr. Johnson' that he is out of town on business for an
undetermined length of time. Then she asked me if I
wanted to be connected with the office of the president.
I hung up.''

"A vice president who doesn't even have an office?
Or a secretary? Who isn't listed on the organizational
chart?'' echoed Corinne, her worst fears coming true.
The man who carried a gun had lied to her, and Corinne lacked all compassion for liars. If she caught a
client in a lie, she dropped him or her immediately, fee
notwithstanding.

"She told me more than she was supposed to, I think.
She hadn't been briefed yet.'' Meg's voice lacked
expression: it sounded wooden, almost mechanical.
"Who do you think he really is, Cory? How can he resemble Stan so closely? Do you think a plastic surgeon
did it for some reason?''

"Not unless he had a plastic surgeon change the location of the birthmark on his back, too,'' Corinne said
grimly. "It's on the opposite shoulder blade.''

"So you've hired a gumshoe in Frisco named Shapiro to find out what your precious Mr. Johnson-Moar
really is up to. I bet he won't come up with as much as
I did with one three-minute phone call.''

Corinne stared at Meg's composed face, aware for the
first time of the light scattering of freckles over the
bridge of her nose and cheeks that makeup hid so well.
"Give yourself another twenty-dollar-a-week raise,'' she
said. "You earned it today.''

Corinne marveled at what a treasure she had found in Meg. And though she hated to lose Meg as her assistant, Corinne knew she had the potential to be so much more. She deserved to be an attorney.

"As soon as you finish with your evening division classes at Butler and get your degree, I'll give you a recommendation letter to IU's law school. Keep up your grades. I'll pay your tuition to law school. When you finish, I'll take you in as a junior partner."

A slow smile crept over Meg's face. "Sounds good to me, Cory. Daye and Krens, Attorneys at law. But be careful. Don't let that carbon copy of Stan work you. He's here for no good reason, I'll bet. I don't trust him."

Corinne's body went taut immediately. The ache in her breasts, the slightest movement of clothing on her skin reminded her of the night she'd spent with the mystery man. She was left stripped of peace.

"You know what I think? I think he's really Stan," Meg said softly, "playing a trick on us."

"Oh, come on, Meg! That's the craziest thing I ever heard!" Corinne shouted angrily. Meg retracted hurriedly and Corinne went to the door, slammed it shut and locked it. She resumed work on the brief but her mind was in a state of chaos after Meg's whispered suggestion. She paced the floor, awaiting Kate's call. Soon it came. Meg was stiff and aloof when she announced who was on the line.

"We accept for tomorrow evening, Cory. One provision. Chris says he can't be at your place before seven-thirty," Kate said cheerfully.

After getting off the phone with Kate, Corinne called the number of suite 1802, tense but thankful when Douglas-Derek answered. "Please come to dinner at my home tomorrow evening, seven o'clock, Doug.'' She gave a detailed description of how to find her place on Stemple Road, a heavily wooded residential section in the far northeast part of the city, close to the county line. She hung up, wondering if Meg had listened in on the conversation. The possibility disturbed her.

Derek had noted the tension in Corinne's voice. Matt Briggs had left a few minutes earlier. Derek wondered what had happened since noon to make her extend the unexpected dinner invitation.

Apprehension filled Derek. The last time he'd felt like this, he'd still been with the FBI. He and his partner, Morey had participated in an attempt to free four hostages being held by a pair of bank robbers. Morey had been killed on the spot by automatic rifle fire, and Derek had been wounded in one leg, which had resulted in a hospital stay and eventually in dismissal from the Justice Department for reasons Derek regarded as not exactly fair.

He considered calling Corinne back with an excuse. He wasn't sure if he wanted to go to dinner after all. But instead, he went out to rent a car. He wanted too much to see her again.

DAY WAS SINKING into a deep purple dusk over Stemple Road. A brick trilevel that had been built in the 1950s by Corinne's parents nestled snugly amid ten acres of trees and was bathed in mauve twilight. A sunset breeze whispered through dense, green outstretched branches.

A welcoming light shone through the window in the kitchen downstairs. In a shallow roasting pan in the oven rested four stuffed cornish hens, and Corinne was checking on them. Penny, an undersized black-and-white Boston terrier, sat close to her, ears raised and expectant, ready to pounce on any scrap of food that dropped to the kitchen floor.

She inhaled the sweet fragrance of the fruit-and-nut stuffing deeply. Oven heat toasted her face. She glanced at the Chinese steamer sitting on top of the electric range and she tested the broccoli with a fork. It was tender and hot. The baked potatoes, wrapped in jackets of aluminum foil, lay in a round pan. A green salad was hidden away in the refrigerator along with the cheesecake she had picked up on the way home from the office.

The wall clock read 7:25. Derek Moar, alias Douglas Johnson, was overdue by twenty-five minutes. Corinne was not impressed.

When the telephone rang, she almost dropped the basting spoon. She shoved the baking pan filled with the small golden birds back into the oven, turned the temperature dial to the lowest setting, dropped the spoon into a dish and hurried to the telephone in the front hall.

Although she no longer trusted the mysterious Mr. Moar, she hoped fervently that he was not calling to express his regrets that he could not attend. Corinne intended to solve the puzzle of his identity, and she thought she already had the answer. It was one she could not quite believe. She hoped the Alberts would prove her wrong.

"The Daye residence."

"Shapiro here. Sorry I'm reporting so late, Ms Daye. The job took longer than I thought it would."

"I'm expecting guests any minute. What did you find out?"

"The address you gave me is an empty apartment. The name Douglas Johnson is on the mailbox, all right.

When I talked to the building manager, he said the apartment had no furniture. No one has moved in yet and it's been three weeks. The management offers weekly maid service as a part of the deal, and the maid told him the apartment was empty.

"He said someone connected with Metro Mega Studios contracted for the apartment on a monthly basis, putting it in the name of Douglas Johnson. A Metro Mega representative even signed the lease. I had to motivate the manager with a C-note to find out that much. Each month's rent has been paid by a check from Metro Mega, too. The manager said he never saw anyone named Johnson. He thought the whole deal sounded funny, since those apartments really cost something. It's a good address. Corporation executives live there. Want me to look up Johnson through other agencies? Do you want me to find out if he has an arrest record?"

"No. You've told me all I need to know," Corinne said, her worst fears confirmed. The man was a fraud. "Send me a bill for your services. You have my address."

"I'll need to be reimbursed for the C-note, too."

"Of course. Thank you for your help, Mr. Shapiro."

"Feel free to call on me again anytime—"

Corinne hung up, too upset to fear being thought rude. Who was this man, this replica of her husband, who had assumed a phony identity? Was he a member of an organized crime syndicate, a con man out to fleece unsuspecting lambs? He claimed to work for Spurgon Corporation, and it looked like Spurgon was trying to cover up for him. Why?

In her frilly white apron covering a long-sleeved apricot-colored silk dress that gleamed in the light, Corinne leaned against the wall and buried her face in her hands. A tremor passed through her. She pictured Stan's look-alike, the tall man with probing blue eyes, a slow magnetic smile, a resonant voice that brought shivers of pleasure washing over her, and a damnable mustache. Although he seemed a copy of Stan, he wasn't. There was much in his manner that was different.

The pounding of the brass knocker on the front door brought Corinne back to her plans for the evening. They were devious plans, but he had been devious also. "Fight fire with fire" had been Corinne's mother's favorite expression. Now Corinne intended to do just that.

At the sound of the door knocker, the black-and-white dog zoomed into the hall from the kitchen and let out a series of high-pitched barks. "Quiet, Penny," muttered Corinne as she untied her apron and pulled it off. She unlocked the new dead-bolt lock—she had decided to follow Sergeant Master's advice—and opened the door.

Her heart skipped a beat. She felt familiar sapphire eyes sweeping over her. "You look beautiful," he said, a smile of longing deep in his eyes as they looked into hers.

"So you did come..." With an effort she made her body go through the usual social motions. "Come in." She couldn't force herself to call him Doug and wondered what she would say to him until the Alberts arrived.

Then Penny saved her. Staring up with alert black eyes at the tall stranger towering over her, she went for his ankles. He froze and eyed the dog distrustfully. She sniffed his ankles, the hem of his trousers and his polished wing-tip shoes, her snub black nose touching his clothing.

To Corinne's amazement, Penny failed even to bark or growl as she usually did with strangers. Instead, she raised herself up on skinny hind legs, in her standard begging position. Her small body, her intent black eyes pleaded for the tall man to pick her up.

"What does she want?" asked Derek, not trusting the terrier enough to take his eyes from her.

"She wants you to pick her up," Corinne answered, feeling faint. In the six years of Penny's life, the only people the dog had ever allowed to lift her without a snarling protest had been Stan and Corinne. She had bitten everyone else who'd tried.

"I don't pick up strange dogs," the man said flatly.

"Stan and I are the only two people Penny ever allowed to pick her up. She can bite."

"I don't like dogs that bite," he said irritably. "That's a Boston terrier?"

"Yes."

"A puppy?"

"No, she's full grown. Six years old."

"Why is she so small?"

"Penny was the runt of the litter. Pedigreed, however. When we brought her home she fit right into the palm of my hand. She won't grow any bigger than she is now. Let's go into the kitchen." Corinne's eyes clung to the man's angular face, and they pleaded, *Drop the pretense, Stan, admit who you are. You didn't fool Penny.*

They walked toward the brightly lighted kitchen that Corinne had remodeled when she and Stan were married. Now it was paneled in wood and contained a small breakfast room off at one side.

"I did some checking up yesterday. Or rather, Meg did. You don't even have an office at the Spurgon Corporation headquarters. In fact, the girl on the switchboard didn't even know who you were." She watched Derek's face drain of all warmth and felt a victory. "The other couple should be here any minute. Would you like a drink? There's Scotch and the mixings for martinis up in the cupboard and there's wine in the fridge."

"Look...I can explain. If we could just be alone for a while..." stammered Derek, following behind her. He had not expected his identity to be challenged so soon. As they walked into the kitchen, they heard the sound of the dog's nails on the gleaming wood floors. "No liquor, thank you. I smell coffee. May I have a cup while we wait?" Derek asked, fighting apprehension.

He was wearing a different suit tonight, a dark navy pinstripe, and a maroon tie bearing a pattern of irregular flecks of silver. Although the body in the suit was impressive—long-legged, slim in the hips and wide in the chest and shoulders—the suit was not up to the standard of elegance Stan always demanded, Corinne thought.

"Surely. Help yourself. Get a cup out of the cupboard," said Corinne, opening the oven door. The heat rose in waves to meet her face.

He stood in the middle of the kitchen, looking around helplessly. "Which cupboard? Where do you keep the dishes?"

"You really don't know?" Corinne felt almost angry. She walked to the cupboard, opened it and pulled out a ceramic mug with an earth-tone glaze. The mug had been Stan's favorite.

Derek failed to recognize the cup that she handed to him. He walked to the automatic drip coffee maker and filled the mug with steaming black coffee. His face looked troubled. He glanced at the dog who was up on her hind legs again, doing a balancing act as she walked two steps forward.

"Does she have to follow me around?" he asked irritably.

"Stan used to slip her something to eat whenever he was in the kitchen. He taught her that begging trick."

"I'm not Stan!" he protested heatedly, on the razor's edge of losing control.

"I guess you're not," Corinne said sadly. For the first time since she had set eyes on the man in the airport terminal, she accepted that truth emotionally. "Stan loved Penny." Corinne bent and gathered the warm canine body into her arms protectively and stood up. "I'll put her in the den while we eat so she won't upset you." Penny snuggled against Corinne's body, enjoying the ride, her front paws on Corinne's forearm.

As Corinne passed the front door, she heard the bell sound its three-toned musical chime. With Penny still in her arms, Corinne stopped to open the door and was grateful to see Kate and Chris on the doorstep, yet at the same time regretted that she had probably let them in for an unpleasant evening.

Penny let out a loud bark and Chris looked pained. "I told you the mutt doesn't like me," he said to his wife as they came in. "Why don't you grow up, mutt?"

Corinne offered her cheek for Kate to kiss. Kate extended two fingertips to lightly massage the dog's head between the ears, where a black dot the size of a nickel stood out against the white fur like a Hindu cast mark.

"She remembers me," said Kate with a smile.

"Hang up your coats," said Corinne, nodding her head in the direction of the hall tree. "I'm putting Penny out of harm's way in the den."

She walked down the hallway, and Chris's voice rang in her ears, "Somebody else is scared of the dog, too, I see." Turning on the light in the den, Corinne gently set the dog on her feet and closed the door.

"Who's here?" asked Kate in a conspiratorial whisper when Corinne returned to the entryway. The nurse's eyes gleamed with delight as she glanced around the immaculate living room filled with contemporary furniture. "There's a man in the kitchen. I noticed his back through the window as we drove up. It must be serious if you want us to give our okay."

"The situation is . . . not what you think," muttered Corinne, compressing her lips into a straight, thin line. One logical possibility would explain the whole mystery of the man in the kitchen: Stan had a brother he never knew about. A twin. And since the Alberts had known Stan's parents since before his birth, she suspected they knew a lot more about Stan than they had ever chosen to reveal, either to Stan or to her. The test would come this evening. Corinne was not looking forward to it.

"Bring him on!" whispered Kate, smoothing a wayward lock of her silver hair. "I'll be the judge of that."

"Remember, you asked for it," whispered Corinne to Kate. A man's measured step moved across the kitchen floor and toward the living room. He paused in the doorway.

Corinne's eyes fastened on Kate. She saw the older woman stiffen and stare and watched her lower lip fall slack in disbelief. Chris Albert responded, too, his hands coming out of his pockets as he took a step backward. Corinne saw Kate turn to her husband, a rare defiance hardening the soft curves of her gently lined face. But she didn't hear her friend whisper, "Chris, for heaven's sake, how could you have been so wrong? You said the other baby wouldn't live longer than a week or two!"

Chris Albert's gray eyes were transformed into flint, flashing sparks of warning to effectively silence his wife of thirty-two years. "Watch what you say!" he muttered in a controlled voice so low that neither the man standing in the doorway to the living room nor their hostess could hear.

"Kate, Chris, I'd like you to meet Douglas Johnson," said Corinne. There was no need to embarrass the man about his false identity in front of strangers. She'd go along with the game for now.

CHAPTER FIVE

OVAL FLAMES STRETCHED HIGH over the tall red-orange tapers and swayed slightly in hypnotic movement. The candlelight glow bathed the faces of the four silent people seated around the Scandanavian teak dining table. On each snowy-white china plate ringed with silver there was a cornish hen, a tender baked potato wrapped in aluminum foil and some steamed broccoli.

Corinne sat at one end of the table while Chris sat in Stan's place at the other end. The stranger sat in half shadows, in the guest's place to Corinne's left, across from Kate. They all concentrated on their food and made no attempt at conversation. Derek Moar was obviously tense, and Chris was grimly silent. Corinne missed the usual display of Chris's dry wit and his jokes about hospital procedure.

Kate began speaking in a bright, clear voice, filling the conversational vacuum. "What is your business in Circle City, Mr. Johnson?" Her lips were drawn into a forced smile and her eyes were almost feverish with brightness.

"I'm vice president in charge of Development for Spurgon Corporation," he answered, looking uncomfortable. "I'm here to investigate profitable video retail stores and video production companies for the purpose of buying. Spurgon is interested in diversifying more widely and plans to open a chain of retail video stores in ten states.''

"Spurgon is already highly diversified. I own some shares. They own a motion picture company, don't they?'' asked Chris, sounding distant.

"Yes, sir. Metro Mega Studios.''

"Your task is an ambitious project,'' Kate commented.

"A lot is riding on its successful completion, ma'am—for many people,'' Derek answered dryly.

"Where did you grow up, may I ask?'' Kate persisted.

"I was born here in Circle City, but I moved with my parents to Chicago when I was four.''

"You were an only child?''

"Until I was six. Then my mother gave birth to my sister, Virginia. I think Virginia was a bit of a surprise.'' He gave a wry grin.

"Why?'' Kate asked quickly.

"Mom and Dad seemed so...surprised. They were happy—don't misunderstand me. They just acted as if they couldn't believe Mom was pregnant. Perhaps she had a hard time when she had me, so they were afraid to try for any more.'' Derek gave a forced smile and reached for the wineglass beside his plate.

A meaningful glance passed between Kate and Chris Albert. Derek sipped his wine.

"Did you go to college, Mr. Johnson?'' Kate asked.

"Northwestern.''

"Your major was Business Administration, I presume?''

He hesitated for a fraction of a second and said, "Of course,'' looking uncomfortable.

You can't lie worth a damn, mister, thought Corinne. *I could make mincemeat out of you on a witness stand.*

"What is the day of your birth, Mr. Johnson?" asked Kate sweetly.

"November first. Twelve-oh-four in the morning to be exact." Derek seemed slightly bewildered at the question.

Chris choked, exploding with an attack of coughing.

"I bet your father is tall like you," Kate said to Derek, barely acknowledging her husband's distress.

"Not really." Derek smiled, and his face betrayed his deep affection for David Moar. "Dad is about five eleven, plenty tall enough. He's a heavyset man. He used to be a wrestler in high school."

"So tell me, Douglas, how is it a handsome man like you hasn't been snatched up yet?"

Derek gave a wry grin. "Well, I don't really know, ma'am. I've dated since my junior year in high school. I lived with a woman for two years." He glanced up quickly at Corinne to assess her reaction. "I assumed Mitzie and I would marry one day, but she found herself a Chicago millionaire instead. I couldn't compete with that."

"A *wonderful* dinner, Cory!" Chris's voice was artificially warm as he praised their hostess, attempting to change the course of the conversation. "You cook as creatively as Kate does. What a delicious blend of flavors in the stuffing."

"Thank you, Chris. I hope you all have room for dessert," Corinne said, rising from her chair. She circled the table, carefully gathering up the dinner plates. She was embarrassed to discover her tall mystery man was following close behind her, helping to clear the table. It was an act Stan would never have considered performing, especially in front of other people. But then, his family had had the services of a professional housekeeper, thought Corinne, seeking to excuse him. Larger families of limited means encouraged children to assume chores. Derek followed her into the kitchen, both hands loaded with dishes.

"How long have those people been married? Do they always act like that?" he asked. He thought the doctor seemed sullen, and the woman, though nice, was trying too hard to be agreeable.

"Thirty-three years," Corinne answered stiffly, disturbed that he was standing so close. She wanted to reach out to touch him. She suppressed the urge. He was devious and a liar, even if he was a replica of Stan, and he carried a gun.

Quickly she pulled the cheesecake out of the refrigerator and cut it into wedges. She placed them on dessert plates and loaded the plates onto a tray. She resolved to have it out with Kate tomorrow. Corinne was certain Kate and Chris knew something about this man and they were trying to hide it.

After the wedges of creamy cheesecake had been consumed, they all left the dining room and went to the den to enjoy after-dinner coffee. Chris had loosened up enough to tell a humorous incident that had befallen his older brother, a pediatrician practicing in Fort Wayne.

"I envy you, Dr. Albert. More than anything, I've always wanted to have a brother," said Derek, pausing in the doorway to the den to let Kate precede him. Kate gave him a stricken look. She laid her hand gently on Derek's arm.

Corinne was puzzled by the change in Kate and Chris. The transformation had begun the moment they had set eyes on Derek Moar. She could feel a hostile current sparking between them. Her suspicions seemed credible now. But she still couldn't believe that Eileen Daye had been so expert in lying all these years. She intended to force the truth from them, but it hardly seemed appropriate to do it in front of this man. The effect on him could be disastrous.

"What a wonderful place to relax!" Derek Moar's voice was full of appreciation as he looked around the den, with its crackling fireplace, leather sofa and comfortable chairs. He let his eyes roam freely from the desk by the window to the walls lined with books, some of which had faded gold lettering. This was the type of house in which he felt comfortable.

"This, the master bedroom and the kitchen are the only rooms we remodeled after we were married. I kept the rest of the house exactly as it was when my mother died, several years before Stan and I married. This house meant so much to her. My father had it built for her when the company he owned was doing well. Then the profits began to drop and the company ran into serious trouble. Of course, the fact that his comptroller was embezzling company funds didn't help the financial situation, either."

"He didn't live long after the company went into receivership, did he, Cory?" Kate's voice was gentle.

"No. He became depressed and he had a heart attack while I was at IU. He didn't live through the attack, as you know, and mother took ill shortly after."

"Influenza, wasn't it?" asked Kate.

"It started out that way. She kept declining and finally consented to tests. By then her condition was inoperable. She had a malignant tumor. So this house and the land were my inheritance. I was able to borrow heavily on it to pay my law school expenses in Circle City. Stan and I borrowed more to do the remodeling after we married. We called the house our honeymoon trip. Then I set up practice and had to start paying off the loans. Oh, boy!'' she sighed. ''What a tight squeak that was.''

''The stocks Bill bought for Stan while he was growing up helped, didn't they?'' Chris asked. ''I assumed Stan sold them to equip his office when he started up his practice.''

''Yes, the stocks were a great help. We were very glad Dad had thought ahead,'' said Corinne.

''Do you need any help in the kitchen?'' Derek asked abruptly. This casual talk of money was making him feel anxious. He had worked while he attended Northwestern, and a scholarship from an association of truckers had helped with his tuition. His father had never owned stock in his life.

''No, thank you,'' answered Corinne, embarrassed. Stan had rarely helped her in the kitchen, and she did not know to respond to offers from a male. ''I'll be right back.'' She left the room and returned in a few minutes, carrying a large tray holding a chafing dish and sundry ingredients.

''Ah, café brulot, my favorite. Cory, you are a sweetheart,'' said Chris, his stern face brightening. She was silently grateful, hoping a mood change in him would save the evening.

In the chafing dish bowl Corinne placed a cinnamon stick, whole cloves, orange peel and lumps of sugar and topped it all with brandy. She lit the candle beneath the chafing bowl. ''It will be ready in a moment. I'll bring in the pot of coffee from the kitchen.''

When Corinne returned with the pot of hot strong coffee, she was astonished to see Penny standing in Derek's lap, her small body stretched upward, her front paws on his chest. Her flattened black nose came close to Derek's chin. She was giving him a swift, sure lick on his cheek while gazing up at the man's wary face with her dark, bulging eyes.

"That's the way Penny used to act with Stan," said Kate in a small, soft voice. "She misses him."

Derek lifted his large hand, hesitated and brought it slowly down to settle on the animal's smooth, short-haired back. He ran his hand slowly from Penny's neck to her rounded rump that lacked a tail.

Corinne closed her eyes momentarily, imagining his touch. Her back tingled. Her breasts suddenly ached.

"With that flat nose, she's so ugly, she's cute," said Derek, gazing down into the small dog's eyes. For the first time that evening, he smiled.

Chris turned away from the scene abruptly and stared into the dancing flames. His arms were crossed over his chest, and his lined face looked stern. Corinne ignited the mixture inside the chafing bowl with a lighted match, and Chris did not even react. She stirred the mixture with a ladle and slowly added the hot coffee. "It's ready now." She poured the café brulot carefully into demitasses.

Chris mumbled his thanks for the coffee but remained standing while holding his cup and saucer. Corinne banished the dog from Derek's lap so he could drink his coffee in peace. She secretly resented Penny's wholehearted acceptance of someone who was not Stan. It seemed a betrayal.

"Delicious as always, Cory," Kate praised her.

Several minutes passed while they all stared past Chris's back, into the fire. Suddenly Kate moved, as if by impulse. She rose to her feet and pulled a snapshot album from a shelf beneath the cabinet on which the tray sat. Before Corinne could stop her, she handed the album to Derek.

"Would you like to...meet Stan?" Kate asked, handing the album to him.

"Kate!" Chris protested. Too late. Derek was opening the album that was a record of a camping trip Stan and Corinne had taken to Yellowstone National Park.

Derek frowned as he turned the pages slowly, his attention focused on his own likeness gazing back at him. He looked at Stan with his arm around Corinne; Stan and Corinne on horseback; Stan with his shirt off, his razor in hand, and shaving lather and a surprised look on his face. They were always smiling, always happy, like newlyweds on their honeymoon. A hot jealousy gripped him.

Derek closed the album and looked up at Kate. The distress on his face could not be disguised. He turned to face Corinne. "I didn't believe you when you told me yesterday how much I resembled your husband. I thought you and Meg were exaggerating. I feel as though it's myself I'm seeing in these pictures. How is it possible?" There was a shocked bewilderment in his voice as he laid the album on the floor beside the Scandinavian leather chair.

"Stan longed for a brother, too, Doug, just as you did. He was the Dayes' only child. Yet Stan wanted no children of his own. Sometimes we argued—" Corinne hastily corrected herself "—discussed the matter after we married. It was the only running battle between us. I tried to persuade Stan I could handle a career and be a mother, too, by paying a housekeeper. But he said he didn't want the responsibility of a child.''

Chris set his cup and saucer on the fireplace mantle. ''I have to call the hospital. I have a patient in the labor room. I'd better check on her. I'll use the telephone in the kitchen.'' He went through the doorway quickly, closing the door of the den behind him, as if to escape.

Kate sat staring at her hands clasped in her lap. Her attractive face was pensive. Finally, she lifted her head and spoke to Derek. Her voice was calm but seemed tinged with regret.

''It just isn't fair. All these years, you two kids living apart, not even knowing of each other's existence. Chris and I are partly to blame. I feel responsible.'' She sighed. ''My husband may never forgive me for telling you what's been buried so long, but my conscience won't let me sleep tonight if I carry on this charade any longer.''

''Tell me what, Mrs. Albert?'' asked Derek apprehensively.

''The resemblance between you and Stan is natural for identical twins. Mirror-image twins, at that,'' answered Kate. She took a deep breath, as if to brace herself. Her voice was even and steady, and she talked slowly. ''Eileen Daye was unable to conceive a child. Her tubes were blocked. When you were born, she and Bill were in Sweden, where Bill was doing postdoctoral studies. A woman came to my apartment. She was already in labor. It was a cold, rainy Halloween. She asked me to help her. I couldn't turn her back out into the street in the rain when she was sick, could I? She was in an early stage of pneumonia, had no physician and had only sixty dollars to her name. She begged me to help her deliver. I heard two fetal heartbeats and I was terrified one or both might be in the breech position. So I called Chris—that was before we were serious about each other—to come to help me."

"One of those babies was...me?" asked Derek, staring at Kate in disbelief.

"You came last, at 12:04 to be exact. Stan—Edward was the name on the birth certificate—came first, before midnight, hale and hearty, yelling up a storm as soon as Chris smacked him on his little bottom. You, son—" she looked at Derek with a maternal tenderness "—Chris could hardly get you to start breathing. When you were born, the placenta was wrapped around your neck and your skin was bluish. Your reflexes weren't normal. Chris thought you were a goner for sure. Or, at least, brain damaged. He called the ambulance to pick you up and take you to General Hospital."

Corinne leaned forward. "General Hospital? Why not Presbyterian?"

Kate looked uncomfortable. "General Hospital was where the charity cases went."

"I see." Derek's jaw tightened. His face registered shock. "I presume my...mother was not married."

Kate clenched her lips into a tight line. "No, she wasn't. But Helen was a very sweet girl. Sweet and pretty. She didn't want her mother to know she was pregnant. She thought the shock of it might kill her. Her mother was not well." Kate sighed. "And you have to remember, social attitudes were a lot different thirty-four years ago. Then it was very rough on young women who bore children out of wedlock in Indiana. Both mother and child were ostracized. Helen did not want that kind of life for her sons."

"So what did she do? Put us up for adoption?" A muscle was throbbing in Derek's jaw as he leaned forward in the leather chair, ignoring Penny, who was pressing against his ankle in search of attention.

The clock on the mantel struck ten times, the clear, golden tones humming in the tense atmosphere of the den.

Corinne sat stunned, unable to believe that the Dayes were truly not Stan's natural parents. Eileen had told such a good story to all her friends—about how she wanted to keep her pregnancy in Sweden a secret and how she had gone to her mother's house to have the baby delivered at home. She had made it all sound credible—the great lie—and no one had questioned it when she appeared in Circle City after a year, smiling and happy, with a handsome infant son in her arms.

"Chris knew William Daye only slightly. He knew the Dayes had consulted a gynecologist about infertility— Chris was completing his residency requirement in gynecology at Presbyterian at the time. He knew Dr. Daye was in Sweden. Bill Daye was already well established professionally in this town. I think Chris was out for brownie points with him, but he was also pleased to be able to help newborns. He found out where to reach Bill in Stockholm and called him from my apartment to tell him there was a mother willing to let him adopt her newborn twins. Bill's attorney was to handle all the details."

"Then the Dayes knew about me?" asked Derek, stunned.

"Yes...but Chris had to be honest, Doug. I overheard the conversation. Chris told them he didn't think your chances for survival were very good and that you might be mentally retarded. He gave them his professional opinion. Eileen…didn't want a baby that wasn't perfect. You know how she is, Corinne.'' Kate's voice dropped to a whisper.

''A perfectionist. Stan had to fight impossible demands all his life,'' Corinne said bitterly.

''Then how did my folks find me? Did Dr. Albert know my folks, too?'' Derek's eyes were pleading for Kate to tell him something of merit about himself.

''No, he didn't. I don't know how they found out about you. Chris was doing his residency then and he didn't follow up on you at General like he should have. He assumed you had died, I guess. You probably entered the state welfare channels and your parents found you through an agency.''

The silence was forbidding.

''How do I find out who my real parents are?'' Derek asked.

''Adoption records are sealed in the State of Indiana. Only a judge can open them, and he has to have very good cause to do so. It rarely happens.'' Corinne spoke slowly, in a daze. She cast a worried glance at Derek. He looked stricken, abnormally pale. His eyes were wide and staring. She felt guilty and also felt pity for him. She had inadvertently set him up for this nightmare. She hadn't expected Kate to open up before him and confess all. She had only wanted to force Kate's hand so that she would bring out her confession in private.

''I've kept in touch with Helen, your mother,'' said Kate. ''Every year at Christmas we exchange letters. She married two years after having you boys, then was widowed. Recently she remarried. She's living in Philadelphia. I can give you her address if you like. I think she would be thrilled to see you.''

"Did she tell you my father's name?"

"No. It was not on either birth certificate. Only your name. Edmund Hersh. And hers. Helen Hersh," said Kate. When she saw him slump forward and bury his head in his hands, her face took on a look of distress.

"More coffee, Doug? How about you, Kate? There's another cup left. I can't toss it down the drain. Somebody take it, please," pleaded Corinne. She suddenly felt feverish.

Both of them ignored her attempt to steer the topic to a safer channel.

"Helen loved your father, Doug. She did tell me that. I could feel it in her. She said his family would disinherit him if he married a girl who had no money. He was attending IU at Bloomington. She didn't want to come between him and his family, and she didn't want to risk costing him his inheritance. She was sure he would end up hating her or leaving her. So she quit her job as a waitress in the downtown restaurant where she'd met him. She claimed he never knew she was pregnant. She quit her job and never saw him again—"

"Kate, how could you!" Chris thundered from the doorway, interrupting her.

They all looked up. The door to the den had been thrown open. Chris's face was ashen, and his lips were stiff, thin lines when he spoke. "We gave Bill and Eileen our solemn word we would tell no one! Bill is my colleague."

Kate's chin quivered slightly. She sat ramrod straight, hands clasped tightly in her lap. "And this man is Stan's brother. I think he has priority over your AMA fraternity. Doug and Cory both deserve to know the truth. Their futures are at stake. Eileen Daye's ego be damned! She's not the only woman in Circle City who's sterile. There's no social disgrace in sterility, for heaven's sake."

"We gave them our word! They are our friends!" he said harshly. "Get your coat. We're leaving."

Kate rose from the sofa with dignity, her petite five-foot-one-inch body as regal as a queen's.

Chris turned to Corinne. "I have to return to the hospital. I'll drive Kate home. It was an excellent dinner, Cory. You were the perfect hostess, as always." He directed a troubled glance at Derek, then grasped Kate firmly by the arm and tried to pull her out of the den and into the hall.

"Let me go!" cried Kate. "I begged Eileen to tell Stan he was adopted *years* ago, remember? And I asked you to check with General Hospital to find out about Edmund's prognosis. Until tonight, I thought you had! Why didn't you tell me?"

"I was finishing up my residency requirements, remember? I had a lot to do," Chris protested.

"No. Your professional opinion was that Edmund would die. You could never face up to being wrong, could you Chris?"

"I'm taking you home," he growled.

"Let go of me. I'm calling a cab." They stood facing each other. Tears shimmered in Kate's angry eyes. "From now on, Christopher Albert, I do what I know is right. We have no right to play God with other people's lives."

Chris fled. The headlights of the jet-black Corvette parked in the driveway flashed on and the car roared away.

Kate telephoned for a taxi and, during the forty-five minutes she waited, scarcely uttered a word. She was comforted somewhat when Corinne embraced her.

"Forgive me, Cory, for not telling you and Stan the truth years ago," whispered Kate as she returned Corinne's hug tightly. "Forgive me, Doug, for not making the effort to find parents who would accept both you boys."

Corinne held her friend close in a sign of forgiveness. The taxi announced its arrival with the bleat of a horn. "It's all right dear. You did what you thought was right under the circumstances. I'll call you tomorrow."

Corinne escorted Kate to the driveway and bade her goodbye, whispering encouragements. She hoped Kate's marriage to Chris would survive her act of defiance. She felt partly to blame because she'd arranged the dinner party.

Deep in thought, Corinne locked the front door and returned to the den. Derek sat slumped in the leather chair, his head in his hands. Penny was cradled in his lap. He looked up as she entered. His sapphire eyes were filled with pain. She paused in the doorway, not knowing what to say next.

"I'm sorry the news had to come out in this way. Oh, Derek, I am sorry." Her distrust of him suddenly faded. She wanted only to comfort him, to wipe away that frightening look on his face. It suddenly occurred to her that this man was her brother-in-law. They were related by marriage. "Kate's gone home," she said softly, her compassionate gaze inviting Derek to unburden himself, even to weep tears of rage.

No curses came. No tears escaped. He only appeared dazed. "I'm a bastard," he said softly, looking up at Corinne as he tenderly stroked Penny's black-and-white back.

Penny was stretched across Derek's thighs, her body relaxed; she had found a home. With her long, curled tongue she licked the back of his hand—the one that lay motionless on the arm of the chair—in a monotonous, soothing rhythm, unconcerned and totally accepting.

CHAPTER SIX

THE CLOCK on the fireplace mantel in the den chimed eleven times. The flames in the fireplace crackled as they danced over smoldering logs. Derek was crouched in front of the fireplace, poker in hand. He was thrusting it between the logs, turning them, when Corinne came in from the kitchen with a freshly brewed pot of coffee.

Strangely, she felt no fatigue, only a dread of tomorrow. The Hawkins trial opened in municipal court room number three at nine a.m. She knew she should be getting to bed soon. She would need all her wits keen and sharp tomorrow if she hoped to obtain justice for Debra Hawkins.

As if he knew what she was thinking, Derek looked up as she entered the room. "I'd better be going. You have to work tomorrow. You need your rest."

"There's plenty of time." She was glad Derek was regaining his equilibrium after the blow Kate's news had dealt him. She placed the tray on a desk and poured hot coffee into a mug.

"Tell me about what you'll be doing at work tomorrow."

"I have a trial. My client is an eight-year-old girl who was injured two years ago while on an amusement ride, one of the ones that whirl you around up in the air. A support arm on the conveyance broke, and the capsule in which she was strapped fell to the cement. She sustained a permanent spinal injury. Can't walk. Probably never will." She watched Derek take a sip of the coffee. "Her father, Jethro, worked as an assembler at an automobile plant, and he was laid off shortly afterward, never recalled. The family is hurting for money right now. I think I've found a job-retraining program here in Circle City for Jethro, though."

"Is that part of your job as an attorney? Finding occupational retraining programs for your clients, I mean?"

She smiled. "No, not exactly. But many of the people who come to me need aid in more than the legal area. So I try to help." She shrugged. "Sometimes all I can do is to refer them to another professional, or listen to them while they talk about their problems. Sometimes a good listener is all they need to be able to get a handle on the situation themselves." She poured herself a cup of coffee and pushed the craving for a cigarette to accompany it determinedly out of her mind. After more than seven weeks of abstinence, the habit of lighting up was losing its grip on her.

"Did you learn this desire to help others in law school?" His gaze was so intense that Corinne felt uncomfortable. The room seemed to shrink, seemed to draw them closer together. The warmth from the fireplace enfolded them.

"No. I think it has more to do with my being female. I can see all my clients as human beings and not just the means to a fee."

The ardor of his gaze matched the warmth pouring from the fireplace. "Don't look at me that way, please!" she whispered. The sudden revelation of the man's true identity as her brother-in-law made the feel-

ings running rampant through her now seem almost in-
cestuous.

"Sorry." He looked away and stared at the leaping
flames. "Where's Penny?" he asked as he poked at the
logs.

"Behind the sofa. Lying down with her head on her
paws," answered Corinne, peering around the back of
the couch and smiling tenderly at the runt terrier. Penny
was the only "child" Corinne had ever had.

"Tell me more. About my brother." His plea was
gentle.

The den filled with languorous warmth as they sat
side by side on the leather sofa, thighs touching lightly,
heads together. Corinne got out the family albums again
and showed him snapshots taken during the time Stan
was courting her, their wedding prints and pictures
taken during brief camping trips. The photos taken
during their wedding anniversary holiday in Jamaica
brought a lump to her throat. Momentarily overcome,
she halted her narration. She had refused to acknowledge to anyone that Stan had changed during that last
year of their marriage. He had been away from home
much of the time and had generally been less considerate, less thoughtful. In some way she assumed this was
her fault. During the Jamaica trip, he'd almost been his
old self again.

"You loved him very much, didn't you?" Derek
asked softly, his angular face shadowed.

"We were...in sync most of the time, you might say.
I could anticipate what he would do next." *Until that
final year.* "His work made many demands upon him.
I tried to be supportive." She wiped her eyes with an
embroidered handkerchief that had been tucked away
in a hidden pocket on her apricot dress. "I accept the

fact Stan is gone now. I couldn't do that before you came."

"Was Stan as altruistic as you? Did he put the needs of clients first instead of his own income? Everybody is out to grab all the money they can, aren't they? Mitzie, the woman I lived with for two years, left me for an older man because he could offer her security. She told mé so." Derek no longer felt bitter. Mitzie seemed a stranger to him now.

"Some people see money in the proper perspective. With Stan, money was not the number one consideration." She smiled gently. "Stan wanted to help people, too. Some of the people who came to him didn't have insurance. He never turned anyone away who needed his skill. He never sued anyone for payment. Most of them paid when they could."

"Weren't you rich?"

She laughed out loud. She couldn't help it. The question was comical. "No."

"All physicians are rich, aren't they?"

She sobered up immediately. "Yes, Derek, we would have been well-off eventually. But Stan was in practice only a few years, remember. After he had a disagreement with his father—" she halted, feeling awkward, then took a breath and started again. "They disagreed about what he should specialize in, so Stan decided to finance his own way through medical school. And I had to borrow heavily on this house to see me through college and law school. So we started our practices and our marriage with big debts hanging over our heads. On top of that, do you have any idea how much it costs to furnish a medical office with a couple of examining rooms? Or the premiums required to carry medical malpractice insurance? No, Derek, we were not rich. We just managed to break even. My overhead runs pretty high, too. In another five years, the financial picture would have improved greatly—if Stan had lived."

She liked being on the sofa with him, being close to him. "Perhaps I should sell this house. It's way too big, costs too much to heat and the taxes are high. Besides, it reminds me of my folks and of Stan every day when I come home. Maybe I need a break with the past and start over. Build a new life for myself." It was the first time Corinne had ever entertained such a thought. She had a feeling of being set free.

"During coffee after dinner, when the Alberts were here, did I hear you say the comptroller of your father's company embezzled company funds?" asked Derek.

She nodded, still gripped with a sadness as she allowed herself to think about the deception that had cost her father his life. "The comptroller poured it all into the commodities market and lost every cent. Dad had trusted him completely. Oh, the man intended to pay it all back when he hit it big in the market. He went to jail, of course. But Dad suffered a heart attack when he learned the news. He never came out of it."

"That was rough on your mother," said Derek.

"Business was not one of my mother's talents. After Dad died, she was confused. The vultures swept in and cleaned her out of what little was left."

"The vultures?"

"The entrepreneurs with get-rich-quick schemes. They prey on widows who are alone and scared." She took a sip of the coffee.

"You lost both of them while you were still in college?" he asked gently, placing an arm around her. She yielded to the temptation to rest her head against the muscular arm, inhaling the pleasant male scent of him. Usually she was the one who listened while others poured out their troubles to her. Seldom did she experience the luxury of someone's undivided attention.

"Yes," she answered in a small, tired voice. "Just a year apart. Our family attorney cosigned my student loans until I turned twenty-one. He and his wife were wonderful to me."

Derek drew her closer. Her eyelids sank closed and her head rolled to his sturdy shoulder. Such waves of intensity rolled forth from him. Stan had projected the same intensity when discussing a patient with a life-threatening diagnosis. Time seemed to stop, to merge, to roll back upon itself.

"You're so much like Stan . . ." she whispered.

The arm suddenly abandoned Corinne. The man beside her leaned forward, and the large hands with the strangely graceful fingers clasped each other until the knuckles were white. She could feel his frustration, his anger as he pulled away from her.

"I'm Derek!" His resonant voice was tight with tension as he stared into the fire.

"I'm sorry, Derek. Please forgive me," she whispered, reality crashing down on her. Now she missed the touch of his hard, muscular thigh and the slim contour of his hip. She ran her hand through her long hair. "It's just...Stan seems to live on in you somehow. You're so much like him—"

"No!" He stood abruptly, jumping up from the leather sofa and facing the fireplace squarely, placing both his hands on the mantel. "I'm not my brother, dammit! I'm *me!* Derek Moar." He gasped as if he were being strangled. "No, I'm Edmund Hersh, according to Mrs. Albert. Whoever I am, I don't want to be a carbon copy of somebody else. Certainly not a man who was such a goddamn paragon of virtue! I can't live up to those expectations. People will have to accept me just as I am. If that's not good enough, that's too damned bad!'' he exploded.

"Derek . . . I'm sorry." Her face burned with embarrassment, and she felt a tension headache starting. "Forgive me. Forgive Kate. Forgive all of us."

"Including my mom and dad?" He turned to confront Corinne, his blue eyes smoldering with pain as he thought about David and Erna Moar. "They lied to me, too."

"Perhaps they were afraid."

"Of what?"

"Afraid you might reject them someday after they poured so much of their love into you. They wanted you very much, Derek, to go through the adoption proceedings. It's a real gift to a child to be wanted so much."

The tall man leaned heavily against the mantel with stiff arms. His head sank. Corinne couldn't help but notice the rounded muscle underneath his shirt and the shoulders that hinted of strength. She yearned to feel those arms around her now. She wanted to comfort him and take away his pain.

He rubbed the back of his neck thoughtfully, as if reflecting on her words. This familiar gesture was almost more than Corinne could endure. "Please don't do that!" she pleaded.

"It's *him* again! Even when I act like myself! How do I separate myself from Stan? From *Edward*, I mean? How do I cut him off without destroying myself in the process?" He looked around the comfortable room as if seeking a path of escape. But there was no way to escape the physical body in which he was trapped, the genes he shared with a brother he would never know.

On impulse Corinne rose from the sofa and slipped her arms around him. She stood on tiptoe and pulled his head down to hers. His body stiffened on contact. Her fingers disappeared into the soft mass of his hair. She could tell it had been coarsened by chemical straightener.

"You're still yourself, Derek. Nothing has changed. Not really."

Slowly she felt him relax in her grasp. "There are two pieces of cheesecake left. Want one?" she asked softly.

A little-boy smile crept over his face. "A great idea."

Feeling strangely maternal, Corinne went into the kitchen and returned with the leftover dessert on two plates. They ate in silence.

"It's getting late. Why don't you spend the night here and get some rest." As she said it, the mantel clock released a single chime.

"One o'clock," he echoed, staring at the clock. They had been talking for hours. It didn't seem possible.

"There's still time. I hope you can trust me enough now to tell *me* the truth, Derek." She freshened his coffee. "Why do you masquerade as Douglas Johnson? Why do you carry phony ID and hold an empty apartment in San Francisco in that name? Why do you carry a gun?" There was a reproachful tone in her voice.

"I have a permit for that gun." He thrust his jaw forward, squared and stubborn. She tried not to look at the hint of a cleft in his chin that was identical to Stan's. "I left the gun at the hotel tonight, locked in my suitcase."

"I'm glad." The sigh was one of relief. "I'm terrified of guns. They're made for only one purpose—to
kill people."

"Or to defend oneself," he retorted stiffly.

"Is Derek Moar your real name? Or another alias?"

He laughed. It was a short, brittle sound that held
more than a hint of cynicism. "My real name, yes. Or
rather, the name David and Erna Moar gave to me. I
have no arrest record. Check if you want. You won't
find even a traffic violation listed under my name. My
record is clean."

"Then why—?" she started to ask, puzzled.

"Didn't it ever occur to you, lady, that I might be on
the side of the law? Special assignment? We can't all be
physicians like my sainted brother and walk on water
and save a sick world. Some of us have to do society's
cleanup jobs, like fighting crime." In his teenaged years
he had wanted to attend medical school but he had
given the idea up. His parents hadn't had that kind of
money.

"You're not an FBI agent, are you?" Corinne's face
reflected the surprise she felt.

Again he paced restlessly, the muscle in his jaw puls-
ing with an ominous beat. The raw power of him, his
lean, taut male body with its muscular arms and shoulders and his brooding, angular face with its shadow of
new beard were elemental in nature. He lacked the languid elegance of Stanford Daye; an unknown x factor
was present in him, a dangerous quality that evoked a
delicious fear deep in her feminine being. He was a copy
of Stan, true, yet he wasn't. A different environment
had made for certain basic differences in Derek Moar.

"I was a special agent," he said in a controlled voice, leaning stiff-armed against the mantel again. "For six years."

"What happened?"

A long moment passed in silence.

"I was terminated. Oh, tactfully, of course. 'Prone to anxiety attacks. Unable to handle assignment stress.' Phrases like that went into my personnel file."

"I see." Corinne really didn't. She was confused. She sensed the steel in this man, the dedication to the job at hand, which was a quality she shared, too. Although his emotions had come to the surface easily this evening, she sensed this was rare. The evening had been an extraordinary one for him. "Who are you working for now? Why did you come to Circle City? Does this man Briggs have something to do with it?" she asked, remembering the name he'd called through the hotel door when she'd knocked.

"I'm not supposed to tell anyone." His angular face was gloomy.

"I'm not just *anyone*," Corinne protested. "My professional occupation involves privileged communication, too, Derek. I won't betray your confidence. I've lived here all my life. I know many people in town. Perhaps I can help you."

She sensed the struggle mirrored in his face as he stared into the leaping flames. Would he trust her with the details of his undercover assignment?

Then he turned away from the fireplace to face Corinne as she sat waiting on the leather sofa. He knew he trusted her. "Matt Briggs is the owner of two video retail stores here in town. He put in a phone call to an association he belongs to, the Video Software Marketing Society, and talked to the head, Sam Shuster, to report that a competitor down the street was selling unlawful videocassette copies of a movie Metro Mega had not yet released to the first-run theaters. VSMS also believes a lot of illegal videos are being sold as authorized studio copies here in Circle City. This town may be a center for a video piracy operation—mass taping and national distribution of those illegal tapes."

"Here? Circle City?" Corinne couldn't believe it. A criminal operation of such scope in this straightforward Hoosier town with its upright Midwestern values?

"That's what I'm here to find out," said Derek.

"You're a private investigator now?" asked Corinne.

"Yes. For almost two years. I get what work I can when I can, where I can. I have to eat." He drained the cup.

"Did you really study business administration at Northwestern?" asked Corinne.

He shifted uncomfortably, setting the cup down and shoving his hands into his trouser pockets. "I earned a degree in law. Never took the bar exam, though. I planned to work for the Justice Department, not go into private practice."

A suppressed excitement began to build in Corinne. He had the same academic background as she did, the same interest. "Study to pass the bar exam and go into private practice now. Give up this Mike Hammer routine," she urged.

"I'd have to take a refresher course."

"So what? Did this woman who left you—what was her name?" Corinne asked irritably.

"Mitzie."

"Sounds like a French poodle. Did her leaving so devastate you that you became unable to take that first step toward shaping a new life for yourself?"

"Don't make fun of Mitzie. She was no French poodle," Derek said stiffly. "She was a beautiful lady and she owned her own beauty salon."

"Had her hair dyed blond, too, no doubt," said Corinne, suddenly jealous. "The voluptuous type, I presume."

"As a matter of fact, yes. Really built." He lifted his hands away from his chest. Then he glanced at Corinne's embarrassed face and let his hands drop. "She was more on the surface, if you know what I mean. She lacked your depth, Cory."

Corinne mumbled a protest, holding up her hand. "Discussion of my depth is overruled. Prepare for the prosecution's leading question. Why did the FBI terminate you? What happened?" She leaned forward on the leather sofa, interested in his answer. The silk dress swirled around her thighs, softly outlining them and the V neck of the dress revealed the deep curving hollow between her breasts.

He was looking down at her, his eyes traveling slowly from her nylon-stockinged feet, up her sheer-clad legs and the line of her thighs to her breasts, which were less than voluptuous but high and well shaped, like ripe pears clinging to the bough. His gaze lingered on the neckline of her dress. As she became conscious of the intensity of his look, her skin warmed. Her throat tingled as his eyes traveled upward. They settled on the pink curve of her soft lips and remained there.

Corinne felt her poise slowly desert her.

"We were born only six minutes apart, yet he had everything," Derek said softly. "He had you!" The clock ticked on, breaking the ensuing silence. "He still does." His voice was little more than a penetrating whisper. "The only reason you...*let* me...the day before yesterday was because you thought I was him."

Corinne could not deny his words. Yet the truth was much more than what it seemed to be. But she couldn't bring herself to tell Derek what she hadn't told anyone—that her marriage had been considerably less than ideal in its final days. She rose from the sofa and went to face him. In front of the searing warmth of the fireplace, she concentrated on a log that was slowly dissolving in the flames. "I don't go around throwing myself at men, no," she said after a long pause. "As long as Stan was here, he was the only man I allowed myself to need. And afterward..." *I gave up a certain belief in myself,* she wanted to say, but didn't.

He turned away from her. His eyes shimmered with hurt.

He wants me. The truth tore through her, making her breathless and dizzy. The room closed in around them, enfolding them in rose-soft petals of intimacy, drawing them closer together with each word they spoke, each ragged breath they drew.

But Corinne had to get some answers. She composed herself. "I want to be your friend, Derek. So we have to level with each other. Why did the FBI terminate you? What did you do?"

"It was almost three years ago. In December. I was on assignment with my best friend, Morey. Two bank robbers had hit a bank, taken four employees as hostages and had taken off over the state line. The missing car was spotted outside an abandoned farmhouse and our office was called." He looked away from Corinne, remembered horror reflected in his eyes.

"Morey and I drew the assignment. We were personal friends, as well as partners. Morey decided to go in through a window in the cellar. I was to climb a tree and gain access through a second-floor window. We didn't know they had an M-16—that's an automatic rifle that fires like a machine gun. I heard it go off downstairs—" His face went pale. He looked suddenly ill. "Morey didn't stand a chance at such close range."

She moved closer to him, wanting to wipe away the look of guilt on his face. She knew he had to be feeling guilty for still being alive while his friend was dead. "Are you sure you want to talk about it?"

"I haven't talked about this to anyone outside." Outside the department, he meant, and she knew that. "When I heard the gun fire, I ran down the stairs. When I saw Morey lying in his own blood, I went blank. I opened fire. Killed the two men at the same time as they landed a couple of bullets on me. One woman hostage was screaming, and one of the men was trying to push her down to safety behind a wooden crate." He closed his eyes and ran his fingers through his hair.

"The money was all there. It was a full recovery. The hostages were scared but unhurt, thank God. None of them had been hit by a ricochet. I was badly wounded in one leg and taken to the hospital. They operated on me. I stayed there three weeks. The leg is okay now." He rubbed his left thigh.

"Why should a success like that earn you a pink slip?" Corinne was puzzled. "You deserve a medal."

"In the hospital something very strange happened to me. I was dozing before dinner was served, more asleep than awake, and this sudden panic hit me, waking me up. I wasn't dreaming. I was instantly awake. Yet I felt as though I were falling through space, while I was just lying in bed.'' He appeared apologetic.

"I started yelling at the top of my voice, yelling somebody's name—'Buzz,' some crazy name like that, and my hands kept pulling back on something, as if I were holding a stick or a wheel of some kind. I kept pulling back and up and yelling.

"Nurses poured into the room, trying to hold me down. Then came a sudden shock. Like a jolt. Everything stopped. There was only a peace, a strange floating kind of peace, like everything was finally all right.'' He gave a ragged sigh and rubbed the back of his neck with his hand.

"The next day a psychiatrist came to see me.'' Derek mimicked a laugh. "He asked me all sorts of questions, gave me a test for the crazies—you know, the Rorschach, with all the ragged ink blots. I told him everything, just like it happened. Next day, another psychiatrist paid me a visit and he went through the same routine.

"When I was dismissed from the hospital and reported to work, the agent in charge informed me I was considered a psychiatric risk. Anxiety attacks under stress—that kind of stuff. Oh, they were very nice. They blamed it on the raid at the farmhouse and Morey's death. They commended me for my years of fine service. But I was out. They didn't think I could be trusted in the event of another emergency. The only job they would offer me was one shuffling papers in Washington, a desk job.

"So I went back home to Illinois to lick my wounds, visited my folks for a while in Brookfield, roamed through the zoo there, then found a three-room furnished apartment in Lincoln Park area of Chicago and became a private investigator. It's been hand-to-mouth ever since." He attempted a grin.

"What was the date in December that this happened at the hospital?" Corinne could hardly speak. A creeping numbness had spread over her during his explanation.

"The eighth. I'll never forget December eighth. Ever. The time was about six o'clock in the evening. Why?" he asked brusquely.

It took a minute for Corinne to speak. "That's the night Henry Perlman's plane crashed near Syracuse. December eighth. Three years ago this coming December. About six in the evening, according to the FAA report. Buzz was the nickname the other physicians called Henry. He was quite fond of that plane." She swallowed hard.

"Somehow, Derek...I think you were experiencing...what was happening to your identical twin... except you didn't know you had an identical twin. And, of course, since you didn't know it, you couldn't inform the psychiatrists and nobody could check out the facts of the incident. That's the shame of closed adoption records, not knowing your true background. For medical purposes, if for no other reason, such knowledge can be crucial at times."

For a long moment Derek stared at her, as if trying to comprehend what she was telling him. "You mean...the moment the plane was falling...somehow I was experiencing it, too?"

"You're identical twins, aren't you? Doesn't one twin know what is happening to the other sometimes? I've read articles claiming it's possible." Suddenly, a trembling seized her entire body. Strong arms wrapped around her quivering form, lending her their strength.

Derek's final description, especially the word "peace," echoed again and again in her mind. Perhaps Stan had found peace after those few terrible moments. Perhaps he was in a state of peace now. She had prayed for that so many times in the past two years.

"How could it be, Cory?" In Derek's whisper was awe, relief and a new understanding. There was a reason behind the strange event. He wasn't crazy after all. Her explanation had set him free from his hidden fears. Derek sensed everything she was feeling, and without words, he drew her trembling body close to his. His strength flowed out to sustain her, and his warm body comforted her. Her face turned blindly upward toward his. He lowered his head.

Their lips met and clung.

Corinne was only vaguely aware of the tickling of his mustache as she sank into the safety of strong arms. The warmth of his familiar body encompassed hers, igniting her. She returned his kiss with a wanton abandon, her tongue boldly probing his mouth. The scent of him was heady, an intoxicating blend of clean pine—his after-shave—and straightforward maleness.

Her senses became muted to everything but him. The crackling flames faded to whispers, and the pendulum tick of the clock diminished as her blood throbbed in her veins. His mouth was warm and moist, fragrant and sweet with the taste of cheesecake; she drank from it greedily.

Loneliness vanished. The separateness of self that kept Corinne an observing stranger in the courtroom, in her office, in a restaurant or at a friend's house was banished in the glow she was feeling. He pulled her hips snugly against his and his male response to her was evident. An exultation filled her. He felt the same way she felt. She was no longer alone.

His hand moved up her back; his fingers crept through her long hair. He cradled the back of her head, and his wonderful lips hardened in a kiss of passion. Against her ribs, her heart beat furiously while every nerve in her body sprang to life, sending electrical tingles fanning outward over her skin.

They didn't say a word. Kisses spoke for them. They clung to each other, minds and bodies opening wide in total acceptance. Their mouths parted as they gasped for breath. He lowered his head and supported her shoulders with his arm. His lips sought the smooth, slim line of her neck, and his lips and tongue and teeth, ever so gently, tasted her, leaving exciting impressions of warmth in their wake. It all seemed so familiar from a time long ago.

"Stan . . ." she whispered.

Derek Moar was suddenly still. His arms dropped to his sides.

He stepped away from her as though she had dealt him a physical blow. His sapphire eyes clouded with pain. She knew instantly that he had tuned her out. She wondered if he would ever open up to her again.

"I'm sorry, Derek," she said, gasping. "I don't know why I said it. Habit, that's all. You're not that much like Stan, not really. In many ways, you're different, a difference I like. It's *you* who turns me on, not a memory. Please believe me." She felt helpless and she knew her pleas were failing to penetrate.

He walked slowly to the doorway of the den. "You have a trial tomorrow. You'd better get some sleep or you won't be worth much. The kid is counting on you.

Do you have a guest room? I'll sleep there tonight. I don't feel up to the long drive downtown."

Corinne burned hot and cold with embarrassment. She would give anything to take back the name she had just spoken. It was Derek she wanted now, not Stan. But could she ever make him believe it?

"This way. The bedrooms are upstairs. The guest room is across the hall from mine." She led the way up the stairway, and Derek followed, a proper guest, leaving a polite distance between them. As they climbed the stairway, there was only the faint sound of the clock on the fireplace mantel in the den. It chimed the hour of two as a black-and-white streak named Penny darted past Derek, unseen by either of them. When Derek opened the door to the guest room, Penny flew in and crawled under the bed, her tailless black rump quickly disappearing.

In fifteen minutes, as a dusky stillness settled over the house, loud, rumbling snores worthy of a drunken sailor rolled with resonance from under the guest room bed. For an hour it continued until Corinne was awakened from sleep by a knock on the master bedroom door.

"What do you *do* with her?" asked a distraught Derek clad only in white cotton briefs, his hands spread wide in an appeal for help. "How can a dog snore like that?" He was wild-eyed with lack of sleep.

"Penny is abnormally small. The problem is an elongated soft palate—you know, the roof of the mouth," Corinne explained. "It flutters over the opening of the larynx and gets in the way. Our vet offered to shorten her palate surgically. He said that would help. I just never got around to having it done."

Smiling apologetically, Corinne wrapped a robe around herself tightly and accompanied Derek to the other room. She sank to her knees beside the bed and wiggled part way underneath, using her elbows. The small, warm bundle of canine flesh tried to evade her, but Corinne was experienced at this type of retrieval operation. She snared Penny and drew the dog into her arms while Derek tugged on Corinne's legs and pulled her out slowly from beneath the bed.

Derek said a curt thank-you, and Corinne walked into the kitchen slowly, her heart aching, and shut Penny in there for the remainder of the night.

CHAPTER SEVEN

ON THE SECOND DAY of the Hawkins trial, a curt and decisive knock sounded on the door of suite 1802.

The man who stood in the hall was familiar to Derek, although he had not seen him since the days they had trained together at the academy. Of medium height and build, with cool opaque gray eyes, Arnold Zinser, special agent in charge of the Circle City regional office, was the kind of man who blended into the background when he desired to do so. None of his features was particularly outstanding. Derek knew for a fact that Arnie had the reputation for being the best of his breed.

Arnie's handshake was friendly and firm. As he entered the room, he removed a lightweight trench coat and draped it neatly over the back of an art deco dining chair.

"Thanks for coming so quickly after my call this morning," said Derek. He went out to the breakfast bar set up in the hall and brought back two continental breakfasts. The door to the balcony was open wide; a cool breeze streamed into the living room. Zinser stood on the balcony, a hand on the railing, looking down at the brick path of the circle on which cars crawled like ants. Always a private man, Zinser seemed lost in thought as he observed the scene far below.

"Breakfast is inside. You still drink your coffee black?" asked Derek.

"Sure. I'm consistent." Arnie turned, his expression of guarded reserve still unchanged. "I haven't changed much in the years since we took training together—except for the wife and kids. Rita and I have been married for six years. We have two little girls, aged two and four."

"That's great! I envy you," answered Derek as his guest came back into the living room. "Sit down, Arnie." The name stuck from training days. "It's great to see you again. It's been a long time."

Zinser complied. It was a leisurely movement; no one pushed Arnold Zinser into doing anything. His gray suit was well pressed and fit just right. The jacket was styled fully enough so that the shoulder holster beneath his arm didn't show. The material was of good quality, yet not the most expensive. In most hotel lobbies he would attract little attention. He took slow, careful sips of the steaming coffee. Finally he looked over the table at Derek, his gray eyes cool and appraising.

"What's holding you back, Derek? Still keeping company with that girl, what's her name? The one you mentioned on one of the Christmas cards you sent."

"Mitzie." Derek sighed imperceptibly. "Mitzie moved out. She went on to bigger fish in the sea. She married a businessman who's made his roll already."

"Oh," grunted Zinser. "Yeh, women like security. You'll find somebody else." He picked up a croissant from the plate and passed it under his nose, inhaling the buttery fragrance. He studied it thoughtfully. "Women and bribes I can resist with ease. But these things... mmmm." He took a careful bite. "When you called the office this morning you mentioned being in town on

assignment for Metro Mega Studios. You have something for me? Should our office become involved?''

"I think so. I have a tape of an interview with an in-
formant named Matthew Briggs. I made a transcript for
you,'' said Derek. He had rented a portable typewriter
while making his video store rounds the day before, the
first day of the Hawkins trial. He had spent most of the
night before typing, transcribing the interview. It had
been a grueling, nerve-racking job. He was not a skilled
typist.

Zinser accepted the typed transcript and smiled
slightly at the white-outs and typos strewn over the
pages. "Not bad for the limited time you've been in
town. We'll assign a man to keep an eye on the salesman.''

"Yesterday I made a tour of video retail stores on the
west side, near the store Briggs owns. The videocassette packaging in several of the stores didn't look right
to me—not like the packaging I examined at the VSMS
office before I came here. I bought twelve different titles I'm sure are counterfeits. I have each one marked
by store name.'' Derek took a large brown sack from the
wet bar and placed it on the table in front of Zinser.

"I'd rather wait to move in on the stores until we can
nail the people responsible for making the counterfeits.
I hate to tip our hand too soon,'' said Zinser, pulling
out tapes and studying each one.

"The VSMS investigator—they have their own, you
know, but all they do is check tapes; they don't do
general undercover work—their man is arriving tomorrow to analyze these and give me his opinion.'' Derek
reached for a croissant.

"If the VSMS investigator confirms that they're fakes, do you think we have enough to obtain warrants?" asked Zinser.

"I think so. Briggs will be a big help. He's willing to testify in court," Derek answered. "That guy is funny." He suppressed a grin. "You'll like him. The way he talks about his wife. You know, Arnie, I had the most fabulous luck. I met a woman—" He hadn't intended to say that. *Do I want Arnie's approval?* he wondered.

"So soon? Fast work. That's a bachelor for you. Shouldn't you be keeping your mind solely on business?" asked Arnie.

"That's easy for you to say. You're married."

Zinser's thin lips pulled into a satisfied smile. "Sure am." He eyed the last croissant but refrained from reaching for it. "The doctor told me at my last physical I needed to shed six pounds, and here I am, eating these things. Who is she?" He made it sound casual as he took a sip of his coffee.

"Her name is Corinne Daye. She's an attorney here in town."

"How did you meet her? On the plane?" asked Zinser, his hand holding the china cup close to his mouth.

"She followed me to the hotel from the airport. By cab."

Zinser choked, coughing violently to clear his throat. The dark level of liquid within the cup rose perilously but didn't escape over the rim. He set the cup in the saucer.

"No doubt you were able to score," Zinser said dryly. His expression became a knowing one. "You didn't tell her who you really are or why you're here, I trust."

Derek's failure to answer gave him away. He reached for the last croissant instead.

"You didn't tell the lady the nature of your assignment, did you?" Zinser's quiet voice carried a tone of warning.

"I did," answered Derek regretfully, intent on the roll in his hand, evading Zinser's reproachful stare.

"You revealed the nature of your assignment to a stranger? She could be one of them, man, seeking you out! You violated the basic commandment of the academy's teachings—to keep your mouth shut! My own wife, Rita, has never heard one word from me about my cases."

Derek flushed, warm with embarrassment. "Corinne is okay. We don't have to worry about her. She's an attorney here and very respectable. Cool down."

"Oh, sure. *You* think she's okay. She's a good lay, no doubt." He jerked a cigarette out of his pocket and lit up. Derek could tell he was upset. Arnold Zinser seldom smoked. Arnie threw the pack down on the round marble table. "Help yourself," he said with tightened lips.

"No, thanks. I haven't picked up the habit again."

Zinser's hand squeezed his knee in frustration. "Somebody dangles a piece of juicy female bait in front of you, and you swallow it. Dammit, man, at the academy you struck me as an intelligent guy."

"Mrs. Daye is not involved with any video pirate operation, Arnie. Take my word for it," Derek argued.

"I don't take anybody's word for anything without checking it out first. Even yours," snapped Zinser.

"Then check her out. It should be easy. She's lived here all her life. Was married here. I bet it's a boring job for you." Derek reached for a paper napkin, no longer intimidated by Zinser. One thing he was certain of was

Corinne's integrity. He wiped fingers coated with a light buttery film on a paper napkin.

"Home address and office address?" Zinser whipped a small notebook out of his jacket pocket.

Silently Derek rose and went into the bedroom, returning with his billfold. He removed Corinne's business card with her home address written on the back.

Zinser raised his eyebrows. "Stemple Road. That's an affluent residential section on the northeast side, close to the county line."

"Her father was Charles Banbury. Owned his own business, but it failed. She inherited the family home. Her practice seems to be going well, but she claims to be poor folk, just like the rest of us."

Zinser grunted in disbelief. "The IRS could tell us something about that. If you confide in anyone else, so help me, I'll drop you flat. I can use you to do some of the legwork right now. More men are due to be assigned to this office soon. When we have to move in on the retail stores selling the counterfeit stuff, I don't want my hard work wasted on charges that don't stick."

The verbal blow struck home. Risking an impression of rudeness, Derek rose from the chair. He thrust his hands in his trouser pockets and walked out onto the balcony, needing to put some distance between himself and Zinser. Since Kate Albert's shocking revelation at Corinne's home, even the dynamics between Derek and Arnold Zinser had changed. He often found himself wondering about who he really was...

Derek watched a cargo van, which looked tiny from this height, wind its way around the brick-paved circle, and he thought of his father—no, David Moar, the man he had always assumed was his father—who had driven a diesel rig over the highways for years to make his living and support his family.

Questions that could never be answered tormented him. What was the man like who had conceived him? A business success? A professional man? An alcoholic? A convict serving time in prison? He knew he was an extension of that physical father, genes and all, just as he was like the identical twin brother he had never met.

He finally spoke from the balcony. "You'll find a typewritten list of the types and brands of industrial electronic equipment needed to do this counterfeiting on a large scale." He knew he sounded stiff and formal but he couldn't help himself. How could he tell Arnie that he no longer even knew who he was? "The list was given to me by an industrial video production company in California. Could you cut some red tape and get someone in the State Department to contact both the Japanese and American manufacturers and obtain the names of American buyers?" he asked Arnie. "Surely these firms have computerized their sales records by now."

Arnold Zinser's eyebrows drew together in a thoughtful frown. "Don't expect instant action if the request has to go through Washington channels," he warned. "But I'll see what I can do." He rose from his chair and glanced at his wristwatch. "Be careful of this woman Corinne Daye." He pointed a warning finger at Derek. "I don't trust any woman who follows a stranger from the airport to his hotel room and lets herself get laid, especially when that man is on an investigative assignment. There may be a leak at Metro Mega Studios, or this man Briggs may have sung his head off to someone. I'd feel better about coming up with a case that'll stick if you promised not to see her again."

Derek left the safety of the balcony and walked past Zinser to the dark marble wet bar. He picked up the typewritten list of electronic equipment and handed it to the FBI agent. "I'm in control of the situation," he said tensely. "Don't worry. I can handle things. You're not my father." A painful ache the size of a fist hit his belly.

Zinser rose from the chair slowly. He folded the list and slipped it into the inner pocket of his suit jacket. "I'll be calling you when I receive an answer from Washington."

Derek didn't answer. He followed Zinser to the door silently, eyes directed to the carpeted floor.

"When the situation involves a woman, Derek, sometimes it's hard to be objective." Zinser threw him a troubled glance. When Derek didn't respond, he picked up his trench coat and draped it over his arm. Derek jerked open the door, as if anxious to see him leave. Tension radiated through Derek's body.

"You were a good man at the academy, Derek. Don't let me down now. Already she's creating trouble between us, and we're both on the same side." Zinser pulled the door shut behind him. He hadn't smiled as he'd said his goodbye.

A HUSH FELL OVER courtroom number three in the municipal building. Twelve jurors sat motionless, having resumed their seats after two hours of deliberation. They stared at hands folded in their laps or at the smooth wooden barrier that set the jury box apart from the rest of the room. The jury foreman stood and cleared his throat. He had thick dark hair and was neatly dressed in a sports jacket and dark trousers, a white shirt and a navy-blue tie.

Corinne sat, quiet and tense, beside Jethro and Amanda Hawkins, Debra's parents. Corinne herself had wheeled in the pretty child with braided hair after the lunch recess had ended and had questioned her gently about the events of the afternoon when the whirling ride that had taken her up into the air had broken loose from its shaft and the capsule had come crashing down to the cement below, rendering her unconscious.

By the time James Gaterow had finished with his brutal cross-examination of Debra, however, the child had been reduced to tears. Amanda's sister, Debra's aunt, had wheeled the child out of the courtroom and taken her home in the special van the family had had to buy to transport her.

The courtroom lacked windows. Corinne longed for a breath of fresh, bright September air and a glimpse of sunlight. She avoided glancing at Jethro and Amanda, wondering if they blamed her for the indignities which their daughter, and Jethro, too, had suffered at the hands of the opposing attorney. Corinne had made repeated objections during the cross-examination, but she realized now that she should have prepared them better for what to expect from James Gaterow.

She herself had been unprepared for the way he had launched into a frightening tirade and intimidated the frail child. He had insisted quite loudly that she was faking her injuries, despite medical evidence to the contrary, and that she had been coached in all her answers by "the rapacious counselor hired by her parents to feather their economic nest at the expense of a respected businessman of the community."

The jury might hold such histrionics against Gaterow, Corinne thought. At least, her mind had been
too occupied to think of Derek Moar. Only now did the
thought of her newfound brother-in-law pop into her
mind. She was glad he had not been sitting in the half-
filled courtroom.

Corinne sat motionless, turning Gaterow's scathing
comments over in her mind, and came to a slow burn.
Trying to relax, she slowed her breathing as the jury
foreman stood to deliver the jury's verdict. The worst
thing Corinne could do for her clients was to let herself
succumb to anger. Anger would render her vulnerable
to anything Gaterow could dish out. She had to keep a
cool head.

She allowed one stolen glance at the defendant's table, where James Gaterow, former high school quarterback, sat with the portly man who was the
amusement park owner. Gaterow's chiseled, granite-
like features were hard and lacked expression, but the
customary cynical smile was missing from his pale thin
lips. He kept his eyes unflinchingly raised to the face of
the jury foreman, as if to intimidate him.

He's worried, thought Corinne. That gave her hope.
The foreman licked his lips nervously under Gaterow's
intimidating stare.

Jethro Hawkins raised an unsteady hand to wipe the
perspiration off his brow. Corinne ached for the poor
man. Gaterow's cross-examination of him had been
brutal. He asked only questions that served to cast suspicion on Jethro's character and on the character of
everyone in Jethro's family back to his grandfather. He
had tried to plant in each juror's mind the impression
that Jethro was a ne'er-do-well drifter who came from
a family of drifters and who was unemployed because

he was too lazy to work. One arrest on a drunken driving charge years before had given Gaterow the ammunition he needed to paint Jethro as an alcoholic, as well.
He had even dragged out Jethro's uncle's record of
mental illness and a suicide committed by a distant
cousin.

Gaterow's rapier verbal thrusts at her gentle client,
whom Corinne knew to be a loving father and a good
man, had made her furious. Jethro had been laid off
from a factory job in an automotive plant and been able
to find only occasional work as a handyman. Amanda
was taking in sewing orders in the attempt to keep their
house and their van from being repossessed.

Corinne glanced at the gaunt man seated beside her.
He had his face buried in his large hands. She reached
out and touched his shoulder to reassure him.

"Has the jury reached a verdict?" asked the judge,
who was dressed in a black robe and was visible only
from the chest up on the raised platform.

"Yes, your Honor, we have," answered the foreman
in a hoarse voice that indicated that hours of argument
had taken place in closed chambers.

A hard knot formed in Corinne's stomach. She closed
her eyes, wishing she could stand up in the crowded
courtroom and tell everyone there all she knew about
James Gaterow, a man who had embezzled fifty thousand dollars from his employer while working his way
through law school. She knew this for a fact. The employer's wife had brought her suspicions and duplicate
copies of the ledgers and other papers confirming her
fears to Corinne almost three years ago. She had wanted
Corinne to bring the papers to the attention of the Indiana Bar Association and have proceedings brought

against Gaterow. She'd also wanted the matter taken to the police.

Corinne had placed the papers in her office safe, wanting time to deliberate on these serious steps. Then Perlman's plane had gone down on a wintry night, and it had been difficult for Corinne to take action on anything. The papers remained in her safe and only Meg was aware that they were there. Then the employer's wife had gone into a hospital and had died, the result of a heart attack. Corinne's one witness was gone.

At that point Corinne had transferred the incriminating evidence from her locked office filing cabinet to the wall safe in the master bedroom of her house. Despite the antipathy she felt for the man, it had been impossible for her to bring herself to strip Gaterow of everything. *At least he's unaware of the evidence I hold against him,* Corinne thought. *Thank God.*

Corinne turned her attention upon the jury foreman.

"We, the jury, decide in favor of the plaintiffs, Debra Hawkins and Jethro and Amanda Hawkins, and recommend that the damages requested, two hundred thousand dollars, be raised to the amount of three hundred thousand dollars."

An electric murmur ran through the courtroom. A reporter jumped from his seat, burst into the aisle and out through the double doors at the back.

Corinne was stunned. Exhausted. Numb. Joyful. Amanda and Jethro sat in staring disbelief, clutching each other's hands. Shining tears sprang into Amanda's eyes. Her daughter's future would be secure.

Corinne curbed her emotions. She knew better than the Hawkinses what still lay ahead. She glanced at James Gaterow. His face was drawn in dark wrath.

Corinne leaned forward, speaking in a low voice to the parents seated with her at the plaintiff's table. "Don't be too elated. Mr. Gaterow has the right to appeal the decision to a higher court, and I'm sure he will. He can tie the award up for another two or three years. We'll continue the fight, of course, and justice will be achieved for your daughter in the end. She'll have an income for life. Just hold on for a while longer."

She watched the light fade from the parents' eyes as the judge's gavel descended, announcing the end of the day's session. Everyone stood while the judge left the courtroom through the special entrance that led to his chambers.

Corinne picked up her father's worn leather briefcase wearily and started to follow the Hawkinses to the aisle leading out of the courtroom. To do so, she had to pass the defendant's table where the portly man sat glaring defiantly at his defeated counselor.

"This will break me! My insurance doesn't begin to cover an amount like that! Couldn't you persuade that bitch to settle out of court?" The portly amusement park owners's voice was strident.

"We'll appeal. I'll tie this up as long as I can. Don't worry," rumbled Gaterow. "You can declare bankruptcy and not have to pay anything. They won't get a cent."

As Corinne passed Gaterow's chair, trying to ignore what she had heard but making a mental note to find a way to thwart the plans of the unholy pair, a grip of steel shot out to grasp her forearm. She tried not to wince when she was brought to a halt.

"Don't spend your fee yet, Toots. I plan to appeal. That bum you represent is not going to take a free ride on my client for the rest of his life." Light-colored eyes containing no warmth slashed through Corinne like shards of ice.

"You have the right to appeal. Your attempts to defame Jethro Hawkins didn't do the job with the jury. By the time this case comes to trial again in a higher court, Mr. Hawkins will no doubt be employed full-time. Too bad, James. You'll have to think up another stinking maneuver. For you, that should come easily. Let me go or I'll yell for the guard." Slowly the pressure on her arm decreased. His hand dropped. "This time you were checkmated, James. I'll give you another chance to play," she said softly.

"Don't be so smug. I'll see you indicted for insurance fraud. Don't think I won't enjoy that," said Gaterow, an unpleasant smile tugging at thin lips.

"What are you talking about?"

"Your husband wasn't killed in that plane crash. He staged it and hid out someplace. Where did you stash the insurance money when the policy paid off? In an unnumbered Swiss account?"

Her worst fears had come true. The rumor was flying that Derek was Stan. How many people had seen him? Of course, she could explain who Derek was to countless numbers of people, revealing the truth about Stan in the process, but right now she was exhausted. "You don't even know what you're talking about."

"A friend of mine saw your husband coming out of a video store in a shopping center on the west side yesterday. She called me. When a man is six two, it takes more than a mustache and hair straightener to change his appearance. I'm astonished you would be so dumb as to let him come back so soon."

Corinne felt herself blush with embarrassment and frustration under the piercing eyes of the overweight client who had said not a word but absorbed everything said. "That man is not Stan. There's a strong resemblance between them but that is all." She started to move away.

"That's what *you* say. We'll see what the authorities have to say about insurance fraud," Gaterow called after her loudly, impressing his client.

Corinne turned, her dark eyes flashing warning. "I wouldn't try anything if I were you! It just might bounce back at you in a way you least expect!" She had in mind the proof of his embezzlement hidden in the safe at home.

"Do I detect a threat, Counselor? My client is witness to that. You threatened me," Gaterow said, leaning back lazily in his chair, making it balance on two legs while pinning her with his cool, hard eyes. The portly amusement park owner guffawed, enjoying her displeasure.

She sailed up the aisle to the double doors, which stood open. She was filled with a righteous anger and a cold fear. In the marble hallway she approached Jethro and Amanda Hawkins, who sat on a bench by the elevator.

"We won, didn't we?" asked Jethro, his brow wrinkling. He wasn't sure.

"Yes, but the battle continues." Corinne let out a tense breath. "Don't worry. We'll win the appeal, too," said Corinne gently, bidding the couple goodbye. She left them sitting on a bench in the wide marble hallway, emotionally exhausted, with their arms around each other.

All Corinne wanted was to have a cup of hot coffee, to relax in a warm bubble bath and to telephone Derek to share the news of her win with him. She took pride in the fact that she had passed through the strain of a trial without the aid of one cigarette, and she wanted to tell him that, too. He'd been right after all. She didn't really need the nicotine crutch.

Her thoughts were filled with Derek now that the trial was over. She realized with surprise just how much she missed his voice and the comfort of his presence.

And to her surprise, she was thinking of him as Derek, not as Stan.

CHAPTER EIGHT

THREE WEEKS AFTER the jury returned its favorable verdict in the Hawkins case, Derek Moar was still in Circle City, still residing at the downtown hotel. Spurgon Corporation had eased up on the two-week limit it had originally set for Derek's expense account. Don Jennings did, however, demand a weekly report from Derek, accounting for his time. A copy of the report went to the studio executive at Metro Mega who had hired Derek for the job.

So on yet another Friday afternoon, Derek fretted over the rented typewriter set up on the dinette table, correction tape at hand. He yearned for a secretary as fast and as efficient as Margaret Krens.

Before tackling his writing assignment this particular Friday, he called Corinne's office. Although he had managed to see her two or three times each week, not so much as a kiss had passed between them since that eventful evening of the dinner with the Alberts. He knew if Corinne called him "Stan" one more time, he would blow up. He kept reminding himself she was his sister-in-law, and he tried to keep his emotions under tight control, but he knew he was growing to love her more deeply each day. He had seen Kate just once, and Chris seemed to be avoiding him.

"I'll take you to dinner tonight," Derek announced as soon as he heard Corinne's cheerful hello.

"You're on! But don't you dare show up until five-thirty. My appointment book for today is full," Corinne said. "I know just the place to go. Le Rocher, the French restaurant on the top floor of this building. We'll watch the lights turn on all over the city."

The conversation left Derek with a good feeling. At about four in the afternoon he finally finished the dreaded piece of business communication and mailed it off to California. He was interrupted from a relaxing shower by the insistent ringing of the telephone on the bathroom wall.

"He's gone!" The woman on the phone was almost hysterical.

"Who is this?"

"Rena Briggs. Matt Briggs's wife." Her voice was strained and high-pitched. The words flew out of her mouth with machine-gun rapidity. "He didn't show up this morning at the east side store. He left the house at the usual time and kissed me goodbye as always. The store manager called me at noon, wanting to know if Matt was ill, if he had any special instructions for her. He's run into trouble. I know it. What do I do?"

Derek felt the hairs on the back of his neck prickle. He was afraid for the good-natured, balding man. "There's no reason for alarm, Mrs. Briggs. Matt probably had a change of plans and didn't think to inform you. Have you notified the police?"

He wished the CCPD didn't have to be dragged into this. If the media focused on the disappearance, the spotlight might blow the case before Zinser was ready to move in.

"I did! They won't file a missing person's report on him until he's been gone twenty-four hours. He could be dead by then." She began to sound panicky.

"Just try to stay cool," Derek said firmly. "I'll get back with you later." He hung up and called Zinser immediately and gave him the news. "Has Briggs been up to the office to see you?" he asked hopefully. Perhaps Arnie had told his chief witness to disappear, stay out of sight. He revealed his conversation with Matt's wife.

"Maybe he just wants a day off to himself without telling the missus every damn move he makes," grunted Zinser. "Maybe he has a girlfriend."

"I don't think so, Arnie. He and his wife are very close."

"He hasn't been here and he hasn't been in touch with me for the past week. By the way, that Tony has done a disappearing act, too. No trace of him. He slipped out past the man we had on duty watching him sometime during the night. The agent we assigned is competent. I underestimated our salesman friend, Anthony. Found out he has a pedigree with the Los Angeles Police Department under two other names. We were able to get a good set of prints off a VCR Briggs was able to get Tony to handle in his store."

"Why didn't you tell me Tony had a record?" asked Derek. The pause at the other end of the line was eloquent. "You don't trust me?" asked Derek, his voice tight.

"I trust *you*, Derek. It's the people you associate with I'm not sure about. Despite my warning, you've been seeing Mrs. Daye two to three times a week."

"You've put a surveillance on *me*?"

"Wouldn't you, in my place?" asked Zinser. "Your friend Mrs. Daye has an interesting client."

"Who?"

"Timothy Greer." There was a long pause as Derek reacted to the name of the owner of At-X Communications, Incorporated, a video-production studio he planned to call on in a few days. He had found out, from scouting around, that At-X was the only video production studio in the county with the equipment necessary to duplicate tapes in large quantities. "You didn't know that At-X was one of her clients, Derek?" Zinser's voice seemed to be mocking him.

"She failed to mention it."

He heard a grim chuckle on the other end of the line. "I wonder why!" asked Zinser. It was a rhetorical question. "You told your lady love about Briggs, too, didn't you?" His voice was accusing.

"I told Corinne about Briggs, yes. Absolutely no one else knows."

"Does anyone else know Briggs made a complaint to the Video Software Marketing Society's national headquarters?"

"Not from me. Maybe he let his mouth run off."

"Maybe he turned tail and ran," Zinser suggested dourly.

"I don't think so. Not Matt Briggs. He's dedicated to getting this piracy ring stopped. Find Tony and I bet you'll find Briggs. Can't you make a call and get the police working on the missing person report his wife made? The least the boys in blue could do is be on the lookout for Briggs's car. Call his wife. You have his home phone number."

"Get *your* ass in gear and get *your* investigation moving! Things are moving on my end," Zinser asserted. "Two weeks ago I made a special trip to Washington. The powers that be okayed our request. A man was dispatched to Japan with an official government request for a printout on all U.S. buyers of the type of equipment on the list you gave me. I just hope we don't find ourselves in the middle of a murder investigation, too,'' Zinser said ominously.

"Call Mrs. Briggs right away," Derek urged.

"Okay. But I hate dealing with hysterical women," Zinser grumbled and hung up.

A MID-OCTOBER frost had turned the leaves on the many trees scattered through downtown Circle City to scarlet and gold. Although a setting sun drenched the buildings, sidewalks and asphalt streets in an orange-gold color, the breeze was no longer languid and warm. It blew cool and steady and brisk, making the steps of homeward-bound shoppers and office workers quicken as they hurried to parked cars or to bus stops.

The air imparted vigor to Derek as he headed toward the Marotte Bank Tower with energetic strides. Arnie could be right, he thought. Matt could have taken off on his own for the day on some private errand. Why assume the worst? Derek was of the opinion that the investigation was progressing satisfactorily, if not at lightning speed. He dreaded the day it would be all wrapped up and he would have to return to Chicago. Would everything come to an end between him and Corinne then? He didn't want to think of that.

Derek's search of all the retail video stores in the metropolitan area had been completed, the reports all submitted. Too many of the stores showed signs of the suspect phony tape packaging to please him. He still had to call on At-X Communications on Monday. The news that Tim Greer, one of the owners, was a client of Corinne's had hit Derek by surprise. *Is she protecting him?* he wondered as he waited at a traffic signal for the light to change. What kind of work did she do for Greer?

He also planned to check back with the airline parcel service at the airport. This had been the other lead that had brought Derek to Circle City: a package addressed to E. L. Haegis with no valid return address on it had been given to E. R. Hargis by mistake by a new parcel-service employee at Circle City International Airport.

A fortunate mistake that was, mused Derek as he waited on the curb, watching the cars pass. When Hargis had opened the plain cardboard carton and found a videotape inside, he'd decided to check it out on a friend's VCR. To his astonishment he'd seen a motion picture made by Metro Mega Studio that had not been premiered yet. The print copies for distribution to the first-run theaters were still being made.

If master tapes were being sent to Circle City airport for pickup, it was logical that the town was also the headquarters for a mass duplicating center. But why had the shipments of master tapes from Los Angeles suddenly stopped? That worried Derek. He would take an afternoon next week and talk to the staff of the parcel service and see what information he could dig up. Perhaps someone remembered "E. L. Haegis" and could describe him.

The light changed and Derek crossed the street, looking up at the tall steel-and-blue-glass structure. He turned his head to glance over his shoulder and wondered which of the pedestrians behind him was Zinser's man following him. *What a waste of time,* he thought in irritation. He would be glad to give Arnie a schedule of his meetings with Corinne just to save the Justice Department money. But Arnie was too stubborn and suspicious to ask him.

Derek mounted the limestone steps of the skyscraper. Office workers, on their way home, were spilling

down the steps, and several of the women paused to give
him lingering looks, their eyes traveling down the length
of his body, taking in his tweed sport coat and tie, white
oxford shirt, dress slacks and polished wing-tip shoes.
The lingering looks made his step quicken, become
more jaunty. At least women noticed him. But he was
interested in the serious attention of one woman only:
Corinne Daye.

Derek was alone in the elevator going up to the
twenty-fourth floor. His footsteps rang hollow as he
walked along the deserted hallway, past locked doors,
his thoughts pounding restlessly in tempo with his
stride.

He wanted to trust Corinne. He did trust Corinne.
She was open, direct, honest and more assertive than
other women he had met. He liked that quality of self-
confidence about her. She could hold her own in any
situation, yet she was feminine, sensitive to his moods
and feelings. A supportive type indeed. She was the type
of woman with whom he could easily live—day in and
day out—for the rest of his life.

He stared at the wooden door with the simple brass
nameplate on it: Corinne Daye, Attorney at law. He felt
angry with himself for feeling so much involved with
her. It was as if he had stepped off a high place and was
now falling, out of control, and had to have faith he
would land on his feet like a cat and survive. He reached
for the brass doorknob, turned it and pushed open the
door.

Meg looked up from her papers as Derek entered the
reception room. Her emerald eyes narrowed and her
pupils darkened. Seductively shaped lips pursed in a
contemplative pout. Instinctively Derek sensed Mar-

garet Krens was attracted to him and was sizing him up. He tensed.

"Is the boss still here?" he asked.

"In there, where else?" Meg gestured a manicured hand in the direction of Corinne's private office. The door was standing open several inches.

Derek wondered how Meg had known his brother and what she could tell him about Stan. "How long have you worked for Corinne, Meg?"

A look of irritation swept across the attractive face, a look that said clearly, "Come on now, let's quit playing games." Then her face turned bland. "Five years."

She suddenly smiled and the pouty face came alive. Her eyes challenged him boldly as his own eyes flicked over the beige woolen sheath dress she wore. The dress was tightly belted and full breasts loomed in tantalizing proportions. The look she gave him was sultry, inviting. "Ah, yes, the good old days," she said cryptically in a husky voice.

Quickly Derek walked toward the door of Corinne's office and knocked on it to inform her of his presence.

"Come in, Derek." Corinne's voice was soft and melodious, devoid of harshness. Mitzie's voice had become quite harsh the last three months she had lived with him. Derek pushed open the door, acknowledging to himself that Mitzie wasn't worth thinking about. He hadn't thought of her in weeks.

Corinne's private office possessed a warmth that reflected the personality of its occupant, Derek thought. It was paneled in a wood that glowed with the golden warmth of clear honey. A beige sofa with soft, inviting cushions stood against one wall, and two leather Scandanavian chairs were opposite her desk for the comfort of clients. Against the third wall stretched a long credenza that matched the walnut of Corinne's contemporary desk. The credenza had nothing on top of it except for a large glass ashtray, which was clean. He smiled to himself. She was really staying off the cigarettes. The fourth wall was a plate of smokey-blue glass, a window yielding an impressive view of the obelisk-shaped monument in the center of the circle that marked the heart of the town, which had been settled in the early 1800s.

"Feel comfortable with that thing?" Derek said, smiling. He gestured toward the computer monitor and detached keyboard on one corner of her desk.

"I've gotten used to it. The public records are on computer now, so it saves us a lot of time when we want to check on the status of deeds or child support payments, etcetera. I subscribe to Westlaw and Lexis, too, the on-line legal research service."

She inserted some files into the cabinet next to the credenza and locked the drawers with one of the many keys on her ring. She slipped the keys back into her purse. "I'll warn you, I'm hungry. I had to skip lunch. A woman wanted a consultation about getting a divorce and the only time she could come to talk was during her lunch hour."

"And what did you advise her?" He gave a wan smile.

"I advised her to think it over very carefully. Two children are involved. I gave her the name of a marriage counselor who has a good track record. He works at Brookman Counseling Center at Presbyterian Hospital. She promised me she would try to get her husband to accompany her and give counseling a chance before she took any action in filing."

"That advice won't net you any fee."

"No, but two children will have a mother and a father to come home to every evening. The food is very good upstairs," she said, pointing toward the ceiling with her index finger, "but it's also a bit expensive. Would you prefer to go somewhere else?" She tilted her head slightly, inspecting his face.

"I'd like to have a leisurely meal and your undivided attention while we look out over the city. It's my treat, too. None of this dutch treat malarky," declared Derek.

"Fine with me. You're welcome to the check. I know when it's to my advantage not to be a liberated woman," she said, chuckling. "Your invitation is gratefully accepted, sir. See, no argument. If you don't mind waiting, though, I'd like to clear off my desk before we leave." She motioned toward her desk, which was littered with sheets of draft paper and opened legal reference books. She called out to her secretary. "You can go now, Meg. Don't you have a class tonight? You won't have time to eat if you don't get a move on." She turned her attention back to Derek. "Meg attends evening classes at a local university," she explained. "She's working on a degree in accounting. Isn't that something? It takes grit to work hard all day and earn a college degree at night." Corinne's voice bubbled with energy. Derek had never seen a woman more beautiful. He hoped her new joie de vivre was due to him.

Meg appeared in the doorway. "I have filing to finish up first."

"Do it tomorrow," said Corinne, a hint of laughter in her silky voice as she came out from behind the desk. She was dressed in a two-piece silk shantung suit of a dusky rose color that complemented her shoulder-length brunette hair. A spotless white silky blouse and black pumps completed the picture. Her figure was so perfect that it made Derek ache. He wanted to unveil her body, to touch it, to elicit its warm response, to experience its pleasure.

"I like to put my things away and lock up before I leave," said Meg, sounding distant. She disappeared from the doorway. "Do you want some coffee, Derek? Boss lady can clear up faster if you're out of there." Her voice came from the kitchenette on the other side of the reception room.

"She's right. She knows me pretty well," said Corinne good-naturedly. "Let Meg give you the grand tour, since she seems in no hurry to rush away to eat. She's never been a clock-watcher. I'll be finished here as soon as I can be."

"Won't we need reservations upstairs?" asked Derek.

"I'll call Le Rocher's maître d' and put the reservation in your name," Corinne teased. Derek swallowed hard and wondered if the ninety-five dollars in cash he had in his billfold would be enough to finance the entire evening. As he approached Corinne's desk, he became aware of the pervading scent of her perfume, an exciting mixture of roses and jasmine as delicate yet strong as she was. "You look worried, Derek. They'll take a credit card upstairs, either yours or mine."

"Matt Briggs is missing, Cory." He spoke in a low voice, aware the door to the reception room was open.

"What?" Alarm registered in Corinne's face. Her hands froze above the cluttered desk.

"Mrs. Briggs called me this afternoon. Her husband never arrived at his east side store this morning. His car's gone, too. She's quite upset."

"That poor woman! What can we do?"

"The police should be on it by now. Cory...did you tell anyone about Briggs?"

Her eyes flicked away from his momentarily. "Of course not!"

"Could your house be bugged?"

"What? Don't be ridiculous! A listening device? For what reason?"

"I don't know. I'm just asking."

Corinne looked down at the accumulation on her desk, as if she had lost all motivation to tame it. She waved her hand. "Go get your coffee. As long as you're in here, I'm at a standstill."

"I give you a half hour." He checked his wrist-watch. "I'll be back in here at 6:15."

The telephone on her desk rang. She bent over and lifted the receiver to speak into it, her dark hair falling in soft waves to partly cover her cheek. A slim hand reached up to brush the hair back. The presence of the slim platinum wedding band and the huge engagement ring—huge to Derek, at least—unsettled him. The metal had to be platinum, the diamond three karats in size. Stan never seemed to do anything halfway, Derek thought with a pang of bitterness toward his dead brother.

As he left Corinne's private office, he heard her say something about filing a bankruptcy. As usual she was soothing someone on the other end of the line. *Does she ever deal with anything but crises?* he wondered as he walked through the reception room toward the kitchen. And did she ever manage to get away from the tele-phone?

Meg was standing in the kitchenette, the glass pot of coffee in one hand, a filled ceramic mug in the other. She replaced the pot on the warming burner and held out the mug, the handle turned toward him. He ac-cepted it.

"Thank you. I'm supposed to take the grand tour," he muttered, taking a sip. Perhaps he could pry some information out of Meg. His conversation with Arnold Zinser earlier in the day still haunted him. What was Corinne's connection with Timothy Greer?

"That's me—tour director, telephone operator, secretarial force, part-time cook and janitor," Meg said lightly. "Follow me to the law library, sir."

He made a special effort to keep his eyes off the well-shaped legs and the feet in high-heeled shoes that were little more than straps. "You have a college class tonight dressed like that? College sure has changed. We wore jeans and sweatshirts; the dingier the sweats, the higher the status," he said laughing. "Your major's accounting?"

"Yes," she answered. "But my class tonight is Urban Society. Sounds fascinating, doesn't it? There's a gentleman in class who has his eye on me. So I like to look nice." She pushed open the door to the library. "Behold the inner sanctum. It also doubles as our conference room."

Three walls of the large room were covered with shelves and heavy law tomes bound in leather with gold lettering. Every set of books he had used in the college law library was here for Corinne's private use. He knew what an outlay of money such a well-equipped law library entailed. "Impressive tools of the trade," he murmured, his glance sweeping the crowded room, with its simple walnut conference table and six armchairs arranged neatly around it.

"I'm curious about someone, Meg. Can you fill me in?"

Her expression altered subtly to one of self-satisfaction. Almost a look of triumph. She closed the library door in order not to be overheard. The intimate gesture disturbed Derek. He preferred the door to remain open.

"Just tell me what you want . . . Derek." That husky quality lurked in Meg's alto voice again. She moved closer, appearing expectant.

"Timothy Greer. What is the nature of his business with Corinne?"

Meg stopped, surprised, her eyes widening. "Tim Greer? The video king? Why do you ask?"

"I'm not asking you to break any of the rules of privileged communication. I know you are just as much bound by them as Corinne is. I just want to know— what does he do? What was, or is, the nature of the legal work Corinne performs for him?"

"Tim owns At-X Communications, Incorporated on East Seventy-first Street. The only major video production house in the county. He's a funny guy, a real riot to talk to," said Meg.

Derek's mouth went suddenly dry. "At-X was on my list to call on. I didn't have the owner's name. Do they do everything in the video production field?"

Meg turned away to put away three volumes that lay on the conference table. "Complete production facilities, tape editing, tape duplication in quantity, hundreds at a time, videoconferencing. Tim once mentioned special-effects equipment, too, but don't ask me about any of that stuff. I don't understand it. When we had an electric typewriter in here, it was all I could do to take out the old cartridge ribbon and insert a new one." Meg straightened and turned to face Derek.

"Who—for whom does Mr. Greer do this type of work?"

"Advertising agencies, I guess. Business and general industry, too. Whoever needs something done. Is Spurgon Corporation in need of such services?" Her smile was mocking him, making Derek feel uncomfortable. He drank from the coffee cup in lingering sips.

"Could be. Good coffee, Meg. Thank you. You still haven't told me what Corinne's connection with Greer is. Why is he her client?"

"She represented him in a couple of lawsuits. I won't tell you anything more than that. I can't discuss clients with outsiders. Although you're not exactly an outsider, are you?"

Meg came close to him, took the cup from his hand and set it on a ceramic tile coaster on the conference table. Without warning she slipped one arm around his neck and the other arm under his, her hand falling close to the gun holster hidden beneath the sport coat. Her lips settled firmly on his and they remained there, insistent, soft and provocative, coaxing his lips to part.

His heart skipped a beat. His breathing stopped. His lips refused to part while his arms remained at his sides. He endured the kiss, not allowing himself to respond to it, because of Corinne. He pushed her away from him. Margaret Krens grudgingly released him.

"I really believe it now. You're not Stan." She said it quietly, almost sadly, her emerald eyes clouding. "I had to be sure. Every man's kiss is different; no two are alike. Stan wouldn't have pushed me away, either. You're different from him in other ways, too."

"How?" Derek cleared his throat and stepped away from her.

"More cautious. You don't take everything for granted the way he did. Stan didn't turn me down when I wanted him. Whenever Stanford Daye wanted anything, all he had to do was open his hand, reach out and take it. The world was his pearl and he knew it.'' The sensuous lips drew into a cynical smile. ''But you—you act as if you don't deserve to have anything. When you could have anything you want.'' Her meaning was clear.

''You and Stan... were having an affair?'' His mind reeled, his view of his perfect brother shattering. How could Stan have betrayed a wonderful wife like Corinne? The man had to be crazy. Or possessed. He felt uncomfortably warm, and the book-lined walls crowded in on him.

''Stanford Daye was mine... whenever I wanted him,'' Meg whispered. Her green eyes were hard and glistened with harsh lights.

''How long?'' Derek's stomach was beginning to react. He felt a sudden heartburn.

''For a year before they went to Jamaica. That trip should have been mine, not hers.'' Her soft purr was pure malice.

''How could you stay with her after... seducing her husband?''

''Stan wasn't hard to seduce. *He* had no trouble making up his mind about what he wanted.''

''I have no trouble making up my mind, either, Ms Krens. I'm just selective about what I go after.'' He reached for the library door and jerked it open.

''What are you? A cop?'' Her voice was devoid of expression.

''Why do you ask?''

''The friend hanging under your arm. Most men don't carry a gun. Of course, I know a lot about you already.'' The green eyes were gleaming with boldness.

''Through Corinne, you mean?'' Had Corinne talked too much, trusting Meg?

"If you tell her, I'll deny everything," Meg murmured in a low voice. "I'll call you a bloody liar. We'll see who she believes."

Derek was on guard, reluctant to say anything to her. His curiosity overcame his better judgment. "You're not married, I assume?" he asked, trying to keep the distaste he felt for her from taking him over.

She smiled contemptuously. "Divorced. Emancipated in California before I moved to Indiana six years ago. I live with a man named Willy now, but you know how that goes." She shrugged her shoulders. "I'm the one bringing in the money. I may kick him out tomorrow. If you ever change your mind, Derek, you know where to find me. Right here. Right here is where I intend to stay."

He was repelled by the hardness in Meg's eyes. He suddenly perceived her as some sort of parasite, taking advantage of Corinne's trusting nature. Corinne praised Meg's work to him constantly.

"I don't need you to keep my coffee warm," he said dryly, flinging the cynical words over his shoulder as he returned to the reception room.

"Is something wrong with the warming burner of the coffee maker?" called Corinne from her office, overhearing Derek's last remark.

"No. I advised Meg to turn it off. Right, Meg?" he said in a loud voice.

Meg's dark red cupid's-bow lips tightened and her pretty face turned into a scowling one as she hurriedly cleared off her cluttered desk and covered up the keyboard of her personal computer. She seemed quite willing to leave the office now, banging file drawers shut.

She locked the file cabinets in the reception room, took her purse out of a drawer in her desk and threw the keys in the top drawer of the desk under the scrutiny of his solemn gaze. She locked the desk last and then reached for her coat and scarf off the hook on the wall. She left without a word of farewell, closing the door loudly behind her. Her heels clicked down the deserted hallway.

After returning his mug to the sink in the kitchenette, he walked into Corinne's private office.

"That was quick. How did you get Meg to leave?" Corinne asked. Then she looked up at Derek, subjecting his face to a long stare. Then her mood changed abruptly. She slammed desk drawers and seemed rigid and withdrawn.

"What's the matter?" Derek asked, puzzled.

She raised her head and pain shone clearly in her velvet-brown eyes. She looked as if she wanted to cry but was refusing to allow the tears to form. She walked briskly out of the inner office and flicked off the light, her cashmere coat draped over one arm, her shoulder bag swinging from the opposite shoulder. Corinne walked through all the rooms, switching off lights without answering.

"What is the matter with you?" he repeated, this time more forcefully.

Corinne whipped a facial tissue out of her handbag, blinking rapidly, fighting the mist gathering in brown eyes dotted with deep flecks of gold. She handed the tissue to Derek.

"You'd better wipe Meg's lipstick off your lips. I wouldn't want people to think it was mine. I don't care for the shade. It's much too red." Her manner was stiffly polite, her tone anything but friendly.

CHAPTER NINE

DEREK WAS FILLED with dismay. He wiped his lips repeatedly. The elevator ride up to the roof was a silent one. Corinne stood as far away from him as the boundaries of the elevator would permit.

"Look . . . I didn't make the pass. She did," he said, desperation in his voice.

"That's your story," Corinne murmured coldly. The elevator doors opened. French doors of glass stood open ahead.

"You have a reservation, sir?" asked the maître d', attired in a two-piece black suit, with a dazzling white shirt and black bow tie. He carried two large scarlet-colored rectangular menus. Beneath his gleaming black shoes stretched a honey-gold floor of parquet tiles. Walls covered with mirrors reflected the light of an ornate crystal chandelier.

"It's under the name of Douglas Johnson," answered Corinne coldly.

"Oh, yes. This way, please, Mr. Johnson. And how are you, Mrs. Daye?" The maître d' gave a restrained smile. Corinne smiled politely in return but didn't answer.

Derek stepped aside to allow Corinne to precede him into the dining room. "I can explain everything if you will allow me," he said in a low voice as she passed him.

"I know. You're irresistible to all women." Her voice was harsh.

They were ushered to a table for four next to a huge window. Over their table hung a soft blue satin swag lamp. The light in the room was dim, and a fat red candle burned in a glass holder in the center of the snow-white tablecloth. Outside the window, dusk had turned to a deep purple night. They both looked out the large expanse of glass at the lights in the buildings and on the streets below.

Instead of sitting beside Corinne, Derek had chosen to sit opposite her, next to the window also. He would force her to look at him. The attractive brunette was ignoring him, staring out the window and down at the peaceful sight below, as if she longed to escape his presence.

"Let me explain about Meg—" he started to say.

"You don't owe me an explanation about anything. If you want to make a pass at my secretary, that's your right."

The prompt appearance of the waiter ended her stilted accusation. "I recommend the chicken breast with sauce, a baked potato with sour cream and Roquefort dressing on the salad," she said primly to Derek in front of the waiter.

"Make that two," Derek told the waiter, putting his menu aside.

"Yes, *monsieur*. Would you care to see the wine list?"

"Your best vintage white wine. I'll trust your judgment," said Derek.

Corinne gave a groan after the waiter left the table. "Talk about giving someone a blank check," she muttered.

"I don't care what the damned wine costs. I do care about getting something straightened out between us!" he answered, careful to keep his voice low.

"There's nothing *between us*. So there is nothing to straighten out," said Corinne, concentrating on the blazing carpet of lights stretched out thirty-two floors below them.

Stan wasn't perfect. He had an affair with Meg. I wouldn't let Meg get to first base with me. That makes me a villain? Derek thought. He couldn't reveal to Corinne what Meg had boasted about to him; he couldn't bear to hurt Corinne. In his dazed mind he began to wonder why Meg had picked this particular evening to test him.

Silence reigned between them until the waiter appeared with the restaurant's choice wine. He filled two wineglasses and left them alone.

Derek raised his glass. "A toast to your win in the Hawkins case. From what you told me about James Gaterow, you must have been resourceful to outmaneuver him."

Derek's praise softened Corinne's inflexible visage. "Thank you," she responded stiffly. "He's a tough cookie, all right, with the heart of an iceberg. A bad public image for all us attorneys."

Corinne took a long sip of wine. "This is good," she conceded. "You certainly know how to order wine, Mr. Johnson." Her lips pulled into a cynical smile. "It's not every evening I have the opportunity to have dinner with a vice president of the Spurgon Corporation." Her dark eyes were mocking, her voice smooth as silk. "Subterfuge is your speciality, isn't it?" she said softly.

"Stop it," Derek said in a low voice, looking around to see if anyone could overhear them. "I have my profession, you have yours. I don't make fun of you."

"You should be on the stage. Will the real Derek Moar please stand up? I probably wouldn't recognize him," she said softly, tipping her glass to her lips again.

"*I did not go after that woman.* She came after me in the library," he protested.

"Oh, sure," said Corinne. "Quit talking against Meg. I trust her implicitly. She manages my office to perfection and no damned male can come between us. She's my right hand."

"Then you better learn to be left-handed pretty quickly," he muttered ominously, closing his eyes to savor the fragrance and taste of the wine and then letting it trickle a sweet, warm pathway down to his stomach.

"Stan used to do that," Corinne said after a pause. Sadness tinged with self-pity was replacing the anger.

"Do what? Kiss Meg?" he asked carefully, opening his eyes.

"Of course not! Close his eyes when he drank a good wine or liqueur," she answered irritably. "Why should I care what you and Meg do?"

He was suddenly alert now, absorbed with her face and hands and every nonverbal cue she was throwing him. "Yes, that's right. Why should you care?" He waited expectantly for an answer, but none came. "How much does Meg know about me and my real reason for being in town?"

"She overheard me calling a detective in San Francisco to check on you. When she asked me what the detective reported, I told her. Also—" Corinne shrugged her shoulders "—Meg took it on herself to check with the switchboard at Spurgon Corporation. The operator reported that you didn't have an office or a secretary and she didn't know who you were, although your name had been added to her list with no extension. Somebody obviously failed to give the operator an important briefing.''

He leaned back in his chair when he saw the waiter approach with a tray. Warm plates of fragrant food were set before them. The waiter gave a half bow and left them alone.

They ate, Corinne paying more attention to the city spread below them than to Derek. Finally she leaned back and spoke, staring at the spread of lights on the skyline and the street below, where cars crept like ants.

''Perhaps you can be reinstated in the FBI. Maybe if you told your FBI friend here about Stan and about your being a twin… It's been said that an identical twin knows when a traumatic event is happening to the other. If the psychiatrist knew all the facts, and was open-minded, he might revise his original opinion about your susceptibility to anxiety states following that shootout in Chicago. Your so-called panic attack correlates closely to the time of the plane crash. Under the circumstances, I might be able to induce the judge to release the adoption records.'' Her voice was quiet, controlled. To his amazement, he realized she was willing to help him even when her ego had just been riddled full of holes.

''I don't want that type of life anymore. Or the type of life I'm living now, for that matter,'' Derek answered.

''What do you want?''

"What most men have. A wife. A child. A dog. A secure living. Nine-to-five hours. To be able to do some good for my fellow human begins. What else is there?"

"You really want children?" she asked slowly, looking at him over the table. She was frowning, as if she didn't believe him.

"Do you think I'm too old to be a father?" he asked.

"Of course not. You're in the prime of your life. You're the type of man who will always be in the prime of his life." A sad half smile illuminated her delicate face. "You could study and take the state bar exam. Dig in and establish a law practice. Did you get decent grades in law school?"

"Of course, I got decent grades," he answered testily, remembering the many nights he'd stayed up studying until two or three in the morning because he'd spent the evening working at his part-time job. It had been a grueling period in his life. He wasn't sure he could manage the same results again, now that he was approaching thirty-five. "Do you think I'm stupid?" he asked.

"I think you'd make a damned good lawyer. That's my woman's intuition speaking, of course," she answered with a faint smile.

"What established law firm would accept me? It would take some time before I'd be earning my keep. I'd need to acquire clients." Despite his protests, Corinne's words were stirring hope in him. Perhaps she was really interested in him after all. He was never sure exactly where he stood with her. Thank God she hadn't slipped and called him by Stan's name since that night in the den.

"Why don't you contact firms in the Chicago area? I'm sure you'd feel more comfortable back home," she suggested.

All hope abruptly faded.

As they took the elevator from the restaurant down at about nine p.m., Derek wondered how long Corinne would punish him for finding the scarlet imprint of Meg's lips on his lips. They were the lone occupants of the elevator in a deserted building. The doors opened to a silent, darkened twenty-fourth floor. Their footsteps rang hollow as they walked in silence toward Corinne's office, where Derek intended to use the telephone.

The key clicked sharply in the dead-bolt lock. They entered the darkened reception room, where Meg's empty steno chair stood guard behind her neat desk. Corinne led the way into her office, switching on the small lamp on the credenza.

Her coolness was almost more than Derek could bear. He walked to the window and looked down at the street below. Traffic was sparse at nine o'clock at night. The height made him dizzy and pulled his attention downward. He could see the lighted fountains spraying water high in the air at the base of the monument in the center of the circle. As he gazed at the street below, he could imagine himself falling in slow motion, and he shuddered, drawing back from the thermal-paned window, which could not be opened.

Derek placed his call to Matt Briggs's wife. Her voice was strained. He could tell she had been weeping. All she could tell him was that she had heard nothing from her husband yet, but the police had called her to inform her they had put out a bulletin to locate his car.

Derek replaced the receiver, frustrated and tense. He stood in front of the telephone, hands buried deep in his trouser pockets while a deep hunger stirred in the core of his masculine being: the need for approval. The need for love. The need for acceptance from the one woman most important to him.

His brother's wife.

"No news?" Corinne asked softly, tenderness making her face vulnerable and beautiful with a silken sheen in the light of the lamp. *He's been under tremendous pressure, finding out about himself. Perhaps Meg did encourage him,* she thought. She knew Meg didn't lack self-confidence and possessed a healthy assertiveness. "I'm sorry, I don't keep liquor in the office, or I'd offer you a drink," she said.

He sighed, every muscle in him drawing taut and ready. "No word from Briggs yet." He paced the floor, rubbing the back of his neck thoughtfully. The silence of the office, of the entire building was working its magic on him. He felt closer to this woman with whom he had shared dinner and wine than to anyone else in his life.

Something deep inside Derek was building, and his attempts to curb it were meeting with little success. He had never felt so vulnerable. What if Corinne rejected him?

Slowly he walked toward her. She held her ground and did not retreat. His hands settled lightly on her forearms. She didn't resist the gentle pressure of his fingers.

"I've known you about a month, Cory. Such a short time, yet I feel as if I've known you forever. How can that be?" he asked softly, willing her eyes to lift to his. Finally they did, and he was surprised to see the hurt in the velvet-brown depths.

Damn Meg! She did this on purpose, he thought.

"I've never met a woman like you, Cory," he said gently, feeling the resistance in her body. She wanted to pull away from him. For a second he thought he would go crazy.

"You're on the rebound from Mitzie. Any woman looks good to you now. Your ego's been damaged. Why don't you ask Meg to go out?"

Corinne's words punished him. "No, it's over with Mitzie. And I'm not interested in Meg. You're the only woman I want. Believe me."

Her face softened, as though she wanted to trust him. His arms moved slowly around her. Her dark wavy hair hung like a cloud about her delicate face, and the fragrance of it compelled him onward. He couldn't stop himself and she made no protest. "I need you, darling. I need you...." He murmured it again and again, enfolding her slim, pliant body into his arms.

She seemed to grow weak, clinging to him. The tick of her heartbeat against his chest was steady and rapid. The warm mounds of her breasts beneath her silk jacket shrank against the hard wall of his chest. He sought her lips and she gave them. They were warm and soft and tasted faintly of wine; her tongue was succulent with the sweetness of chocolate.

He drew her close and joy raced through his burning veins. She was giving her tacit consent, yielding to him without a murmur. He hoped that she wanted him as much as he wanted her. The soft purrings from the depths of her throat as they kissed passionately added more fuel to the fire burning within him and brought his manhood to life.

He wanted only to be close to her, to merge with her. He wanted to draw her into himself as he became one with her. He wanted to protect her and take care of her the rest of her life.

"Let me . . . let me . . . please," he whispered, intoxicated by the scent and pleasing softness of her. The force within him was gaining momentum, and he wasn't sure he could stop it now if he tried.

"Yes . . ." came her answer.

Exhilaration exploded within him with such force that he could feel all his muscles tighten.

"The effect you have on me, Derek . . ." she murmured. It was not a complaint, just a bewildered comment.

He felt joy burst through him. This time she had addressed him by his own name and not by the name of his brother. This time she was responding wholly to him.

With trembling hands he began to undress her, urgency making him clumsy. A beautiful smile was on her face, and her eyes were misty with tears as the undergarments slid down to the carpeted floor. Only the dim glow from the lamp on the credenza and the silver moonlight flowing in through the wide expanse of window illuminated the office, revealing the soft curves of her nude body. Her breasts rose high and firm, the nipples hard and eager to his touch. Her satin-smooth skin and the pleasing roundness of her hips beneath his roaming hands made a delicious warmth course through his veins. He was ready for her.

"I need you, too," she confessed in a low voice. She blinked as if to hold back tears. Slowly he began to undress, and then she helped him. Embracing, they sank to the sofa on their knees, his tongue passing over her lips, then paying homage to her beautiful breasts, with their hard, exciting peaks.

They sank into the cushions, entwined tightly. Her warm body rose to accept his, and the warmth of her response was pure joy to him. They moved in an exquisite, synchronized rhythm, and then the fire within Derek suddenly exploded and was followed by a blissful peace. She lay very still beneath him, her arms and legs around him, the valley between her breasts damp. Her eyes were closed, and her nose was pressed tenderly against his cheek.

She gave a sigh of contentment.

Tears of happiness burned his eyes. Words failed him. He kissed her lips gently again and again, certain she would recognize his declaration of love. Did not his every movement, his every breath, his every thought center around Corinne? Surely she sensed it.

Derek Moar had never felt so happy, so complete. He had found a woman of complete integrity, one with whom he could spend the rest of his life....

DEREK WALKED into his suite later that night to an angrily ringing telephone. "Where have you been?" barked Arnold Zinser when Derek answered.

"Ask your man. What did he tell you?"

"I called him off. I needed him elsewhere. I know you went to her office late this afternoon. That's all I need to know," growled Zinser. "They found Briggs."

Derek's heart stopped for an instant. "Alive or dead?"

"Alive. Walking around on the far north side, badly beaten and scared to death. Two cars had run his car off the street when he was on his way to the store this morning, and two hoods pulled guns and took him to an abandoned farmhouse. They roughed him up a little and warned him not to talk to any law enforcement officer again. The police found him wandering around and had a hell of a time even coaxing him into a police car to take him home."

"Thank God he's all right," said Derek.

"He's lost to us as a witness," grumbled Zinser, displeased. "We have more to go on, though. I just received a computer printout of the names of all the U.S. customers who, during the past three years, bought the specialized electronic equipment needed to duplicate video cassette tapes in quantity." He sounded hard and tough. And pleased. "A distribution amplifier and fifty units of Panasonic VCRs, the industrial model, were delivered last year to 10978 Grant Road here in Circle City. That's on the far northwest side of town, over the county line."

"Good work, Arnie! Give me the buyer's name." Derek was feeling excited as he jerked a small spiral notepad out of his jacket pocket along with his pen and wrote down the Grant Road address. He knew this report would make the Metro Mega executives happy. Now the FBI might have a case.

"Corinne Daye. You know her home address. Stemple Road," answered Arnie.

CHAPTER TEN

"CORY, WHY WOULD SOMEONE be following you?" Kate Albert sat across from Corinne at the oak trestle table in the cheerful alcove off her kitchen. Beyond the window, the trees on the other side of the driveway had turned to flaming scarlet and brilliant yellow. They were now drenched in the hearty sunshine of a Saturday morning in late October.

"I don't know. All I know is that a plain black Ford is always behind me when I drive to work in the morning and when I come home at night. And I see the same man at Ramir's delicatessen when I go to lunch. He sits at a table where he can keep an eye on me."

"That sounds slightly paranoiac, Cory. What does he look like?" Kate spoke carefully. It was evident to Corinne that her friend did not accept her suspicions as credible.

Corinne sighed. "He's hard to describe. He's so...ordinary. Nothing outstanding about him at all. He fades into the wallpaper, so to speak. But I know his face. Oh, do I know his face by now."

"You look awful, Cory. I'm sure you have been working too hard." Kate refilled Corinne's empty cup with fresh coffee. She seemed to enjoy mothering the distraught woman.

Damn her. Why won't she take me seriously? thought Corinne in desperation. To make matters worse, some-

one had gained access to her office the night before last.
When she had come to work yesterday morning, she'd
noticed that the handblown glass paperweight on her
desk had been moved three inches away from the ink
stain on the blotter, the spot where Corinne always kept
it. Of course, the cleaning woman could have moved it
when dusting the desk, but she had never touched anything on Corinne's desk before. The telephone had been
shifted slightly, too.

"You've been under a lot of strain ever since you
were released from the hospital, Cory. Want to know
what I think?" Kate asked gently.

"Please tell me." Corinne's lack of enthusiasm for
her friend's opinion was apparent. At the moment, she
was too bothered to care. She had been careful to keep
Derek's secret. Kate and Chris did not know his real
name or the real reason Derek had come to Circle City.
Only Meg knew, and Corinne knew she could trust her
assistant.

"I think Douglas Johnson's appearance has put you
under a terrific strain. You see Stan in him. You want
him to *be* Stan so much—"

"That's not true! He's unlike Stan in certain subtle
ways. Besides, I haven't seen . . . Doug in a whole week.
The last time was the night he took me to dinner at Le
Rocher."

Surprise registered on Kate Albert's face. "I'm sure
he's been busy."

"Too busy even to telephone me?" Tears sprang into
Corinne's eyes. She lowered her head and pressed her
hands over her eyes. She concentrated on taking deep,
slow breaths and felt herself begin to calm down a little.

"Did you two have a fight?" asked Kate, perplexed.

"No. Everything was . . . wonderful the last time we were together." *I'll never trust another man again as long as I live,* thought Corinne. She felt betrayed. She swallowed hard, fighting the lump in her throat.

Kate took a sip of coffee from her cup, looking thoughtful. "Are you telling me everything about this man, Cory?" Her dark eyes were upon Corinne, unflinching in their directness. But her look changed to one of sympathy when she saw the pain in the younger woman's face. "Is Doug really a corporate officer of Spurgon?" she asked gently.

Corinne stared at her friend. Kate looked too knowing. "What makes you think he isn't?" she asked, her breath catching in her throat.

"Chris had a chunk of money to invest and he looked up the Spurgon Corporation's annual report after meeting Doug. Doug's name was not listed as one of the vice presidents on the corporation brochure. Doesn't that strike you a bit odd?"

Corinne swallowed hard. Kate sat, alert, awaiting an answer. For years Corinne had confided in Kate Albert; she knew about the fights with Stan, the frustration she'd felt when she wanted a child and Stan didn't, and . . . the change that had come over Stan during the last year of their marriage. Kate had listened patiently, nodding her head and reminding Corinne of the pressures a surgeon endured. She had heartily approved the idea of the trip to Jamaica, a second honeymoon.

"Douglas Johnson is not his real name. His real name is Derek Moar. He's a private investigator here on an undercover assignment," Corinne confessed. "That's all I can tell you. I shouldn't even be telling you this much," she said in a low voice.

"Derek Moar? A private investigator?" Kate's voice rose in surprise, her eyes widening. "Does he know that the police think someone sabotaged your car?"

"I never told him."

"Why not, for heaven's sake?"

"The subject never came up. Sergeant Masters may have been mistaken, anyway. It was just his theory. I'm probably imagining the black Ford behind me, as well. The driver is probably someone who lives on Stemple Road and leaves for work and comes home the same time I do." Corinne gave a sheepish smile.

"You know what I think is *really* bothering you?" Kate asked in a conspiratorial whisper, leaning forward. Without waiting for Corinne to answer, she said, "In my day women were trained to wait for the men to call us. Things are different now. A woman can make the first move. If Derek Moar hasn't called you, why not call him? Or do you want *me* to call him and arrange a dinner at my place, all four of us?"

"No!" Corinne said quickly. Kate looked crushed. "It's Chris, not you, Kate. Did you and he make up after that evening at my house?"

Kate's lips drew into a thin, determined line. "After a few days. Chris Albert is a man who likes things his own way, but I intend to be my own woman from now on. I'm returning to nursing, part-time at least. I can't allow my husband to dictate to me. We shall discuss things and reach amicable solutions."

The two women talked some more, and Corinne felt a little less anxious. She spent a pleasant weekend puttering around the house, and by Monday she'd screwed up enough courage to slip downstairs to the bank building lobby and call Derek's number from a pay telephone. She suspected her office telephone was bugged. This, too, was probably paranoia at work, but nevertheless, she couldn't shake the feeling.

At nine in the morning, there was no answer in suite 1802. Why was he avoiding her?

"HERE'S A GOOD PROSPECT. We may have found our man," said Arnold Zinser, throwing a small file card with a business name written on it down onto his cluttered desk. He was in an unusually good mood for 9:10 a.m. on a Monday morning. He leaned back in his desk chair. "Mrs. Daye has a connection with that outfit, as I told you. I'm not surprised she chose not to discuss this client with you."

Derek picked up the handwritten card. On it was the name of At-X Communications, Inc., the same video production company Derek knew was Corinne's client.

"You think this is where the duplicate tapes are being made from the master?" asked Derek, subdued. He perched on the corner of Zinser's desk, one foot swinging in air, the other foot planted firmly on the office floor.

For the past week he had not been sleeping well. He had hidden in his comfortable suite of rooms and had avoided paying that call on Tim Greer that Zinser expected him to make. Derek was scared of learning the truth—that Corinne Daye might not be the honest, wonderful woman he thought she was.

If she's just been playing with me, stirring up my emotions and watching me dance to her tune...using me...like she used me as a substitute for Stan the day she followed me up to my hotel room... Derek's thoughts were nagging whispers of doubt.

"Derek, did you hear what I said?" Zinser asked sharply.

"Sorry." He managed an apologetic half smile.

"I said, Greer has all the facilities for mass duplication of tapes. It says so right in his ad in the yellow pages," said the man behind the desk who sat comfortably in shirt sleeves, his suit jacket on a hanger suspended from a hook on the wall of the agency field office. Arnie wore his shoulder holster, the revolver nestled beneath. "She never mentioned her connection with Greer to you?"

"No." Derek stood up rigidly in front of Arnie's desk.

"She represented At-X in a lawsuit to collect a chunk of money a customer owed them and failed to pay. That was three years ago. She's been on retainer ever since, I suspect."

"You had a check run on all court cases to find every one she's been connected with?" A chill passed through Derek. Zinser had been thorough, indeed.

"Her phones are tapped, too, so be careful. Don't call her," Zinser warned him. "She wins a high percentage of her cases. She must be raking in the dough. She's sure not keeping the money in her bank account, though. Fifty industrial VCRs and a distribution amplifier, whatever the hell that is, represents a huge chunk of money. I'll recommend to the IRS that they do an audit on her back tax forms."

Derek sank down again, one hip on the corner of Zinser's desk.

"You can't have a real case against her yet, Arnie. All you have is the record of the purchase of a couple pieces of electronic equipment," Derek argued.

"A couple of pieces? Come on, Derek! One distribution amplifier and fifty industrial VCRs? Hardly the kind of stuff you buy for your house! If you or I had

that kind of money at our disposal, we could retire tomorrow.''

Zinser pointed to the card in Derek's hand. ''Mrs.
Daye is involved, all right! Why they didn't move the
new equipment into the At-X facility instead of building a place clear out in the country, I can't understand.
Whichever location is being used, I think we've found
our piracy ring, and she's a definite partner. Maybe
even the brains. We've had this At-X place under surveillance the past week. Business must be good!'' The
faint smile on the thin lips was loaded with meaning.

''Go on,'' Derek said tensely.

''They worked late last Saturday night. Lights were
on until two in the morning. A Ford station wagon
showed up and parked in the service alley and one man
loaded cartons into the back of the car. When the car
left, one man locked up and went home. That man was
Tim Greer himself, according to his license plate.

''Why did only one man work? Why not run everyone on overtime if it's a legit rush job? That's your job,
to find out. Get Timothy Greer to accept your story and
confide in you. Metro Mega will be demanding a complete report soon, and it'll help you keep the Spurgon
Corporation off your back and the expense money
rolling in if you come up with some answers.''

''You're centering your investigation around Corinne Daye now,'' Derek argued. ''But all the evidence
you have is circumstantial. You may be sniffing up the
wrong tree.'' Derek wished he were more sure of that.

''I'll lay you odds she's the brains behind the whole
operation. She may be giving Greer his orders.'' He
reached for a cigarette, first offering Derek one. He refused it with a wave of his hand. ''That's right, you quit

smoking, didn't you? You're a damn martyr," Arnie grunted, blowing out the match.

"No, I finally got smart! And I'm not going to hang around you and breathe the air you pollute," Derek said sourly, sliding off the corner of the desk.

"That woman's sure gotten to you! You used to have a friendly disposition. I'm going to nail her, Derek. I'll give the judge enough to send her up for five years with a fine that will bleed her dry." Zinser leaned forward in his chair. "She knows the law, and she's violating it with impunity, raking in the dough by committing a felony and cheating our government out of the taxes she owes. Such a lawyer deserves the full penalty of the law and should be disbarred."

"She's also innocent until proven guilty. That's what I was taught in law school. Have you had a directive from the Justice Department to supercede that philosophy on which our judicial system is supposed to be based?"

"You're not funny, you know that?" growled Zinser. "Do you know how many times I've risked my life because I *do* believe in the constitution and our judicial system?"

"I'm sorry, Arnie. You do a good job. You're thorough, you leave nothing to chance and you know how to handle the agents in your charge. But you're dead wrong about Corinne." Derek spoke with a bravado he did not quite feel; for he, too, had been trained to regard hard, cold facts as more important than personal intuition. So far, all Derek had was his intuition, and he was plagued with doubts. He *wanted* to believe Corinne was innocent. That didn't mean she was. He *wanted* to believe she was being honest when she made love, but the idea that she might be using him threatened all the faith he had in himself.

"If you cover up any facts, I'll have you sent up as an accomplice, Derek. We may be friends, but that cuts no ice in my report," warned Zinser.

"My reports, of which you get one copy and Spurgon the other, are complete," said Derek. "What more do you want from me?"

"Your loyalty, as a former agent," answered Zinser.

A long silence passed between them. "You've got it," said Derek. "I'll run out to Grant Road and look the place over after I pay a visit to At-X."

"Derek, I understand what you must be feeling right now." Zinser's voice dropped and his cool gray eyes betrayed an unusual compassion. "Keep in mind that as soon as you arrived in town, the shipments of master tapes from L.A. stopped. And as soon as you met this Daye woman, the method of operation suddenly changed."

The gazes of the two men locked. Derek broke first. Without a word of farewell and eager to escape the acrid odor of cigarette smoke, Derek Moar left the FBI office. Like it or not, Douglas Johnson was on his way to pay a visit to Timothy Greer.

AT ELEVEN O'CLOCK, Derek stood on the sidewalk outside At-X Productions, Inc. The image of a top executive for a large corporation was reflected in clean plateglass window. A new gray wool suit, maroon silk tie and gold-plated cuff links, a small diamond in each, created the illusion.

He stared at the sign in gold letters on the window.

3/4" & 1" Facilities * Production * Editing *
Duplication * State of the Art Equipment *
Trained Personnel * Services to Industry,
Business, Schools & Advertising Agencies

Closed venetian blinds blocked a view of the interior.

Derek pushed open the door. He walked into a cozy reception area. An attractive young blond woman sat at the desk, opening mail. An electric typewriter sat at right angles to the desk and a white Touch-Tone telephone sat close to her elbow.

"Yes, sir. May I help you?" she asked in a businesslike tone, looking up.

"I'd like to see Mr. Greer on a matter of business. Here is my card." Derek thrust forward the business card of Douglas Johnson, vice-president in charge of Business Development for Spurgon Corporation.

"If you're selling supplies, we have companies we deal with on a regular basis—" she started to say. When her glance fell to the card extended toward her, a slight flush of embarrassment spread over her pretty face. "You didn't make an appointment, did you, Mr. Johnson?"

"I didn't call for one. I'm sorry. You were recommended to me by Corinne Daye. I'm seeking a video production firm in the Midwest for a possible purchase by the Spurgon Corporation."

"Mr. Greer just hung up." The blinking white light on her telephone had just gone off. The receptionist seemed flustered. "Please be seated." She pushed a button. "Tim, Douglas Johnson, vice president with Spurgon Corporation, is out here to see you. Shall I send him in?'' She listened intently for a moment, then hung up. "He'll be right out. Please wait."

"Is my information correct? Mr. Greer is one of the owners as well as the manager?"

"That's correct."

"Good!" The emphasis he gave the word seemed to unnerve her. The blond head bent over the mail as she deliberately ignored him.

A wiry, smooth-shaven man who was about five feet nine inches appeared in a doorway. He was dressed in plain trousers and a sport shirt open at the neck and looked comfortable. Derek silently envied him and swallowed against the knot of the silk tie.

"Tim Greer," said the smaller man with a smile, approaching Derek with his hand extended. He moved with ease and brisk energy, and his handclasp was firm and trustworthy.

"Doug Johnson," answered Derek, maintaining his poise.

"Can we do a training or employee motivation film for you?"

"May I talk with you privately, Tim?"

The smaller man was instantly alert. "Sure. Hold my calls and take messages, Sue," he instructed the receptionist before leading Derek down the hallway to a small office with a cluttered desk.

TIM GREER TREATED Derek to a tasty luncheon at a seafood house. Derek allowed his reserve to melt slowly. They discussed football and the NFL and the best big-ten basketball prospects for the coming season. They also discussed the virtues of Tim's business, to which he was dedicated heart and soul.

"Spurgon is willing to pay us *that much* to take us over and then allow us to continue to operate the business for them at a salary?" His hazel eyes were bright, his face intent.

"Your facilities and your customer goodwill are worth a tidy sum, Tim. Of course, I'll need to see your ledgers and report back to California before I can make you a firm offer. I need to know *all* your sources of income to have a fair picture to present to the front office."

"You want to see the books?" He frowned at the unusual request. "You say Ms Daye recommended us to you? She's one hell of a fine lawyer." Approval chased away the frown.

"I assume Mrs. Daye has money invested in your company. For the purchase of new equipment, perhaps? Is she a silent partner? I notice you have forty industrial VCRs in your tape duplicating room." Derek was referring to the quick tour Tim had given him before they left for lunch.

"You counted them?" Greer looked surprised. "No, Mrs. Daye is not connected with our place in any way but as our attorney. She handled one lawsuit several years ago to collect money due us by a large company for past work. We put her on a small retainer to handle our collection work. No, sir, there are no silent partners around our place. Just me and Rex—and Rex is anything but silent!" Tim chuckled.

"I have to have a *complete* picture of your operations, understand? The bottom line is all that matters to Spurgon," Derek said softly. His meaning was clear.

Tim Greer's hazel eyes were studying Derek's face. "That philosophy could get you into a peck of trouble if you bump heads with the law, couldn't it?"

"I wouldn't know," Derek said stiffly. "We all go into business with one objective—to make money. Do you work your employees often at night? I'm thinking of overhead expense."

Tim Greer's face assumed a careful expression. "No. We never work at night. Rex doesn't like to pay out overtime."

"Never?"

"Never," asserted Tim.

Derek threw caution away. He had to glean information that would exonerate Corinne. "I drove past your place about two in the morning the other day on the way to my hotel. I saw a Ford station wagon there in the alley, and the back door was open as though someone was loading the car."

Tim Greer's face closed shut, and the friendliness fled from it. He seemed to sense Derek's tension. "There could have been a car back there. We have a no parking sign in the alley but people sometimes ignore it. There's nothing I can do about that." He glanced at his watch. "I have to get back."

The two men returned to the hallway in front of Tim Greer's office, and the man seemed suddenly wary. He refused to show Derek the ledgers. "Look, I don't mean to be rude, but a client is due any minute. I've got your card. I'll talk your deal over with Rex. This is Tuesday. Call me on Friday. I can't guarantee we'll be interested."

"Tim, there's a call on line one for you. It's important," Sue called down the hallway from the reception room.

"Excuse me," Tim said abruptly, and went into his office and slammed the door.

Say **YES** to Romance

Say YES to free gifts
worth over $20.00

Say YES to a rendezvous with romance, and you'll get 4 classic love stories—FREE! You'll get a lighted makeup mirror and brush kit—FREE! And you'll get a delightful surprise—FREE! These gifts carry a total value of over $20.00—but you can have them without spending even a penny!

MONEY-SAVING HOME DELIVERY!

Say YES to Harlequin's Reader Service, and you'll enjoy the convenience of previewing four brand-new books delivered right to your home months before they appear in stores. Each book is yours for only $2.50—25¢ less than the retail price.

SPECIAL EXTRAS—FREE!

You'll get our monthly newsletter, *Heart to Heart*—the indispensable insider's look at our most popular writers and their upcoming novels. Now you can have a behind-the-scenes look at the fascinating world of Harlequin! You'll also get additional free gifts from time to time as a token of our appreciation for being a home subscriber.

Say YES to a Harlequin love affair.
Complete, detach and mail your
Free Offer Card today!

FREE—Lighted Makeup Mirror and Brush Kit. This lighted makeup mirror and brush kit allows plenty of light for those quick touch-ups. It has its own on/off switch and operates on 2 easy-to-replace batteries and bulbs (batteries not included). Holds everything you need for a perfect finished look, yet small enough to slip into your purse or pocket (4-1/8" x 3" closed).

DETACH AND MAIL CARD TODAY

BUSINESS REPLY CARD

First Class   Permit No. 717   Buffalo, NY

Postage will be paid by addressee

Harlequin Reader Service

901 Fuhrmann Blvd.,
P.O. Box 1394
Buffalo, NY 14240-9963

NO POSTAGE
NECESSARY
IF MAILED
IN THE
UNITED STATES

Derek went into the men's room next to Tim Greer's office, sick with apprehension. He checked the thin lead wire that ran from the miniature microphone in his tie clasp, down under his shirt and through a slit in his shirt to the miniature tape recorder hidden in a pocket sewn into the lining of his suit coat. Tim Greer's words were on tape, and even the subtle nuances of inflection were revealing.

Derek was displeased with himself. He had had the man eating out of his hand until he'd mentioned the late-night activity. Could he have phrased the question differently? Despite Greer's assurances, Derek feared Corinne was involved with some illegal activity going on in this place.

He leaned wearily on the white enameled sink in the washroom, his sandy head bowed, his stomach upset by too much shrimp and crab-stuffed flounder and a bad case of nerves. He heard the receiver slam down on the cradle in Tim Greer's office beyond the thin partition.

He heard the man's voice sound faintly through the wall. "Sue, get Mrs. Daye's office on the phone as soon as this joker leaves. If she's in court, tell her secretary that Mr. Johnson's been here and describe him to her. Find out what in hell the secretary knows about him. He's been asking a lot of questions. I want to know why."

CHAPTER ELEVEN

CORINNE GLANCED UNEASILY into the rearview mirror of the automobile she'd been leasing since her release from the hospital. Two bright headlights glared in the dark, but the car was maintaining a discreet distance.

Her hands tightened on the steering wheel. In the darkness, the dashboard lights glowed softly, the speedometer held steady at fifty, and the clock read 8:10.

Corinne fixed her eyes to the black two-lane winding ribbon of road ahead. At this time of night her street was like a country road, devoid of traffic. Only an occasional street lamp illuminated the night, and dark clumps of shadowed trees lined the road.

Corinne turned into the lane that led to the circular driveway in front of her house. Glancing into the mirror, she saw the headlights mysteriously vanish. She stepped hard on the accelerator and plunged ahead into the black void bordered by trees, fighting the fear that rose in her throat.

Ahead of her an automobile sat motionless, a dark silhouette in the driveway, blocking the way into the garage. Inside the parked car was a formless shadow.

Corinne did not activate the automatic garage-door opener. She sat motionless, with the car's engine running and the headlights fixed on the shadowed form sitting in the car.

The beat of her heart was frantic, the lump in her throat growing thicker by the second. Then she recognized the tall male form that unfolded itself from the compact car. She turned off the engine, gave a sigh of relief and rolled down the car window.

"Derek! How long have you been here? Why didn't you let me know you were coming?"

"I decided against calling you at the office," he answered, his voice tight. "I've been waiting here over an hour." As he walked toward the car, moving in a gait slightly out of rhythm, she wondered if the leg injured in the shoot-out in Chicago was bothering him.

"I'm sorry. I was late getting away from the office. I was in court until four. Then I had a new client for a five o'clock appointment. She needed to talk."

"So I see." He bent down and put his hands on the window frame. His sapphire eyes were brooding. "We need to talk, too," he said, his resonant voice tense.

"Have you had any dinner?" asked Corinne.

"I didn't think about eating. I was anxious to get here." His voice was laced with fatigue.

"I'll drive into the garage. Pull your car inside, too. There are leftovers in the fridge. I haven't had anything to eat since morning."

The garage door slid noiselessly upward, and the garage lights flooded the driveway with a harsh glow. She drove into the right-hand side, leaving space for Derek's leased compact car on the left. As soon as his car was in place, the headlights extinguished and the motor turned off, the garage door slid silently downward and locked automatically with a solid click.

On the other side of the door to the kitchen a warning growl sounded, then a high-pitched bark. "The lock looks new,'' commented Derek as Corinne inserted a key into the dead bolt.

"It is. I had new locks put on every outside door of the house after I came home from the hospital.'' Corinne didn't tell him why. She flipped the switch in the kitchen, and a cherry light bathed the tidy room. Penny stood up on her scrawny hind legs, placing her front paws on Corinne's knee to have her head rubbed in greeting. Then the tiny terrier ran to Derek, pausing to sniff his ankles first, before beseeching him for attention in the same way.

Derek stooped and carefully lifted Penny, cradling the six-year-old pup in his arms.

Corinne studied Derek. Something about him had changed. He seemed almost a stranger—withdrawn and taciturn. Shadows clung beneath his greenish-blue eyes and his face looked leaner than when she had last seen him over a week ago.

Her body trembled imperceptibly as he helped her off with her lightweight cashmere coat. "Do you know anyone who might be following me?'' she asked, trying to sound casual.

He didn't answer, but seemed to sink deeper into the gloom that was enshrouding him. She interpreted that as a positive answer. "I'll whip us up a quick dinner from leftovers,'' she said briskly. "Let Penny outside for a minute, will you? She's been shut up in the house all day.''

"Come on, pup.'' Derek led the dog out through the kitchen and used the small door in the rear of the garage. They both disappeared into the back yard. Soon they returned, Penny following obediently at Derek's heels.

"I'll help. You've worked all day," Derek said. He removed his down-filled jacket and draped it over the kitchen stool. He went to work making the coffee.

Corinne took the remains of a huge stewing hen from a bowl, placed the chicken in a baking pan and slid it into the oven to warm. Leftover rice and vegetables joined it on the oven rack. She started to make a salad.

"I'll help you," he murmured, washing his hands at the sink. He found a spare paring knife and began to slice carrots.

"I know that Tim Greer called you today," Derek said quietly, applying the small knife to the carrot he held in one hand. Thin yellow-orange rings fell into the bowl.

Corinne glanced up, surprised. "He did? How do you know? Meg didn't tell me. I was in court this afternoon." Corinne paused. With the paring knife she was using poised in midair, she asked, "How did you meet Tim Greer?"

"What does he have to hide, Cory? And why are you the first person he calls when the heat is on?" Derek demanded to know.

"How the hell should I know?" Corinne froze, staring at him. His face was inscrutable. "People often call an attorney when something goes wrong. He's my client. He keeps me on a small retainer."

The knife in Derek's hand slipped and sliced the skin of his thumb. Bright red blood oozed from the cut. He put his thumb to his lips and sucked it.

"Here," she murmured, tearing off a piece of paper towel and taking his hand. She wrapped the toweling around his thumb tightly and held the makeshift bandage in place with firm pressure.

"The FBI is following you," said Derek.

She stared at his troubled face. "That's a terrible joke, Derek. Not one bit funny," she declared.

"Who's joking?" His face was haggard.

"What have I done?"

"Don't pull that goddamn innocent routine with me, Cory! For once, just once, level with me! This may be the last chance you have. Tell me everything and perhaps I can get you time off for being cooperative." His jaw was tense. A tiny pulse throbbed at the side of his neck.

"Time off? For what? So I'm guilty until proven innocent, am I?"

Her hand was shaking when she removed the paper towel from his thumb. The bleeding had stopped, and the paper was covered with dots of blood.

"Look, Derek, it's been a tough day! I'm so hungry I'm not hungry anymore, and I don't want to quarrel with you. First we have a cup of coffee, then a meal. Then we talk. You can explain to your heart's content what this is all about. The FBI suspecting me of something... That's the craziest thing I've ever heard of!" Crisp pieces of celery fell to the cutting board. She chopped mechanically, numbness creeping through her. "Go light a fire in the den, why don't you? We can eat in there."

He obeyed and walked toward the den, moving as if a heavy weight lay across his shoulders. Once there, he knelt in front of the fireplace and arranged the logs and crumpled newspaper. Then, he struck a match to ignite the paper. When Corinne came into the den, carrying a tray loaded with plates of steaming food, the fire was already catching. Tendrils of smoke wafted up from the logs, filling the room with the scent of pine.

Penny ran to Derek and thrust her head insistently under his arm, waiting to be petted.

"I'm not your daddy, dog. Go away," mumbled Derek.

The dog refused to leave his side, attempting to bury her flat nose into the opening of his pocket and nuzzling his hip. "I'm not Stan, dammit!" he shouted, jumping to his feet. The tiny dog cowered and gazed up at him with sad, dark eyes.

The burning wood crackled in the silence. "She thinks she did something wrong," said Corinne in a sad voice.

Derek bent, contrite. He reached out and pulled the dog close to him. He closed his eyes as if he were in anguish, and he rested his wide forehead lightly on Penny's smooth, black-and-white back. "I'm not mad at you, Penny. I'm not taking it out on you, babe," he murmured. The dog licked his cheek.

"First we eat. Then I want you to explain to me why the FBI is interested in me. If you think it will help, I'll go to see the agent in charge myself and get things straightened out," Corinne said, pretending a self-confidence she did not, at the moment, feel.

Derek stared at her. Hope ignited in his sapphire eyes. "That will surprise Arnold Zinser, all right!" he muttered before digging into the food on his plate. The aroma was too tempting to resist.

"I haven't done anything wrong," she asserted quietly. Though she had little appetite for food, the coffee was hot and invigorating, and she managed to wash small bites down. Her thigh touched his lightly as they sat side by side on the leather sofa, balancing round trays on their lap.

After dinner she opened a can of fruit and served the fruit over ice cream. When she surveyed her empty bowl and the second cup of coffee beside her, the restless ache for a cigarette returned to haunt her.

As if he knew exactly what she was feeling, Derek gave a little smile. "You don't need a cigarette. It takes a while for the habit to extinguish itself. Substitute something in its place." He pulled a package of mints from his pocket and offered it to her.

"You still suck these things?" she asked, accepting the gift. She was beginning to feel a peace in his presence, a peace she had never felt with the perfectionistic Stan. She had always been so concerned with pleasing him that she had rarely relaxed enough to please herself.

"No. I bought these mints for you. Today. I knew you'd still be fighting the craving. You're winning, Cory. Don't give up now, when you're almost there."

The round peppermint tablet was cool and soothing to her tongue. His small act of thoughtfulness touched her.

Derek took the tray stacked with empty plates and bowls into the kitchen, rinsed the dishes quickly and arranged them in the dishwasher before returning to the den. As he entered the room, Corinne braced herself for the coming ordeal.

"If it's okay with you," he started out by saying, "I closed Penny up in the kitchen since her bed is in there. I left the light on, and gave her fresh water. We need to talk seriously, and Penny is a distraction."

"She loves you, Derek. She can't stay off your lap. But you have my permission to incarcerate my dog." She gave a weak smile. The word *incarcerate* left an unpleasant taste in her mouth. "Okay, Derek, what does your friend Zinser have against me?'' she asked quietly.

"The Justice Department was able to obtain lists of customers who bought commercial electronic equipment in the past three years from Japanese and American manufacturers. You were listed as having ordered one distribution amplifier and fifty industrial VCRs. The shipping destination was 10978 Grant Road.''

Her eyebrows rose. Fifty industrial VCRs? She didn't even have one in the house. And what in the hell was a distribution amplifier? She searched Derek's face for a hint of smile, in vain.

"A distribution amplifier? Tim Greer may be my client, but he never discussed equipment with me. What is it?'' she asked.

"I don't know. Something used in tape duplication for boosting the video signal and power levels to the VCRs.''

"That sounds expensive! I'd sure know if I wrote a check for that sum, wouldn't I? Well, I didn't! I can show all my past bank statements to your friend, Mr. Zinser.''

"I'm not sure he's my friend anymore. He's accusing me of being your accomplice because I'm still seeing you.'' His angular face looked pained. "I'm considering sending in my resignation to Spurgon and Metro Mega Studios and giving up the investigation.'' Derek had decided nothing could make him testify against Corinne, even if she was guilty—even if she was playing him for a fool.

"Give it up?'' She felt a sudden sense of loss. What if he went back to Chicago and she never saw him again? The thought brought sudden pain. "So...there's been a computer error somewhere in the sales records.

My name was put down by mistake,'' she said, feeling suddenly drained of all energy. Warmth poured forth from the fireplace, yet her skin felt chilled.

"The list gave your home address, your office address, your office phone number, the 'ship to' address of the building on Grant Road and the numbers of the bank cashier's checks in payment," he said harshly, raising his voice. "Bank cashier's checks!"

"On what bank?" she shot back, also raising her voice.

He frowned, trying to remember. "Avisco Trust, I think."

"I never use Avisco Trust's services. No particular reason. I always use the bank in the building where my office is located. And I don't make transactions using bank cashier's checks. I only write checks on my personal account or my office account so that I have a receipt with each cancelled check," she explained.

He rose from the sofa and paced the floor restlessly.

"By using cashier's checks the transaction wouldn't show up on the bank microfilm record of your checking account. You know that. But the amount of withdrawal would. Corinne, stop lying to me! I suppose you don't know anything about the building on Grant Road, either."

"What building?" asked Corinne, almost hysterical.

He stopped pacing and turned to face her. "Dammit, Cory, quit the big act! You're not helping yourself one bit with this useless charade!" Heartsick that Zinser might have been right and that he had been wrong about Cory all along, he'd almost shouted the words.

"Then *you* tell me about this place on Grant Road. Where is it, for Pete's sake?" Corinne almost shouted, too, the cleansing surge of anger purging the apprehension momentarily.

"Ten thousand nine hundred seventy-eight Grant Road. A cinder-block building. Painted white. No windows. About three thousand square feet in size. It's a one-story building on a big patch of ground surrounded by a tall barbed wire fence. Only a number on a rural mailbox. No company name, no sign of life when I was out there. Now, you tell me what's inside that building. I bet it's fifty VCRs and a distribution amplifier, for openers." He glared at her defiantly.

"I don't know! I know nothing about it!" She was on the verge of tears, but she refused to let one escape. Her nerves were on edge, and her temper was slipping out of control. "It's not *my* electronic equipment, I tell you! I know absolutely nothing about electronics. How would I know what equipment to order? How would I run it?"

Derek paced the floor, an ominous look on his face. Suddenly he halted and whirled on his heel to face her. "Maybe that's where Tim Greer comes into the picture. He's part of this video piracy operation, isn't he? Tell me! I can get you off with a lighter sentence if you'll turn state's evidence."

"Video piracy operation?" Corinne looked at Derek in horror. Tim Greer was as straight as they came; she would gamble her life on it. Tim was under suspicion, too? The whole world was going crazy.

Corinne rose from the sofa, too agitated to sit still. She faced the fireplace, holding her hands out toward the fire, trying to warm herself. The chill of fear was spreading all the way through her. It appeared Arnold Zinser had some kind of circumstantial evidence that she'd committed a felony. That could mean a punitive fine, disbarment proceedings, even a prison sentence. Her career would be over.

All her life, she had believed in the principle of justice. So much so, in fact, that she was devoting her life to obtaining justice for others. The irony of it was tragic. Where was justice for her now?

The faint pendulum tick of the mantel clock synchronized with her labored heartbeat. Corinne whirled around to face Derek.

"You think *I* am capable of being involved with something like this? Me?" Perhaps that was the worst hurt of all.

"If you're not involved, Cory, then none of this makes any sense," said Derek.

Her breath caught as she stared at him. He looked awful, even ill. This crazy thing was taking its toll on him, too. She gripped the fireplace mantel for support.

"Nothing that's happened to me lately makes any sense. First, somebody tries to kill me by tampering with the brake-fluid line in my car—"

"What?" cried Derek, eyes widening. "All you told me was your brakes failed..."

"I couldn't believe the police were right. The department impounded my car and examined it. One of the sergeants told me that the brake-fluid line had been sabotaged during the day while I had the car parked. The leak was a very slow one."

"Who would want to kill you? Why didn't you tell me?" He was staring at her.

"And then there were the thirteen red roses delivered to the hospital without the name of the sender on the card. That made no sense to me, either. Only Stan ever sent me roses. An even dozen. Never thirteen. That seemed like some ghoulish joke. That gift makes about as much sense as my name being on a list of industrial VCR buyers—'' Her voice broke. ''Oh, Derek, Stan couldn't still be alive, could he? Wanting me dead? Or trying to drive me out of my mind?'' she whispered, wide-eyed.

Derek moved swiftly just when she needed his strength most. His arms went around her, and she crept into them, hiding her face against the hard wall of his chest. She felt the steady beat of his heart against her cheek.

''I'm sorry I ever doubted you, Cory. I should have known. There's someone behind this. But who?''

''I don't know,'' she wailed. ''I haven't made any enemies that I know of. I thought Sergeant Masters was exaggerating when he advised me to get the locks changed to dead bolts on all the outside doors.''

His rough cheek settled reassuringly against hers. He pressed his lips tenderly on her cheek. ''We'll find out,'' he murmured. ''Don't worry.'' He planned to bring Sergeant Masters and Arnold Zinser together, tomorrow if possible.

''Don't worry? Who in hell would go to such lengths to implicate me? They'd have to be crazy. Stark, raving mad! Or spiteful. Heartless...'' The tears were winning, filling her eyes. One escaped.

''Don't cry.'' Tears seemed to alarm him. His strong arms pulled her more firmly against his lean, taut body. Even Derek's embrace seemed so different than Stan's, she thought. Derek's had a sweet fierceness Stan's had never had. The coarse hair of his mustache grazed her cheek as his warm lips pressed against it.

''Maybe Meg will have some suggestions. She's amazingly resourceful when she wants to be. Maybe if the three of us put our heads together...." Corinne said, sniffing.

Corinne felt his body stiffen. "Don't tell Meg anything. Nothing! Understand?" he ordered. "Did she ever tell you about Willy, the man who lives with her?" asked Derek.

Corinne lifted her head. She stared up at him. "No. How strange," she mused, bewildered. "She told you she lived with a man? When?"

"That evening in your law library." He felt Corinne go rigid in his arms. He responded by pulling her closer. "So, for the time being, tell Meg nothing. Keep all conversation confined to what she needs to know to do her job. Nothing more! Okay?"

Corinne's head dropped. She nestled her forehead against the hollow where his neck met his shoulder, and she knew peace again. "Okay," she said in a soft voice, feeling protected and cared for. At the moment she desperately needed that kind of reassurance to keep everything from overwhelming her. "I'm sorry I raised my voice, Derek."

"I'm sorry, too, darling," he whispered. "I'll never doubt you again, I swear it."

He sought the hollow beneath her ear with his warm lips and tasted her skin with his warm tongue. The subtle scent of his skin, the invigorating roughness of his five-o'clock shadow filled her senses. Her heartbeat quickened as her hands roamed his broad back and found the muscular forearms hidden beneath the soft material of his shirt.

She sensed he wanted to speak, but all words became lost in the kiss he gave her. A large pop sounded in the fireplace as the flames licked a knot in the log. A golden cascade of velvet warmth enveloped Corinne in the snug circle of Derek's arms. No more was she wishing it was Stan she was embracing. Such intensity, such earthy firmness as she felt in Derek was foreign to Stan. She sensed a blend of consideration and tenderness in Derek, sensed that he was holding in check a passion that could careen out of control.

All within her responded. She wanted him desperately. She let him know it with kisses that held nothing back. "Derek . . . Derek . . ." Between kisses she whispered his name over and over, in wonder.

Urgency poured through his hard thighs, his groin, his muscle-layered chest. Need quickened his heartbeat and his breathing, making his skin damp beneath his shirt. They kissed without pause, lingering kisses, devouring kisses. She sensed he was drawing something vital from her through her mouth, and she offered it willingly to him as she caressed his searching tongue with hers.

"Oh, Derek, I don't want to go to prison and lose everything I've worked for!" she murmured, her eyes shut tight, the taste of his mouth in hers. His arms drew her closer. His strength was becoming hers.

"Hush," he commanded. "We'll find a way out of this." He kissed her again. She felt her confidence and hope revive. She was ready to face Arnold Zinser on her own initiative, on his own ground. She was innocent and somehow she had to convince Zinser of it.

"You're trembling," Derek whispered, moving her gently closer to the warmth of the fireplace. "These past days without you, Cory, have been pure hell." His whisper was fervent, his lips moist as his large hands stole upward under the wide skirt of her dress and pulled her panty hose down.

"You'd make a wonderful father, you know that?" she whispered, nuzzling his stubbly cheek.

"You'd make the perfect mother." Sapphire eyes shone in the soft firelight.

A strange elation swept through Corinne, making her giddy. She felt joyful. A child someday. That would be a dream fulfilled.

His hands cupped her bottom and lifted her slowly upward. Then, raising his leg and resting his foot on the edge of the leather sofa, he gently lowered her so that her soft, feminine warmth was resting on his hard thigh. She clung to him, her heart beating fast, her head tilting slowly backward to expose her throat. Warm lips, warm tongue, tips of gentle teeth made firm contact with the slim, silky-soft column of her neck in delectable sucking and nibbling motions while his arms pressed her firmly down upon his hardened thigh.

The telltale pressure between her legs left no doubt as to his state. Lightheaded from the kisses raining on her face and neck, Corinne felt the long zipper at the back of her dress move slowly downward. A delightful shiver rippled over her as her dress slipped down and her bra was released. The soft wool dress sank into thick folds around her slim waist. The warmth from the fireplace settled over her chest and back.

He encircled her bared waist with his hands and pulled her body slowly backward and forward over his hardened thigh. A wave of sheer delight radiated up through her abdomen at the gentle friction.

A haze of passion clouded his sapphire eyes. His resonant voice was husky. "I want you with me forever."

"Forever...forever..." she whispered, her words lost in a searing kiss. Her head moved in gentle rhythm with his as his hand moved in a starburst motion across her warm, full breast. The coarse hair on his upper lip was brushing her own upper lip in a coaxing tickle. She found the sensation pleasurable and exciting.

She was filled with languor and her nipples became turgid as his fingertips continued to work their magic. A shiver of delicious anticipation swept all the way through her. The echo from the pressure point where she balanced with parted legs on his thigh sounded deep in her pelvis.

The fingers of his other hand were making feathering movements parallel to her spine, circling sensuously at the base of her neck, along her delicate, rounded shoulders then back to her neck, down her spine and ending their journey low on her back.

Every nerve in Corinne came joyously alive in tingling trails. What little calm objectivity she had managed to retain fled, abandoning her to an elemental drive.

"Now. Please," she murmured. He lifted her, lowering his leg. She stepped out of her dress and half slip, letting them fall beside his clothes.

Tears of happiness sprang into her eyes. She held her arms open to him. As they sank to their knees on the thick area rug, she pulled the decorative pillows from the sofa for their heads and hips.

Her arms opened, locked about him and drew him down upon her chest. Her legs parted as her kiss triggered a fierce reaction in him. Her body arched to meet his, and her heartbeat merged with his tempo. She succumbed completely to the warmth that radiated around them and, like him, became driven by sheer desire.

Suddenly they both fell still. The den was silent except for the tick of the clock and the crackle of logs being slowly consumed by flames.

Corinne could not move, possessed by wonder at the miracle his body represented, so different from her own and yet so beautifully compatible. She pressed a tender kiss against his rough cheek. After a languid moment he rolled away from her, spent. Her worries seemed far removed, and the peace spreading through her deepened quickly to sleep as Derek threw a brightly colored afghan over her. She snuggled against him and yielded to the need to rest.

MORNING CAME, stealing over the trees surrounding the house, floating on the chill breeze of the last days of October. They awoke at the same time, both a bit stiff from the night spent on the floor of the den.

Dressed in a lilac-colored velour robe, Corinne hurried down the hall to the master bedroom. Derek was in the bathroom, taking his shower. She heard the steady spray of water. She planned to shower later. Before dashing down to the kitchen to prepare their breakfasts, Corinne wanted to run a comb through her hair. She looked around for Penny, then remembered. Derek had shut the dog away in the kitchen last night.

Strange. The master bedroom door was closed. Corinne distinctly remembered leaving the door open the morning before when she'd left for the office. She had not been in the room since. Her body still ached from spending the night on the den floor, snuggled close to Derek.

She opened the bedroom door, immediately detecting a strange odor that was sweet and sickening. Her mind reached back to her college days and laboratory classes. She recognized the disturbing smell. Chloroform. Yes, that was it.

Then she detected short, narrow legs and tiny white feet with dark nails. Corinne froze. She dropped to the floor and reached out for the limp dog. Penny's eyes were open only a tiny crack. Her eyes were not seeing, Corinne knew.

Her heart beating wildly, she gathered the limp form into her arms and held it against her. She placed her ear against the smooth white chest speckled with dark flecks, searching for a heartbeat. Corinne blinked rapidly; the dog reeked of the sweet, sickening odor of chloroform. She detected a very slow, very faint heartbeat.

Corinne's stricken glance swept the room. A cold feeling stealing through her, she got to her feet, still cradling the dog close to her body, as if to keep it alive by means of her own will. A landscape painting, an original oil by a Hoosier artist who had been a friend of her mother's, hung crookedly on the wall. Supporting the dog in one arm, she lifted the painting clumsily off its hooks.

The door to the small wall safe was ajar. With her free hand, Corinne released the painting and jerked the door of the safe open. It was empty. The papers implicating James Gaterow of embezzlement, a crime committed fifteen years before, were gone.

"Derek!" she screamed. She ran from the master bedroom and headed down the hall toward the closed bathroom door.

"Derek!" she shouted through the door, kicking it. The dog's body, limp in her arms, seemed heavier than twelve pounds.

"What's the matter?" He jerked the door open. His sandy hair was dripping wet and matted, and had a bit of a wave now, since he hadn't used hair straightener on it recently. Rivulets of water streamed down his naked body. "What happened to Penny?"

"She's been chloroformed! Someone broke in last night and stole evidence from my safe in the bedroom," raged Corinne, her face looking wild. "We must get her to the veterinarian right away. I'll explain everything later."

While Derek hurriedly toweled himself dry, Corinne laid Penny on her cushioned bed in the kitchen and dialed the home number of the veterinarian who had cared for Penny since the day Corinne had brought her home, barely weaned, a mite of a puppy that had fit in the palm of her hand. The veterinarian was shocked by Corinne's description of the dog's condition and agreed to open up the office and see what he could do. Corinne dressed hurriedly.

Derek was stunned when he surveyed the kitchen, dressed in the same clothes he had worn last night. "The dead bolt is locked. The windows are locked. How did the SOB get in?"

"Check the other doors and windows—no, there isn't time. We'll do that when we get back," said Corinne. They got in his compact car, and while Corinne held Penny on her lap, Derek drove frantically because a life was at stake. They were both too tense to talk. Corinne only gave him directions to the veterinarian's office.

Derek stood silently with Corinne beside the examining table while the doctor checked Penny over. "She almost got a lethal dose. She's such a small dog. I think she'll be okay, but I'll keep a close watch on her in case. Leave her with me. Call me later on in the day for a report," said the doctor.

On the way home Corinne explained how the papers had been brought to her by the widow of Gaterow's one-time employer, and Derek listened thoughtfully.

When they returned to the house on Stemple Road they went over every window, every door. There was no sign of forced entry anywhere. Derek double-checked everything.

"Who else has a key to the place?" Derek asked, tense.

"No one. I had dead-bolt locks put on the first week in September. I've given no one a key," Corinne answered angrily. There seemed no answer to her attorney's mind except one. Corinne's head recoiled. She wanted to throw china against the kitchen wall, scream bitter accusations.

Had she been wrong about Derek all this time? Was he capable of being bribed? Could James Gaterow offer enough money to buy Derek's soul? To do such a terrible thing to a little dog who loved him just to keep her from barking and awakening her . . .

Corinne's tormented thoughts whirled in furious circles. Derek had managed to break the combination to the safe, steal the papers and hide them in the compact car parked in the garage. She felt betrayed and abandoned. Her adrenaline surged.

"You won't get away with it, mister! Hand over the keys to the car or I'll call the police and press charges. We'll see how you like spending time in the lockup downtown." Her voice was harsh and ugly.

He looked dumbfounded as he dug into his trouser pockets and produced a small ring of keys. He tossed them to her with a look of bewilderment.

Corinne went into the locked garage, opened the trunk of Derek's car and dragged out the spare tire, scattering tools and letting the tire bounce to the garage floor. Nothing was hidden there. Her face grim, she opened the doors and started to yank on the seats with her bare hands as strength she never knew she had welled up within her.

"Stop that, dammit!" He caught her wrists and held them with a grip that threatened to crack the frail bones. "This is a leased car. I won't have you damage it."

"Then give me what you stole out of my safe!" A controlled fury blazed from her eyes. How could he have used her in such a way last night, making her trust him? That was worse than any theft. "And Penny..." Tears blinded her. "How could you do that to Penny?"

If she had hit him in the abdomen with doubled fists, his expression could not have shown more shock, more pain. "You think I could do such a thing to Penny?" He could barely speak. "You don't know how I feel about that little dog?" His eyes were flashing now, his jaw hardening into stubbornness, his breathing harsh. "What's with you, anyway? You've let that damned Meg turn you into some Jekyll and Hyde. Maybe Arnie was right!"

He jerked open the garage door, sending it careening upward on its rollers, dumped the tire back into its well in the trunk and slammed down the trunk lid. The compact car rocked on its tires. "Don't worry! You won't be bothered with me ever again!" He folded himself into the car in one abrupt motion, slammed the car door and revved the engine. The car shot backward, made a turn at the end of the driveway and sped out of sight, leaving Corinne standing alone in the entrance to the garage.

She stood alone, too numb to shed tears. A cool breeze rustled the leaves. A large grayish-brown rabbit leaped from a crouching position in the thick, short grass and landed in the middle of the driveway. Rising on muscular hind legs, it stared down the driveway after the vanished car, its dark, shiny nose wrinkling, its whiskers twitching, as if it had detected the scent of a lover's spat in the brisk autumn air.

The rabbit was no stranger to Corinne. It came regularly from the woods surrounding the house to pick up tidbits of food Corinne left for it. It often goaded Penny to chase it, and they would speed around the yews and the junipers until Penny suddenly reversed course and let the rabbit chase her. The rabbit would lope along, frustrating Penny when it would catch up with her and pass her to disappear into the dense brush.

Now, the rabbit turned on its large hind legs and stared directly at Corinne, its body stretched tall and vertical, paws held up before its chest. It looked so comical, so expectant that Corinne was caught off guard. Her anger sputtered, fizzled and vanished, leaving only a vague aching throb somewhere in her midsection.

She started to smile—a sad smile—despite herself. Beady black eyes remained fastened upon her while long whiskers twitched.

Penny has to live, thought Corinne. *The rabbit will miss her.*

"Penny can't play today. She's sick. Come back in a few days," Corinne told the rabbit. It dropped from its hind legs and obediently hopped away, disappearing into the brush.

CHAPTER TWELVE

CORINNE SAT STARING at the monitor of the personal computer on her desk. The cursor, a small green rectangle, kept flashing before the green letters, Margaret R. Krens.

Corinne had just entered the computerized public records. Margaret R. Krens was listed as the sole owner on a deed to three acres of land at 10978 Grant Road. The property was free of lien; the purchase date, eighteen months ago. A quick check of the records had revealed that a building permit had been issued to Margaret Krens fifteen months ago, permitting a one-story cinder-block building, comprising thirty-two hundred square feet of floor space, to be erected at that same address. Purpose of the building: to house a television repair shop.

Where did Meg get the money? thought Corinne, stunned. On the twenty thousand dollars a year Corinne paid her, Meg supported herself and dressed well. She often admitted to a weakness for nice clothes. Meg had also bought a Datsun 280 ZX automobile.

There was no doubt in Corinne's mind that the Margaret Krens in the public record was her secretary. There was only one M. Krens listed in the white pages of the Circle City telephone directory. The name was not a common one.

Too many questions remained unanswered. Papers and books lay strewn all over Corinne's desk. She was preparing a brief. Now her mind refused to focus on the task at hand. The questions kept intruding. Why had Meg failed to mention a live-in lover named Willy? Was she financing a television repair business for him? If so, that was harmless enough and not Corinne's concern.

Corinne's cheeks burned as she remembered the stinging accusations she had hurled at Derek that morning. Now that the cloud of emotion had lifted, and she'd spoken to the veterinarian, whose report on Penny was encouraging, Corinne's suspicion that Derek had committed the foul deed seemed foolish.

When Meg walked in without knocking, Corinne quickly turned the monitor off, not wanting her secretary to see what was on the screen. Fortunately, the two personal computers in the office were not linked. The one on Meg's desk was used only for word processing.

Meg leaned against the edge of Corinne's desk and crossed her arms over her chest. "I can't believe you'd stand up a wealthy old man and two very successful businessmen to stay home with a sick dog," said Meg. "What's wrong with the terrier? Doesn't your vet make house calls?"

The harsh noon light fell in slanting rays across the fair-skinned features of Margaret Krens, highlighting her curly cap of auburn hair and emphasizing the golden flecks in her emerald eyes. Dainty gold circles dangled from her pierced earlobes and swayed gracefully with each movement of her head. In the revealing light, her smattering of freckles, almost hidden by a very artful application of makeup, was clearly visible. Freckles also dotted the back of Meg's hands.

Derek's warning to Corinne to tell Meg only what she had to know to do her work effectively, and nothing more, flashed into Corinne's mind. *It might be a warning to heed,* Corinne conceded grudgingly. Only Meg had known about the papers implicating Gaterow. Only Meg had known that Corinne had taken the papers home to keep them in the bedroom safe. Yet Corinne's sense of loyalty remained strong. She refused to make assumptions about her without proof.

"Is everything okay?" asked Meg. "You looked uptight when you came in this morning. Is the trouble really the dog? Has Derek done something?"

She was definitely fishing. Corinne decided to play a cautious game, although she longed to come right out and ask Meg about the property on Grant Road. The moment had to be right; Meg had to be in one of her expansive moods, ready to talk.

"No trouble. Everything's fine. Why shouldn't it be?" said Corinne, stretching in her leather chair and suppressing a yawn. A crazy plan to test Meg had just popped into Corinne's mind. "Catch the telephone, will you?" Corinne asked, rising from the leather desk chair. "I'm going down the hall to the little girls' room."

Corinne left her shoulder bag on the floor beside her desk, as always. Sometimes she left it open, the snap unfastened, as she did today. She didn't take her bag with her to the ladies' lounge as she preferred to freshen her makeup at the mirror in the kitchenette. "Actually, Meg, the main reason I'm late is because someone broke into my house last night and robbed the safe. I called another locksmith to have the dead-bolt locks changed right away. I had to wait for the locksmith to come."

She headed for the doorway leading to the reception room, hoping the lie sounded convincing.

"Was something taken?" Meg asked, almost indifferently.

"The embezzlement evidence implicating Gaterow," said Corinne, pausing and glancing back. Meg's face showed no response whatsoever.

"You can't report a theft like that to the police, can you?" asked Meg. "Besides, the papers didn't belong to you; they belonged to that old woman who brought them to you."

A chill swept over Corinne at the unemotional response. Had Meg changed so much in the past five years or was she merely being more open to Corinne now?

"It would be hard to explain, yes. Without the papers as proof, I don't dare say a word about Gaterow. He could sue me for slander. Oh, by the way, I'll be back in about a half hour. I want to pop into Andy's place down the hall. I may need his help at tax time next year." Andy was a new accountant in the building, a personable young man who had sent several new clients to Corinne.

She closed the door to the office, her high heels clicking noisily down the hallway as she headed toward the ladies' room. Just short of it, she halted and leaned against the marbled wall, her eyes on her watch. Corinne was not subject to logic now. Gut-level feelings were what guided her. Despite the seriousness of the occasion, she smiled to herself, wondering what her favorite law professor, Dr. Berne, would think of her actions at this moment. He would disapprove of a lawyer playing detective, she was sure.

On tiptoe she moved back up the hall to the door of her office. Slowly she turned the knob. The door opened without a sound. Slowly Corinne closed it, quietly. She tiptoed through the reception room and peered through the half-opened door to her inner office.

Meg was behind Corinne's desk, leaning down toward the floor where Corinne's shoulder bag rested. Meg picked it up. She stood with it in her arm and pulled open the inside zipper. There was the slight sound of metal clinking. Something gleamed in Meg's hand.

Corinne's ring of keys.

Her heart hammered in her chest. She darted back to the door and slipped through it swiftly. Then she ran on tiptoe to an office door bearing the name of an insurance company, opened the door and darted inside, leaving the door open a mere crack.

The front door of Corinne's office opened. Meg glanced quickly in both directions. She locked the door and headed toward the elevator with Corinne's ring of keys in her hand. Corinne continued to peek through the slit until she heard the elevator doors open and close.

"May I help you, ma'am?" asked the woman at the desk behind the partition. "Are you interested in a life policy or medical coverage? Our agent can see you now."

Corinne started, her hand still clutching the doorknob. "Uh, I'll be back to see later. I forgot something." She threw a wan smile, ran out the door and took the next elevator down to the shopping level, her heart beating wildly against the tender wall of her rib cage. Wasting no time, half running, she headed for a shop with the name Angelo in gilded letters over the plate-glass window.

Meg was inside, at the rear of the store—the key duplicating corner. The sign on the wall said, Keys Made

While You Wait. Mr. Angelo was bent over his vise, grinding a duplicate, while his wife checked out a customer who was buying a can of hair spray.

Corinne turned away from the hardware store and ran back to the elevator, catching the next one going up. She ran to the office where Andy had his accounting business, next to Meg's office, and burst inside. "May I wait in here? I'm locked out of my office," she told his office girl. She then sank into a chair and waited for Meg to stroll by the long, vertical section of glass. From the corner of her eye she saw Meg walk by but pretended not to notice her. After a five-minute chat with Andy's secretary, Corinne left a vague message for Andy and got up and walked out.

Returning to her office was the difficult part. Corinne could feel the beginning of a tension headache. For the first time, she was fearful of Meg and wondered if her trusted alter ego was on the payroll of James Gaterow, too.

When Corinne entered her office, Meg was busy filing. Corinne's purse was beside her desk, just as she had left it. It did not appear to have been touched in her absence.

"Andy went to lunch early. Arlene said he would be back any minute, so I waited. I gave it up finally. Anything happen while I was gone?"

"I was here the whole time. Didn't even go to the john. Nothing much to report. I'm going to lunch now," said Meg. Her face was completely controlled. Nothing about her conveyed a shred of guilt or uneasiness. For a dizzying second, Corinne wondered if she had imagined the whole episode. She watched dazedly as Meg took her coat from the wall rack in the reception room and left.

Corinne sat motionless in the leather chair behind her desk, stunned. Many things now assumed new significance. How a thief had gained access to the house during the night while Derek and her had been sleeping on the floor of the den and how her Buick Regal had been taken from the indoor parking garage and returned were questions that were now easily answered—duplicate keys.

Corinne closed her eyes and leaned her head against the high back of the chair. She wanted to weep, but she was beyond the sweet release of tears. Never again would she lose her temper. Never again would she unleash razor-sharp words to cut another human being to the quick. Once the words were out, the damage was done and the words could never be recalled.

Corinne feared she had driven Derek away with her own foul temper. She felt the loss of him more keenly than she had ever imagined possible. There was a black hole in her life now, gaping and ominous. She had lost a lover, and she had driven away a dear friend, one who understood her even better than Kate Albert did.

And what made matters worse, Derek had been right about Meg.

CORINNE HAD NO INTEREST in food as noon came and went. But a voice from the past whispered in her ear a thought long forgotten and now remembered. It was her mother's voice repeating one of her favorite sayings. Whenever another child would push Corinne down, or when the boy behind her in class sprayed her with ink from a fountain pen, her mother would say, "Fight fire with fire."

Meg returned from lunch at exactly 1:57, one hour after she'd left. At two o'clock, after her one o'clock appointment had left, Corinne called Meg into her office and gave her a research job to do in the library. Ordinarily Meg enjoyed these breaks in the usual routine.

"Please look up these cases for the brief I'm preparing now," she asked Meg. "Then run me off duplicates of each case." The list was staggering in its length. "I'm promoting you to the status of paralegal soon. You need to be thoroughly familiar with this type of research," said Corinne.

Meg shot a withering look at her employer, but she accepted the scribbled list.

"I'll be working in my office. I'll keep the door to the hallway locked until my next appointment at four. You won't need to worry about covering the reception room. Enjoy yourself." Corinne couldn't help rubbing it in a little.

With a sullen face Meg went into the library, taking a hot cup of coffee with her. Corinne closed the door to her office, took the telephone receiver from its cradle and laid it on the blotter to keep the instrument from ringing. She then walked out to the reception area and breathed a sigh of relief when she saw her secretary's purse on the floor underneath her desk.

Holding her breath, Corinne opened Meg's handbag and surveyed the contents. She knew the ring of office keys was kept in the center drawer of Meg's desk during the day. The leather case of keys in the purse had to be Meg's personal keys. One of them, Corinne thought, might be the key to the mysterious building on Grant Road. Taking the leather case in which there were eight keys, including an ignition key for a car and a gas-cap key, Corinne replaced the bag on the floor, aware of the pulse beating in her ears. She quietly opened the door to the hallway, then closed it softly behind her.

Then she ran on tiptoe, as if demons pursued her.

She reached the elevator and leaned on the down button, cursing every second until the light came on over the set of closed doors. She rode down to the basement and ran directly to Angelo's.

A heavyset man stood behind the counter.

"I hired a new housekeeper and she needs a duplicate set of keys to the property," Corinne explained, pulling each key off its metal holding and handing the key to the person she assumed was Angelo. He asked for no explanation and seemed bored with the one she offered him. "Can you please hurry the job? I'm due back upstairs."

As he returned each master key to her, she replaced it on its holder in the key case with trembling hands, praying she had remembered the order the keys had been placed in so Meg would not be alerted.

Her heart pounding so hard that she could feel her pulse beating in her temples, Corinne rode back up to her office. Holding her breath, she eased open the door leading from the hallway. Meg was nowhere to be seen, presumably still in the law library on the other side of the kitchenette. Corinne returned the case of keys to Meg's handbag, then opened the door to her inner office and darted inside. She closed the door softly behind her and replaced the telephone on its cradle. She took a tortured breath and let out a sigh of relief, sinking into her chair behind the desk.

The faint noise of the duplicating machine sounded in the small room on the opposite end of the kitchenette. Meg was finishing up the assigned task, which had been only an excuse to keep her occupied long enough for Corinne to visit Angelo's.

Corinne leaned forward in her desk chair, trying to look absorbed in what she was writing on the yellow legal pad when Meg opened the door to the inner office. Corinne's hand was unsteady. Her vision was blurred from tension.

"Here are the copies of the cases you wanted." A sheaf of duplicates lay in Meg's open hands. "What are you doing, for God's sake, appearing before the Supreme Court?"

At ten minutes to four, Corinne made the excuse once again of visiting the ladies' room down the hall. This time she took her shoulder bag with her, for in it was a small manila envelop containing Meg's duplicated keys. She took the elevator to the lobby. From the pay phone she dialed the number of At-X Communications, Incorporated. She couldn't take a chance on Meg picking up the phone in the reception room and listening in. She also suspected a listening device had been attached to her telephone by the FBI.

"Sue, put me through to Tim right away. This is important. I'm Corinne Daye."

"Hello, Corinne. What can I do for you?" It was Tim's pleasant voice.

"Tim, I need your expertise." She had to trust him. There was no one else to trust but Derek, and Corinne doubted he would speak to her, not after the way she had talked to him that morning. "I want you to accompany me tomorrow on an important matter. I'll pay for your time. It should take about two hours. I'll pick you up at your shop at one o'clock tomorrow afternoon."

"Can't. Got a job to finish. Make it two sharp. What's this all about?"

"I'll tell you when I see you."

"Where are we going? I want to have a talk with you, too, about this guy named Douglas Johnson. He smells like a phony to me," complained Tim.

"We're going to Grant Road on business. Bring your portable camera with you. And, for heaven's sake, Tim, don't tell anybody where we're going. Don't even tell Sue. Whatever you do, don't tell my secretary!"

AT THE SAME MOMENT Corinne was making her date with Tim Greer over the telephone, Derek Moar opened the door to the Circle City FBI field office and walked toward Arnold Zinser's desk.

"I'm on my way to the airport. Maybe someone at the airline parcel service office can give me a description of A. E. Haegis. If so, I'll get it on tape. Haegis may be an alias used by the salesman who called on Briggs," said Derek. He knew the man named Tony was still missing.

"This is the salesman, Anthony Newell, alias Tony Sapenza, alias Tony Katten. Take a good look," said Zinser from behind the cluttered desk. He reached into a manila file folder and pulled out a five-by-seven color print of a man playing basketball with some teenaged boys in an inner city park. The image of a dark-haired lanky man dressed in jeans and a soiled gray sweatshirt was sharply in focus. In the photograph, he was playing basketball, and his hair was ruffled by wind, his mouth open in a gasp for breath. His features were sharp. His body was stretched in a leap toward the basket, his arm raised high, the ball released and inches away from his hand.

"We had the man under surveillance for two weeks," said Zinser. From experience, Derek knew Zinser's man had been in the back of a truck parked across the street and had used a telephoto lens.

"No sign of him yet?" asked Derek. Zinser only gave him a fish-eyed stare. "Has Briggs changed his mind about testifying in court yet?" Derek asked. His jaw was tense. The muscles across the back of his neck were knotted with tension from the scene with Corinne in the garage that morning. His temper had cooled a bit. He realized how worried she must have been about Penny, and he was worried about the dog, too.

"No. Briggs is still scared. He wasn't seriously injured by the beating the two punks gave him, but they made a threat against his family. Might be a bluff. Who knows? We'll give him more time to reconsider," Arnie answered. He eyed Derek thoughtfully. "You look like you've had a rough night."

"Someone entered the Daye home during the night, using a key, and stole evidence against a certain person of prominence in town. The bastard also chloroformed the dog, so she wouldn't bark and alert us. He even had the nerve to carry the dog upstairs and dump her in the bedroom where Corinne found her. By the way, how long have you had Corinne under surveillance?" Derek asked sharply.

"How long have you been sleeping with her?" Arnie countered. "I warned you that you could be implicated as an accessory. But no, you have to go barging right in when a doll crooks her finger—"

"She is not a 'doll.' She's my sister-in-law."

Zinser caught his breath. "Since when did you have a brother?"

"Since thirty-four years ago when our mother gave birth to identical twins. The nurse who was there at the birth told me the truth shortly after I arrived in town. The Moars adopted me. I never knew it."

Zinser let out an audible sigh and leaned back in his seat. "So you can't be objective about this case. No wonder." The toughness in his face softened momentarily to an expression of compassion, embarrassing Derek, who looked away.

"Check with Sergeant Masters of the Circle City Police Department," he said grimly. "Corinne had an auto accident in mid-July. CCPD examined the car. The brake-fluid line had been tampered with. He warned her to be careful, that someone might be out to get her, and to change all the locks on the doors at home. She did. There was no indication of forced entry. Someone had a key."

Zinser glanced up sharply. "In-fighting among the gang members. Happens all the time," he said dryly.

Derek chose to ignore the comment. "Her safe was robbed. The only item taken was evidence implicating a prominent attorney in town of embezzlement during his college days, about fifteen years ago."

This time Arnie sat up, all attention. "What attorney?"

"James Gaterow." Derek watched Arnie scribble the name on a scratchpad in his indecipherable handwriting.

"So she was blackmailing Gaterow—"

"No! The papers were left with her by the employer's widow, who died. She wanted Corinne to institute disbarment proceedings against Gaterow and take the evidence to the police. Corinne was reluctant to take the man's livelihood away from him, even under those circumstances."

Zinser leaned forward, forearms on the desk. "You really believe that story?" he asked quietly. He made a harsh sound, then leaned back abruptly. "My advice to you, buddy, is to get off this assignment. Disqualify yourself. Spurgon Corporation and Metro Mega are not receiving their money's worth if you're trying to shield the number one suspect. We'll have enough to get warrants in a few days. Then Ms Daye had better call in a good lawyer herself."

"Corinne is innocent."

"How do you know?" Zinser reached for a cigarette, frustration clouding his gray eyes. "Because she's the girl next door who married your brother? I need a better reason than that."

"I've resigned from the case. I've written a letter to the executives at Metro Mega who hired me." He patted the long envelope sticking out of his suit jacket pocket. "I want to be free to pursue this on my own."

"For *her*, you mean?" Zinser's gray eyes were cold shards of ice impaling Derek.

"Not for her. For justice, Arnie. For the principle that prompted me to apply to the Justice Department's training academy in the first place."

DEREK SHIVERED as he locked the doors of his rental car and walked toward the airport terminal. Although the sun was bright, the chill wind held no warmth as it blew against him. Something in Derek was hardening to the changes of season, to Corinne's angry outbursts, to Arnold Zinser's warnings.

Once inside the terminal, he dropped the letter of resignation into the wall slot at the post office. The die was cast now. No more expense checks would be arriving from California. He was on his own. He was also a free agent. He planned to stay away from Arnold Zinser until he had proof of Corinne's innocence. He knew Arnie to be a fair man in the presence of evidence.

Lost in his thoughts, Derek failed to notice a man carrying a suitcase who had passed him, glanced at him and stopped, an incredulous look on his face. "Stan. Stan, wait!" the man shouted.

Derek came to a halt, icy prickles stealing up his spine. He turned hesitantly to face a gray-haired stranger walking toward him, suitcase in hand, shock engraved on his lined face.

"Is it really you? God, I don't believe it. The newspaper said you died when Perlman's plane crashed. Where have you been, man? Why haven't you come back to the hospital? Were you injured?"

Derek stared at the stranger with hostility, yet he remained polite. "I'm sorry. You have the wrong man. I don't know you."

The man stared at Derek as if he had lost all his faculties. Across the patrician face flashed a fleeting look of fear. "Gordon Randolph. The anesthesiologist who assisted you. God, man, don't you remember?"

Derek broke into a run, wanting to put as much distance between himself and the stranger as possible. The stricken look in the older man's eyes was more than Derek could bear. At the moment he hated the brother he had never seen and would never meet. He hated the resemblance to Stan that now tarnished his life. And he felt guilty to be alive while his brother was not.

"Stan, come back! Come back!" The older man's voice faded as Derek ran farther away. His lungs strained for breath and blood pounded in his ears as he broke out in a sweat. He sped down the corridor in the direction of the airline parcel service.

He stopped in the men's room to sponge his face with cool water and run a comb through his hair. As he looked into the mirror, he imagined how his face would look without the mustache and with the natural wave restored to his hair. Already this was beginning to happen. He had neglected to order an application of hair straightener during his last haircut.

"No," Derek muttered to himself in the empty room as he stared into the mirror. He was more than a clone of his brother. He was a unique individual. He was himself, and for the first time in his life, that uniqueness was precious to him. He would surrender it for no one.

The pickup counter of the parcel service office was in a small clean room with white walls. "I'm Derek Moar, working for Metro Mega Studios." Derek produced identification, grateful to be able to be himself again. "I'm checking on some parcels sent here from the Los Angeles airport. We think the property shipped was stolen from Metro Mega. Do you or anyone else here remember helping a regular addressee named A. E. Haegis?"

The young man wearing a name tag with the name Roger on it reacted. "Yeah, I remember him. Kinda hard to forget a man like that one."

"Is it all right if I record our conversation?" asked Derek.

"Sure, why not? I bet you're with an insurance company, aren't you?"

Derek gave an enigmatic smile. The young man beamed, considering himself a good judge of character. "Cover for me for a minute, will you, Jeff?" Roger called to a serious-faced older man at the other end of the counter. Jeff shot him a sullen glance but nodded his head.

Roger led Derek to the opposite end of the counter, and Derek turned his small tape recorder on. Roger identified himself with his full name, address and home telephone number. They both kept their voices low.

"How many times have you helped this patron with a parcel pickup?" asked Derek.

"Three times, at least, maybe more. I heard some of the other guys mention him, too. They've all waited on him at some time."

"How would you describe A. E. Haegis?"

Roger squinted at the floor, as if trying to call the man up in his mind's eye. "He struck me as kinda... well, you know... effeminate."

"Go on," Derek said tensely.

"About five-seven. A short guy. Same suit each time. Bluish gray, with an oxford shirt, plain blue or brown tie and a bulky raincoat, even in the middle of summer when there wasn't a cloud in the sky. And leather gloves." His eyes twinkled with merriment as he smiled. "Always wore a black fedora, too, the brim turned down. Oh, I remember the guy all right. Real campy."

"Did you notice eye color? Hair color?" Derek asked.

"The fedora covered the guy's hair completely. Usually he looked down at the counter, but once, when I couldn't find the parcel right away, he got mad. He looked up, and his eyes were burning holes right through me. Mad as hell."

Derek swallowed hard, remembering Corinne's anger when she found Penny beside the bed, her tiny body limp and reeking of chloroform. "Were his eyes brown?" he rasped.

"No, more like green. A deep green. Eyes like that on a woman would be terrific." The young man shrugged his shoulders, letting them express his disappointment.

Derek let out a slow breath of relief. "Any other identifying characteristics? Moles, scars, voice?"

"He never talked except to state the flight number, ticket number and arrival time. He never even said 'Thank you.'" The young man sounded resentful. "His voice was kinda high for a man, although it would have been low for a woman."

"Do you think you could identify it if you heard it again?" asked Derek.

"I think so. I'd sure be able to identify the freckles."

"Pardon me. What did you say?"

"You know...freckles. Over his nose and cheeks. The way the hat threw a shadow over the guy's face, they didn't show up too good, but they were freckles, all right."

"Did he wear lipstick?"

Roger cast a look of contempt at Derek as the tape continued to spin. "Of course not. He was a guy all right. He just walked and gestured kinda...you know. He probably can't help it."

"Have you seen him lately?"

"No, not for a month or more."

"If he comes in again, stall him, will you? Act like you're having trouble finding the parcel. Call this number immediately while he's here." Derek handed the young man a number he knew Roger could recognize immediately.

"This is the airport security office," said Roger.

"I've already talked to the head man there. Two armed guards will come down to escort Mr. Haegis to the security office while FBI agents are summoned."

"FBI? Gee," said Roger in awe. Fear flashed in the clear, honest eyes. "What's in the packages? Drugs? Explosives? He's not a terrorist, is he?"

Derek pushed the stop button on the recorder. "I'm not permitted to say. Just be careful. He has friends who play rough." He was thinking of the unfortunate experience of Matt Briggs.

Roger backed away from the counter, the paper with the telephone number on it clutched in his hand. "I'll give this to the manager. He can tell the other clerks when they come on duty." His face was somber.

"Thanks. We need cooperation from all of you men, Roger."

As the leased car sped along the interstate toward downtown Circle City, Derek recalled the encounter with the anesthesiologist and was once again plunged into gloom. Only now did the full impact of his similarity to his unknown identical twin truly register. To everyone, he appeared as a carbon copy, aside from the mustache, which made for a superficial difference.

Yet he knew how different from Stan he truly was. He had surmised from the information he had gleaned that Stan had been endowed with an ego of prodigious proportions and was a perfectionist in his standards, besides which he had to have been a poor judge of character. He had walked into Meg's web of deception, eyes wide open, and had deceived a wonderful wife.

He was stupid, mused Derek, his jaw set as he took the exit ramp and headed toward the indoor parking garage that adjoined the hotel where he was staying.

He took a sack of groceries from the back seat of the car and carried them up in the elevator to the eighteenth floor. He had to conserve money now in every way he could since he was no longer on an expense account. The bill was his to pay from now on, and his bank account in Chicago was limited.

He thought about calling Corinne, but not at the office where Meg might listen in on the extension. He would wait until later when Corinne would be at home. She had had the afternoon hours in which to cool off and come to her senses. So he hoped.

As he thrust a frozen dinner into the microwave oven, Derek accepted the hopelessness of the situation and grieved. What chance could there be that Corinne would learn to love him for himself, as Derek Moar?

It struck him as soon as the buzzer sounded, announcing his dinner was ready to eat. *Am I Derek Moar?* he asked himself. A personal identity so long taken for granted, that of Derek Moar, son of a truck driver and a homemaker who worked as a volunteer at the local hospital, was suddenly shattered. His genes came from a man and a woman, neither of whom he had never seen.

I'm Edmund Hersh, he thought, stunned. *And my brother was Edward.*

Derek took his dinner out to the balcony, needing the crisp wind to nip his face and cool his heated brow. He yearned for a sense of self. He needed to know his roots, who he really was. A tremor passed through him as the wind hit, and he looked down at the rush-hour traffic,

in which people who knew who they were pressed
homeward.

CORINNE LINGERED before the public telephone in the
lower level of the bank tower. Her pride had gotten lost
in her concern for Derek. Stan's brother had lived and
was probably hurting from all he had learned about
himself in such a short time. This morning she had only
added to that burden.

*A woman can retain her pride and still have the good
grace to say 'I'm sorry!' if love lives in her heart.* As
Corinne perceived this truth, the light of it blinded her.
She reached for the pay phone and punched the number of suite 1802, having memorized it, as she had
memorized Derek's voice, walk, facial expressions and
the soothing touch of his hand.

"Hello?" He was no longer identifying himself as
Douglas Johnson, she noticed.

"Derek . . . it's me," she said in a faint voice.

"Corinne?" He didn't dare believe it.

"I'm so sorry about everything I said this morning," she said in a rush. "I went crazy when I found
Penny. She's the only child I have, Derek."

"What does the vet say?"

"She'll be all right," she said, sniffling, "thank God.
He'll keep her overnight for observation just to be sure.
He told me not to worry."

"I'm glad."

"Derek . . . please forgive me for the way I acted. I
know now how the burglar got into the house."

"It had to be with a key."

"Yes."

"How did he get it?"

Corinne let out a long sigh. She wanted to confide in him, tell him the whole story about the trick she had played on Meg this afternoon and her plan for tomorrow. Yet she feared that if she did, he would oppose her plan and another argument would break forth. She didn't dare take the risk.

"I'll tell you later. Don't call me tomorrow. Don't call me at the office at all anymore. Meg can't be trusted. I don't know her connection with Gaterow yet. I may know more after tomorrow."

"What's tomorrow?" he asked, tense.

"Do you forgive me?" she asked.

"Always," he answered to her relief. "I couldn't stay angry with you if I tried. Can you finally trust me?"

"Oh, darling, I trust you." Her voice shimmered like a sparkling waterfall, cleansing all his fears.

"Come to my suite. I brought in some food. I cook a great frozen dinner."

His invitation was appealing. Derek's place was only a few blocks from where she was phoning. *I've done enough damage to him already,* she thought, feeling guilty. First, she had introduced him to the Alberts, opening the door to Kate's shocking news. She had also cast the light of suspicion on him due to his involvement with her. His friendship with Zinser might be over now, and if she failed to clear herself, Derek could be charged as an accomplice to a felony. His professional status would be ruined.

The most loving act Corinne could do for Derek now, she knew, would be to stay far away from him. They were probably both being watched by Zinser's men.

"I ... can't," she murmured, hesitating. "I'll try to contact you tomorrow evening—if I'm able." She hung up quickly, afraid she might weaken and tell Derek her plan. If she did, she knew he would try to stop her and bitter words would fly.

Her hand still clung to the receiver of the public phone. She was barely aware of the voices behind her as people passed through the lobby on their way home.

Corinne was afraid to go home, afraid of what might await her there. She longed to be with Derek, to feel safe and loved.

CHAPTER THIRTEEN

THAT NIGHT Corinne slept sitting up on the leather sofa in the den, fully dressed, with her sharpest, longest butcher knife by her side. Meg had believed her story about getting the dead-bolt locks changed, Corinne knew. That was why she had gone to all the trouble to have another set made. Of course, the keys would be identical, which Meg could not help but notice if she took the time.

Corinne didn't know what to expect in the darkness of night. The house, without Penny, was as quiet as a tomb. When the pale blue light of dawn broke, Corinne felt more secure and dozed a bit. She awakened to the electronic bleat of the alarm clock she had placed on the desk.

She stayed home that morning, telephoning Meg to inform her she was ill with flulike symptoms, had a fever and wouldn't be coming to the office. When she asked Meg to cancel her appointments for the day, Meg made no protest.

"It isn't like you to be ill, Cory. Stay in bed and take it easy." How solicitous Meg sounded. "Do you want me to come to your house after I close up the office? Do you need anything?" Meg seemed genuinely concerned.

"Oh, no," Corinne said hurriedly, "you have enough to do, keeping things going on that end. I'm going to

bed now and maybe tomorrow I'll feel better. You'll put
in a full day as it is, with the brief to type on the Ern-
sten case. I'm so glad I have you to count on!'' Corinne almost choked while saying it. She was becoming
a pretty good liar, too. *Fight fire with fire.*

Corinne hung up, bewildered. The woman on the
telephone had sounded like a true friend.

She went to her purse, took out the small envelope
and felt the hard shape of the keys that were the duplicates of those on Meg's key ring. Her one hope was that
one of the keys opened the door of the mysterious
building at 10978 Grant Road and another unlocked the
gate.

The black Ford was behind her as she drove into town
to pick up Tim Greer. She was determined to lose it in
traffic, and after swerving a few times to make left turns
at changing lights, she finally left it standing at a red
light. She imagined the driver fuming.

When Corinne pulled up in front of Tim's place of
business at exactly two o'clock, he was waiting in the
doorway, the collar of his jacket turned up to protect his
ears from the autumn chill and a video camera in his
arms. A cardboard carton containing two lights was on
the sidewalk beside him.

''I haven't seen the script on this shoot yet. Fill me in,
Cory,'' said Tim as he settled into the front seat of the
car. She decided to give him the news straight out as she
pulled away from the curb. ''You and I are under suspicion by the FBI.''

The thin, wiry man let out a strangled sound. He was
staring at her as if she had lost her mind. ''For what,
dammit? I'm a loyal American. I even go to church.''

She smiled sadly. ''We are not being investigated for
subversive activities, Tim. We're under suspicion for a

felony charge. I suspect I dragged you into this on my coattails, because you're my client.''

"That guy Doug Johnson is mixed up in this in some way, isn't he? I had the feeling he was putting me on. What is it you and I are supposed to be doing that's illegal?''

"Video piracy. Violation of copyright laws. Mass duping of videotapes of feature films and then selling the dupes to the public for profit. Depriving the motion picture companies from their legal royalties. That's violation of Federal law since 1982.''

"Piracy?'' Tim's voice echoed plaintively within the car.

"That's the plot of the script,'' said Corinne.

A stunned silence followed. He was staring out the windshield, but Corinne suspected he was not aware of anything around him.

"Our company doesn't do that! We've never done anything outside the law,'' he protested.

"Your place has been under surveillance, Tim. Derek—I mean, Doug Johnson—told me so. You made a tape run on a Saturday night, loading a station wagon about two or three in the morning. An FBI agent informed Doug.''

Tim hit his forehead and swore under his breath. "So that's what he was hinting at.''

Corinne turned the car onto the ramp leading to the interstate. "What were you doing there until three on a Sunday morning, Tim?''

She glanced at her passenger after the car had merged with the flow of traffic. He was looking uncomfortable. She had an uneasy feeling. Was Tim connected with Meg and Gaterow in some way? *No, dear God, please let it not be!* she silently prayed.

"We needed some quick cash. The landlord jacked the rent up on us without warning, practically doubled it, the bastard. A guy came to us who had some adult films he wanted duped. He owned the rights to the films; he was the producer. They were made on a Pacific Island. 'Art films' he called them.'' Tim gave a derisive guffaw. "He wants to ship them overseas."

"Tim! You? Accepting a job to dupe porn films?"

"I ran each one of them through first, Corinne. No violence, no abuse of women, no bondage—nothing like that. I wouldn't touch filth like that. The films this guy wanted duped were just good, clean sex. Nothing perverted, just hot and heavy. If my wife ever finds out I accepted that job...whew!" He shook his head. "But I wasn't breaking any law! Was I?" he asked weakly. "Maybe I should have called you first to check."

"I have the feeling you'll have to tell the FBI agent just what you've told me and give him the name of your client to prove it," Corinne said grimly. "I hope he backs up your story."

Tim muttered an oath under his breath and turned to look out the window. The wind blew raw and chill, and thick gray clouds threatened ominously.

In just two days it would be Halloween, Stan's birthday. Corinne tried not to think of it. Her life with Stan was beginning to seem unreal, like a dream, and now she had awakened. It was Derek, mustache and all, who was ever-present in the background of her mind.

They drove in silence, the speedometer staying at an even fifty-five miles per hour. Her seat belt was securely fastened around her. She glanced at Tim, who had asked no questions concerning their destination. He seemed to trust her.

A green sign appeared overhead. Grant Road 1 Mile. Within one minute, the car had taken the exit and was winding down a ramp onto Grant Road. Gingerly, Corinne tapped her brakes, relieved when the car slowed. She knew she would never be free from the memory of the accident.

They passed through terrain that had once been countryside but was now yielding to scattered subdivisions. They passed groves of trees. Scarlet-and-gold leaves sailed through the air, torn from limbs by the relentless wind. As the car headed north on the two-lane road, leaves scuttled across in front of the car and scrunched beneath the rolling tires. Others whipped through the air like drunken birds, dipping and looping, and smacking against the windshield.

"Why are you under suspicion? Hell, you don't know a thing about electronics." Tim broke the long silence, turning to look at Corinne.

"My name turned up as a customer on the sales list of a company that sells tape-duplicating equipment. It is alleged that I bought fifty industrial VCRs and one distribution amplifier, whatever that is," she muttered. "All the units were delivered to a place on Grant Road."

"That's where we're going now," he said, sounding surprised. "And who do we meet when we get there?"

"I don't know," Corinne said faintly, thinking of the thugs who had kidnapped poor Matt Briggs and administered a beating to him and threatened his family. She felt guilty as she glanced at the wiry frame of the man who sat beside her. She knew she should have warned Tim what he might be getting into. She wondered how the short man would fare in a fight.

Tim Greer frowned, gazing out of the window at the open expanse of fields. There was a gray cast over everything that rendered the scenery lifeless. Real estate signs indicating land for sale dotted the area they were passing through.

When Tim spoke, he sounded thoughtful, as if he were talking aloud to himself. "You know, Corinne, there ought to be some way to put an electronic signal on the tapes that the VCR hardware would recognize— if the manufacturers would just cooperate. Were that signal absent, the screen would remain blank. No picture, no sound." Tim chuckled. "The customers would get so mad at being rooked out of their money, they'd converge on the stores that sold the counterfeit copies to them and bust heads. The retailers of illegal goods would go out of business pretty quick. The customer is still king."

Corinne nodded her head in agreement, her eyes intently scanning the road on both sides ahead. The region was lonely, hardly a likely spot for a television repair shop. She spotted a rural mailbox beside the road with the number 10978 on it. She slammed on the brakes.

The cinder-block building was formidable looking, like a windowless Spanish fortress in the middle of flat acres of former pasture land. Behind the building was an air-conditioning unit and a huge propane gas tank. An eight-foot-high barbed-wire fence surrounded the property, just as Derek had described.

"Holy Toledo. What have we here?" Tim commented, staring at the scene spread before him. The car was halted in front of a gravel driveway. The driveway was blocked by a closed gate with a padlock securing it.

Corinne let out a nervous sigh. The palms of her hands were damp from nervous tension. At least no cars were in the parking lot inside the gate. The place appeared deserted. What if Willy were inside? She tried not to think of him. She pulled the small stiff envelope of keys out of her purse and got out of the car, leaving the engine running. With trembling hands she tried the smallest key first, the one Angelo had had so much trouble finding a master for.

The key fitted in the padlock. With a sharp twist of her wrist, the padlock dropped open. Corinne swung open the gates and returned to the car.

"You got the keys to this place?" Tim sounded incredulous. "How?"

"I'd rather not tell you. I'm not proud of the method."

As the car drove slowly up the driveway, the stones crunched beneath the tires. They came close to the entrance of the building, a metal door, and she pulled to a stop and shut off the engine.

Timothy was giving Corinne a guarded look. She could just imagine what Tim would say when questioned by Arnold Zinser. "She had the keys." She gave a deep sigh. She was in too deep now to turn back.

The fields around them were silent except for the sporadic moans of a brisk wind. The billowing clouds were so low that Corinne was tempted to reach up and touch one.

"I'll explain everything later, Tim. You have to trust me for now."

"You ever been here?" he asked.

"No."

"Then how come you got the keys?"

"I can't take the time to explain now. I'll tell you when we're finished and on our way back to your place."

"Okay," he said, shrugging. "You're the customer. What's the purpose of this shoot?"

"I want you to film whatever is inside. If there's nobody in there to stop us, that is."

Tim threw Corinne a startled glance. Then he pulled open the back door of the car and pulled out the video camera, balancing the unit on his shoulder while he carried the lights with one hand.

Corinne tried every key in the envelope, one by one, on the lock in the metal door. None fit. Feeling as if it was full of cotton, her mouth went suddenly dry, and her heart began to pound. Chill blasts of wind penetrated her lightweight wool suit. She started trying them again. At last, with a little jiggling, one worked. She pushed open the door, weak with relief.

Inside the large room it was cool and dark. She groped along the wall for a light switch. Finally she located one, and overhead fluorescent lights came on.

"Look at that, will you!" Tim said in a slow, silky whisper as he scanned the room.

Freestanding shelving units, five shelves high, lined two walls of the room. Black boxes—industrial VCRs, Tim explained to her—sat on the shelves in military order, in vertical rows of five. She counted ten vertical rows. Fifty VCRs. A machine about seven feet tall with meters and dials on its face and several separate components stood guard on one side of the shelves.

"That's the distribution amplifier. It boosts the video signal so the power level to the machine is constant," Tim explained.

"These VCRs all run at the same time, then," she said, a little awed by the sight of the equipment that she had ostensibly ordered and for which she had allegedly paid. *With what?* she wondered.

"Yes. There are master machines and slaves, regulated by routing switches," explained Tim.

Tim glanced slowly around the room, squinting. "This place is as well equipped as the one Rex and I have. Out here in the country! This is the equipment you're being accused of buying? Hey, Corinne. Let's go into business together!" Tim said jokingly, his thin lips twisting into a nervous grin.

Corinne threw her cohort a dark look. Tim wandered to the other side of the vast room, his camera propped on his shoulder.

The other two sides of the room were filled with worktables. Unopened cartons were stacked against the wall and empty cartons stood on the floor next to a long table. Tim picked up a blank cassette from one of the boxes.

"Where do they get all these tapes?" He swore softly under his breath. "I buy all my blank tapes from one of the top American companies, and I'm allotted only a certain number per month. They're in short supply." He bent down to scrutinize the top of one carton. "Hong Kong. That figures," he grunted, straightening up.

Corinne had noticed a camera mounted on the ceiling at the rear of the room, the lens facing the door, but she was so relieved to find the place empty that she gave the camera little thought. Tim was so engrossed as he wandered around, examining boxes and opening closets and storage cupboards, that he noticed little else. His hand dipped into another carton and emerged with an empty package, a five-by-eight-inch VHS plastic jacket bearing a four-color picture of three astronauts in space suits, two male and one female, and a bearlike creature from outer space. The colors were slightly untrue, the outlines not sharp. "The packaging was probably done in Hong Kong, too," he muttered. "This movie is big stuff right now. Came out five months ago. I bet these crumbs are undercutting the price of the legitimate tapes by half." He let the jacket drop in disgust. "My kids would love to see this!"

"Could a woman run an operation like this one, Tim?" asked Corinne.

Tim's head jerked around. "Not alone. These machines require regular maintenance. In my place, I take five VCRs off the shelves every night to clean heads and do lubrication. Preventive maintenance is essential. Of course, a woman could be trained to do that. Several people work in here at one time, I would guess by the way the work areas are arranged. They probably work at night."

Corinne shivered as she glanced at her watch. The time was already past four. "Shoot the interior of this room, Tim, so we have it on tape, and let's get out of here before the swing shift reports to work."

"Why make a tape?"

"To give to the FBI. But make me a copy first." She gave a wan smile. "I may have to serve as my own defense."

"You think these people may pull out of here in a hurry?"

"It's a possibility. Or they could blow up the place and escape. We could be left holding the bag, and the FBI might have enough circumstantial evidence to send us to prison. While you do your job, I'll collect a few samples of recorded tapes and blank tapes and empty jackets." While he arranged the lights, she walked around and collected her samples. She went so far as to rip the return addresses from the boxes from Hong Kong and placed them in her shoulder bag.

"Hey, they'll know we were here," Tim warned her as he heard the label rip from the cardboard.

"They'll know sooner or later." Corinne had a feeling everything would come to a head soon. How would she come out of it? Never in her life had she taken such a risk. All or nothing. A future as a lawyer or years in prison, with punitive fines heavy enough to bankrupt her.

Tim's video camera began to roll, slowly scanning the room and coming in close on equipment. Corinne checked the two closets. In one of them a man's bluish-gray suit hung neatly on a hanger along with an oxford shirt, two plain ties—blue and brown—a bulky rain-coat with leather gloves sticking out of the pocket and a man's black fedora. Corinne held the fedora in her hands and looked into the crown inside. Removing tweezers from her purse, she retrieved several short hairs from inside the fedora and slipped them into an empty white envelope. She gasped. Against the white of the paper, the strands of the hair were reddish brown— the color of Meg's hair.

"Come on. Let's get out of here!" Tim sounded suddenly nervous.

"What's wrong?"

"See the camera up there? It's activated. Probably got a wide-angle lens in it that covers the whole room. When the front door is opened, the switch is tripped. If I take it apart and take the film out, they'll know somebody was here, but at least they won't know who."

"Do it!" urged Corinne.

As Tim started to climb on the table just underneath the camera, the distant crunch of gravel on the driveway froze them both. Fear showed in Tim's eyes. ''Come on! Let's get out of here!'' he said, picking up his video camera and heading for the door.

Corinne was right on his heels, switching off the light, slamming the metal door and locking it. A large sedan was in the driveway, slowly backing up. Four people—two men and two women—were in the car. After a distraught driver got a look at them both, the car swung around and headed out of the gate and sped down the road at top speed.

''Come on, let's go!'' Tim growled, jumping into the front seat of Corinne's car while still holding the camera. Corinne slid behind the driver's seat and was out the gate in a flash, the gravel crunching as she slammed on the brakes. She got out, pulled the gates of the fence closed and locked the padlock.

As she walked the few steps to the car, she glanced across the road. The dark shape of a car blended with the trees, almost indistinguishable from them. The front of the car faced the cinder-block building. She blinked and rubbed her eyes. The car was so far away she could not see if anyone was sitting in it. And Tim did not give her time to reflect on it.

''Come on, Corinne!'' he said impatiently. ''They must work here. They'll probably come back when they calm down.''

She slid behind the steering wheel, and the car shot out of the driveway, spraying a shower of gravel in its wake. The grove of trees in which the car was hidden across the road quickly dropped out of sight in the rearview mirror. She tried not to think about it. The car could have been abandoned. Or it could have sheltered a man watching the building through binoculars. One of Zinser's men.

If so, there was one thing of which Corinne was certain. He had taken down the license number of her car.

CHAPTER FOURTEEN

IT WAS THE MORNING of Halloween in Circle City. A chill hung in the air. A gray sky threatened rain.

In his suite at the fashionable downtown hotel, Derek made an important telephone call. He held a slip of white paper with the name Helen Custere and a suburban Philadelphia address and telephone number written on it in Kate Albert's neat, precise handwriting.

All Derek intended to do was to call—to hear his mother's voice once. He didn't know what words, if any, would come to him. He simply felt compelled to reach out just this once. He had to make the effort to try to erase the many question marks in his mind.

He hadn't expected to hear such a dignified voice. In the back of his mind, he still thought of his natural mother as nineteen, the age at which she had delivered him. He knew she had married again recently, a man named Brent Custere. Kate's information stopped abruptly at that point. She had seemed afraid of furnishing too many answers too soon. Kate was leaving the answers to Helen.

The woman on the other end of the line gasped when she learned Derek's name. "I'm Edmund," he said. "My name is Derek Moar now."

They talked awkwardly for a bit. Then she said, "Kate Albert phoned me. She said she'd told you about me. Edmund—" she paused "—my husband, Brent, is your father. He's in the hospital. The doctor thinks he's dying of pneumonia. He's not responding to any of the antibiotics they've given him." Her voice caught, and then she went on, while Derek listened, astonished. "Brent's first wife, Mary, passed on four years ago. Did Kate Albert tell you that? Mary was Brent's second cousin. Both families had always assumed they would marry one day. Brent's parents have been gone for many years now. He tracked me down, after Mary died, through the IU alumni office. He knew it was my dream to attend school at Bloomington one day, and he assumed I had. I managed it after my husband decided to attend school there, too. We both found jobs." She paused. "Is there any...possibility...you might come to Philadelphia, Derek?"

"No, I don't think so. I have...business in Circle City, and I can't get away now."

"Oh." Her voice trailed away.

"Perhaps I can come sometime soon, when my business here is finished."

"That might be too late." She began to weep very softly, as if she was embarrassed.

"Please, don't...." He didn't know what to call her. Helen? Mother? That tag didn't seem to apply. She was only a fragment in his mind, a disembodied voice. It was a lovely voice, however. "Even if I were there, what good would it do? For him, I mean?"

"He would meet his only living child. Brent had no children with Mary. She couldn't carry a child past the fourth month. You can't forgive us, can you? That's why you don't want to see us."

"There's nothing to forgive. You did what you had to do."

"Brent doesn't see it that way. Brent takes everything—" she sighed "—upon his own shoulders. He's that kind of man. A very good man, Derek. I wish you could see that for yourself. You're a part of him. When he's gone, that part of you will always be missing because you never had a chance to know him.

"It would mean so much to Brent to see you, even once, to see the kind of man you've become." She was pleading, but with dignity. "Please don't turn your back on your father now."

Derek stood beside the art deco sofa and stared at the balcony door. Today was Stan's birthday; tomorrow would be his. Was she thinking of that now?

The answer came from him, simple and direct, before he had a chance to analyze it. "Yes, I'll come," he said.

Derek heard her gasp. "Thank you," she said, but the way she said it conveyed a wealth of meaning. "Call this number when you're ready to board your flight. If I'm at the hospital, talk to a man named Sherman. Tell him your arrival time. He'll be at the airport to meet you."

When Derek hung up, he knew he would not be quite the same man anymore once he'd met Helen. He dreaded telling Corinne he had to leave her now. Would she understand?

DEREK MADE THE TRIP to Stemple Road after he'd called the office and Meg had informed him coolly that Corinne was at home in bed with the flu. He wanted to tell Corinne in person that he had no choice. He had to fly to Philadelphia immediately.

To his surprise, he found Corinne quite well. To his relief, she understood and confirmed his decision to make the trip. "You can't not go, considering the circumstances," she said.

He let the warmth of his embrace speak for him. He hoped the tenderness, the longing in his kiss would tell Corinne all he wanted her to know. "You have to go to him, Derek. Stan used to say a patient's will to live can be the crucial factor. Medication isn't the entire solution. For your own peace of mind, too, you have to make the trip."

"May I take the albums and show Helen and Brent the pictures of Stan?" Derek asked.

"Of course." Corinne led him into the den and gathered up all the photo albums, including one from Stan's childhood that the Dayes had been willing to part with.

"Is there anything I need to know, Corinne?"

She told Derek about seeing Meg remove the keys from her purse and about following her downstairs to Angelo's. She told him about the visit to Grant Road that she'd made with Tim. "He's making me a copy of the videotape so that I'll have a record of exactly what's inside." She told him about finding the clothes in the closet and the bits of auburn hair inside the crown of the fedora.

"I don't want to leave you alone! Who knows what that pair might do?" Derek cursed under his breath.

"A couple of days won't make any difference, darling." The endearment was one she never used with Stan. "I'll stay with the Alberts. Gaterow and Meg won't try any funny stuff if I'm there."

Corinne clung to him, needing his strength, afraid but still smiling. "One thing, though. I don't think I can play dumb with Ms Krens much longer. I want to bob her in the nose!" declared Corinne, clenching her hand into a fist.

"The only chance we have is to get a confession from one of them," said Derek.

"Huh! Fat chance of that!"

"Did Stan ever keep a gun around the house?" asked Derek.

"No. Why?"

"I'll leave you mine. With some ammunition. Just remember, if you shoot, aim to kill."

"I don't know how," she protested. "I don't think I can."

"If you're close enough, you don't have to be an Annie Oakley. You're about to have your first lesson in marksmanship. Put on the coffee and come outside with me," he ordered.

They bundled up against the cold, took every empty can from the trash in the garage and lined the cans up in front of some trees. With a patience that bordered on saintliness, Derek repeated each lesson again and again: how to load, how to unload, how to brace herself, take careful aim with both hands and how to hit the mark.

It was the most intensive two-hour lesson Corinne had ever had. By the time it was over, she was hitting the riddled tin cans two times out of three, and she'd knicked the bark on a dozen trees.

"When I come back, we're taking all your information to Arnie. He should have met you long ago. I'll be gone only two or three days at the most. Stay away from the office, whatever you do. Don't be alone with Meg. Stay out of trouble. Do you promise?"

"Me? Get into trouble? How can you entertain such an idea?" she asked mockingly. Then she smiled and whispered, "Happy Birthday tomorrow. We'll celebrate when you get back." She accepted the revolver from his outstretched hand and slipped it into her jacket pocket.

"Remember—either stay with Kate or barricade yourself at home with a chain on the door until I return," warned Derek.

Corinne promised and watched the compact car speed down the lane and disappear into the trees. Her hand crept into her pocket and she felt the weight of the firearm there. She was filled with dread.

THE MANSERVANT WHO MET Derek at the Philadelphia airport was dressed in a conservative suit and his manner was formal. His name was Sherman Park. He was white haired and sixty and had been trained in a special school in Great Britain to serve nobility. He had been with the Custere family for thirty years. Derek discovered all this during the drive to the suburb where Helen lived with her husband of three years, Brent Custere.

Sherman had seemed surprised when he'd first seen Derek, who'd been clutching a large gift-wrapped box, a present for his hostess. The man's eyebrows had risen and his eyes had fixed on Derek's face. He'd looked astonished, and then he'd frowned. In a second, however, the mask of polite control had slipped back over the dignified, lined face, converting it to proper blandness.

"You are wearing a red carnation in your buttonhole, sir. I am instructed to ask you if you are Mr. Derek Moar. I am Sherman Park," he had said with a British accent carefully retained for the thirty years he had lived in the United States in the service of the elder Mr. Custere. Sherman had led Derek to a silver Mercedes that was seven years old but immaculately clean and polished, even to the rearview mirror.

As the flat, monotonous countryside rolled past them, Sherman was careful to ask no questions. He spoke only when Derek addressed him first, and then his reply was terse and to the point, leaving Derek little to say.

When the Mercedes rolled to a stop in the curved driveway before a stately brick mansion, Derek was stunned to realize Helen's good fortune. The house sat in the middle of an estate protected from the outside world by a brick wall that seemed endless and a gate composed of iron bars with wicked points on them. At least the gate stood open in welcome, Derek thought.

Sherman slid out from behind the steering wheel and carried Derek's worn leather suitcase through the front door. He had brought his best suit and a spare shirt, dress shoes and pajamas and toiletry items. He also had Corinne's family photo albums with him. He wanted to introduce Stanford Daye—no, Edward Hersh—to Helen in the only way available to him.

Derek hadn't been this nervous since he'd taken his final exams in law school and had paced the hall, awaiting the posting of grades. He yearned to be accepted.

Sherman set Derek's bag down on the wood parquet floor of the foyer. "I'll tell madam you're here, sir. She's waiting in the library." Sherman disappeared down the hall while Derek surveyed the tan-colored, textured wallpaper. A pier table was a focal point in the hall, over which hung ornately framed pier glass. A stairway to the left curved upward to the second floor.

Built in the previous century and passed down from father to son, the house was still and cool, with high ceilings. To Derek the house was formidable. He much preferred Corinne's, or better still, the cozy two-story brick house in which the Moars lived in Brookfield, Illinois.

He saw a woman come toward him. She was hurrying down the hall—Sherman was nowhere in sight—a vision of purity in a white satin tunic top with long sleeves that fluttered gently as her arms moved, and white satin long-legged pants that rippled as she walked. Her slim, graceful bare feet were in high-heeled silver sandals with straps.

Derek's heart stopped for a perilous moment. The woman was beautiful. Her sandy hair hung in soft waves frosted with silver. Her face was smooth, her skin lustrous and soft like precious porcelain.

Is this my mother? Derek asked himself in wonder. She came to a halt just a step away, seemingly shy. Greenish-blue eyes with serene depths gazed up at him. A mist of tears slowly formed in those eyes as they locked with his.

"Derek..." She spoke his name in wonder, like a caress. "Is it really you...my son?" she whispered. "You're tall. Built just like your father. You look just as I hoped you would."

They stood staring at each other, each straining toward the other and each afraid to see the first sign of rejection. Derek swallowed hard, determined not to lose control. "There were two of us."

"I know." The mist of gathering tears shimmered more brightly in her eyes.

"I brought pictures of Stan."

"We'll take them to the hospital. Your father will want to see them. We told the doctor all about you. He wants to be present when we arrive."

"Do you want to go now?" His voice was thick, his self-control beginning to slip. He had not been prepared for the sight of this lovely, gracious woman who seemed so caring.

"The cook has been holding dinner until you arrived. We mustn't offend her. Perhaps you can manage a bite or two?"

"I'm really not hungry."

"Coffee perhaps? Your father is a fiend for coffee."

A chuckle broke free from him. "So that's where I got my habit."

"He has many good habits, dear. You are fortunate to have inherited his genes. He is a man above men!" She spoke proudly.

Helen moved a step closer, and that was all it took. Derek opened his arms to her. It seemed the natural thing to do. She moved into them gratefully, and her arms went around him.

"I was so afraid when you called me, Derek." Her voice trembled as her face lay against his chest. "I'd prayed for that phone call for so many years, hoping Kate would tell you boys about me someday, yet knowing it might be better for you never to know."

Derek drew his arms more firmly around her.

"Kate and her husband, Dr. Albert, assumed you were dead, you know. The ambulance came to take you to General Hospital. You looked awful. We didn't think you had a chance." Her body gave a shudder. She lifted her head and stars of wonder shone in her eyes. "But look at you now! So handsome, so fit."

Her eyes closed when Derek bestowed a kiss on her wide, smooth forehead. Her hands gripped his upper arms, the grip as strong as a man's.

"Come on, dear. We mustn't keep Clare waiting. She's a wonderful help to me. She baked turkey with oyster dressing, just for you."

After they had eaten, Helen changed clothes and Sherman drove mother and son to the hospital.

Seated in the back seat of the Mercedes, with Sherman Park behind the steering wheel, Derek received the impression that the dignified man served as a bodyguard, as well. He wondered if Sherman's dark, boxy suit hid a shoulder holster. Mother and son were careful not to say anything too personal in front of the older man who spoke not a word but was, no doubt, listening to the conversation in the back seat.

"Kate didn't have time to tell me much over the phone. What is it you do?" Helen asked Derek.

"I have a degree in law. I was with the FBI for six years."

Helen's eyes widened. She was clearly impressed. "The FBI? Why did you leave?"

"Leg injury. Confrontation with bank robbers in Chicago," he answered tersely. "I'm a private investigator now, on assignment in Circle City. That's how I met the Alberts—through a mutual friend."

"Your sister-in-law." Helen smiled. Kate had told her the important things over the phone the day she'd called Helen to let her know her son was in town.

"We met by accident. I knew nothing of Stan's existence. To be truthful, she mistook me for Stan." The hurt, though diminished, was still there.

Helen's smile faded. The car pulled into the visitors' lot of a Catholic hospital, and Sherman opened the rear door. He touched his cap in a gesture of respect for the young man's FBI connection. Sherman ranked the FBI as high as Scotland Yard.

"You were married before you and Brent got together again. What happened to your husband?" Derek asked Helen as they entered the hospital lobby. Sherman remained with the car.

"He died. An auto accident. He drove like a fool. I was widowed for seven years. Never wanted to marry again. Once was enough. Until Brent tracked down my address. I had kept my maiden name as my middle name on my college records and on my degree. He wrote me the most exquisite letter, telling me his parents were gone and his wife had passed away. He asked me to come to Philadelphia to visit him, and I did. Nothing had changed between us, not really. We had a quiet ceremony with just a few of his friends present."

"How did Brent find out about me?" asked Derek in a low voice as they waited for an elevator.

Her answer surprised him. "I told him. As soon as Kate met you and realized who you were, she telephoned me. She thought Brent and I should come to Circle City to see you. That was the plan. So, of course, I had to tell Brent about the birth of you boys so he would understand why I was so set on making the trip."

"You see, Brent never knew I was pregnant," she said in a very low voice to avoid being overhead. "I ran away, left the restaurant where I was working, moved out of my furnished room and left no forwarding address. Brent didn't know where to find me since I had never given him my mother's address. We lived in a run-down part of town, and Brent's family was rich. He drove a sports car and didn't have to work while he attended classes on Bloomington campus. He had told me a bit about his parents. They expected him to marry a second cousin. The money would stay in the family that way."

The elevator doors opened to admit them. During the short ride up, they said not a word, but instead, stared at the elevator numbers that lit up in succession over the folding doors. They reached the proper floor and filed out with the others.

"Brent agreed to come with me to Circle City and surprise you. He was angry with me at first when I broke the news about you boys, but he understood why I had to give you up for adoption. His parents would have disowned him, and all their money and factories would have gone to a distant cousin. They were harsh people.

"Then Brent came down with a sudden case of the flu, just after I'd ordered tickets for the flight to Circle City. It was a virulent attack from which he didn't recover in the usual week. Pneumonia set in. Every antibiotic the doctor tried failed to get results. He declined so fast. That's when I called Kate and asked her to give you my phone number, praying you would call me."

They entered a long hallway bordered by patients' rooms, and an unsmiling man greeted them outside the door of one of them, identifying himself to Derek as Brent Custere's physician. "He is putting up absolutely no fight at all, and that man is a fighter. I know. I treated his family for years. He told me his wife recently informed him about you. Where's your brother?" He was looking about the hallway.

"He's dead. Almost three years ago."

The doctor's eyes clouded. "I see. Too bad. I was hoping that if his sons rallied around him, his biochemistry might take a turn for the better. His body's resistance to whatever we give him seems psychosomatic. I know he's devoted to Helen. It's almost as if he feels guilty about something. And he found out about you a very short time ago. It all seemed linked."

"I'm here. I'll do what I can."

"He's very weak. Don't talk to him too long. Let him know you care. That's the best medicine. I'll look in on him later."

He left them and strode down the hall. Helen took Derek's hand and led him into a private room with a crucifix over the inside doorway.

The drapes were drawn tight. Helen opened them to admit the light of day. The man in the bed was long and lean, his angular face, with a hint of a cleft in the chin, filled with the look of physical suffering and fatigue.

"Brent, dear, I've brought him. Derek. Derek is here. Open your eyes, darling." Helen's voice was steady as she took the motionless hand on the man's chest.

Derek watched the two of them as he stood back from the bed, uncertain what to do, and felt the wave of love and affection that passed back and forth between the two of them. In that respect, they reminded him of David and Erna Moar.

"Derek? Is that you?" The head on the pillow moved, and the eyelids in the ashen face slowly opened. The man's eyes were the clearest blue, the color of an unspoiled mountain lake. "Happy Birthday," said the older man faintly, as if it took a great effort to talk. Only then did Derek realize the date. In a few hours it would be November first and he would turn thirty-five.

"Thank you, sir." Derek moved to the side of the bed, taking the proffered hand and feeling self-conscious in doing so. A silent appeal to create a miracle concentrated in the glance Helen threw him.

"Has your life . . . been tolerable?" Brent seemed to be having great trouble breathing. Derek noted the oxygen tank at the head of the bed. "I wish . . . I could have raised you . . . provided for you as you deserved. If only Helen had told me at the time, instead of running away...." His accusing gaze shifted to his silent wife. As if he'd noted her suffering and had been appeased, Brent let his eyelids sink closed.

Derek's grip on the man's hand tightened with the strength of forgiveness. He wanted his own energy to flow into his father's body through the bond of flesh and blood. "Mother only did what she thought was best at the time."

Helen looked across the bed at Derek. On her face was an expression of wonder at the name he had just called her.

"Don't run out on us now, Dad. Not when we're finally together," said Derek, his voice thick.

"No word from Derek?" asked Kate. She let the copy of the morning newspaper drop to the kitchen table. A whine sounded from the vicinity of her knees. She looked down. Penny was standing on her hind legs, her front legs propped on Kate's thigh, her bulging black eyes staring fixedly up at her hostess for the past week.

"Penny, get down. Don't beg for food. You've had your breakfast," scolded Corinne. The dog didn't move.

"Oh, a tidbit or two won't hurt," said Kate, holding up a bit of leftover bacon from breakfast and rising from her chair. The aging pup walked backward on two spindly legs, her round barrel chest elevated behind relaxed front paws. She began a slow pirouette, dancing around and around in circles beneath the food held over her head.

Then the bit of bacon dropped into her open, waiting jaws. Immediately the dog dropped to all fours and worked at tasting and chewing with great enjoyment.

"Derek may not be coming back," said Corinne. "He checked out of the hotel the day he left for Philadelphia."

"I have Helen's phone number. Give him a call." Kate was feeding Penny the rest of the bacon in tiny bites with the hope of getting a repeat performance.

"I can't."

Kate paused and glanced at Corinne sharply. "Why?"

"Don't you see? He's finding himself. He's finishing the picture of who he really is. I may not fit into that picture now," said Corinne.

"Why not?" Kate dropped the rest of the bacon in the dog's small, stainless steel bowl. Penny chased the bacon bits around inside the bowl.

"He's still in a stage of self-discovery," said Corinne.

"Well, Derek can't be that much different from Stan. After all, they have the same genes—"

"But they were brought up in different environments, Kate. Stan was the center of attention all his life, adored by two wealthy people, while Derek had to learn to share with two younger sisters. Stan had everything given to him. Derek had to work for everything. He earned money from a newspaper route so he could buy a bicycle, worked as a stock boy in a supermarket so he could buy his first car, and he had chores to do around his home. Derek told me about those years. We talked a lot. More than Stan and I ever did."

"You and Stan had a good marriage, Corinne," protested Kate.

"It could have been better. The last year, Stan changed. We were both wrapped up in our separate careers, actually. I guess I was changing, too, at a different rate. We just weren't changing together. Am I making any sense?''

Kate sank back onto the chair she had just vacated, her eyes fixed intently on Corinne. She sensed she was about to hear something she didn't want to hear. Yet she was friend enough to listen.

"I was too proud to consult a marriage counselor," Corinne confessed. "Even though I always recommended to my clients that they seek one out when trouble develops in a marriage."

"Would Stan have consented to see a counselor? I doubt it, Corinne. Stan was never one to admit there was a problem of any kind, personal or otherwise. He took after Bill Daye in that. He took after Bill Daye in his quest for perfection, too. I imagine that was hard to live with, wasn't it?''

Silence reigned. Penny was licking the bowl so vigorously that it rattled in its metal frame.

"There was someone else that last year. I'm sure of it," said Corinne.

Kate fell silent, and riveted her attention on Penny, who sat on her haunches, quietly waiting. Penny's pointed black ears were fully raised as she stood at attention while her gaze passed back and forth between the two women.

"Stan took you on a trip to Jamaica for your fifth wedding anniversary. He must have felt something for you, Cory."

"I had such hopes for that trip, Kate! A change of scene always seemed to do something for Stan. And it was great—like the early days of our marriage. But as soon as we returned to Circle City, his mysterious absences began occurring again. I even considered divorce."

Kate was stunned. "Then the plane went down and you were stricken with guilt. You took all the blame on yourself. When you saw Derek at the airport, you thought you'd been handed a second chance to be the wife you should have been. Am I right?"

Corinne stared at her older friend in wonder. "Yes. How did you know?"

Kate leaned over and clasped Corinne's arm. "Give yourself credit. You were a good wife. Don't make the same mistake with Derek. Don't let him drift away from you. You do love him, don't you?" Kate asked anxiously.

Corinne's hands went to her head and she massaged her temples. "I'm not sure he loves me. He resents Stan so. He can't accept being like him at all! That feeling would always come between us. I'm not sure I want to risk it. I'm not sure what I feel. Sometimes I feel I'm being disloyal to Stan when I think of Derek so much. Does Derek love me, do you think?"

"You'll *know* if he loves you, Cory. He'll lay himself right on the line. He's that kind of man. When that time comes, grab hold of him and don't let go."

Penny whined, crouched low on her belly and stretched. It was a sign that she wanted to be picked up and held. Kate obliged, holding the dog in her arms like the indulgent grandmother she was.

Corinne stared at the silent telephone on the wall. Derek had the Alberts' phone number, yet he hadn't called once. He was already caught up in a new life. Having found his new identity, had he discarded his old one already?

What am I waiting for? Corinne wondered. She watched Kate massage the dog's back. Penny was stretching as far as she could, enjoying the sensation and laying her ears back. Corinne had to smile at the sight.

"Kate, I truly appreciate all you've done for me, but I'm leaving today. I want to be in my own home. I'm through hiding. If Zinser has a warrant to serve on me, let him serve it and be done with it. And if Gaterow's ready for a showdown, let it come."

She had to get on with her life...with or without Derek Moar. Over Kate's protests, Corinne put her suitcase and her dog in the back seat of her leased car and went home to Stemple Road. The house stood lonely in the midst of a pseudo-forest. Leaves blew all around, and the chill of winter hung in the air.

CHAPTER FIFTEEN

THE NEXT MORNING Corinne answered the impatient ring of her telephone. Nine days had passed since Derek had left Circle City, and no word had come from him. Ten days had passed since she had last gone to her office. She was afraid to be alone with Meg.

"The office was broken into last night. Files were all over the floor when I came to work this morning. I called the police, and a policeman is here now. You have to come down and fill out a report."

"What's missing?" The hair prickled on the back of Corinne's neck. Confidential material aplenty was in those files.

"The petty cash money. Over a hundred dollars. The cash box is gone."

"Were any files taken?"

"I can't tell. I'm still trying to put things away. I need your help in evaluating possible loss."

"How did they get into the office?" Corinne asked Meg suspiciously.

"A hole was chopped right through the door." Meg paused significantly. "I'll bet your Moar is behind this in some way."

"Derek isn't in town. He left—" Corinne wanted to bite her tongue for letting the secret slip out.

DEREK'S WARNING to avoid Margaret Krens vanished
from Corinne's mind as she hurriedly dressed and sped
downtown. The condition of the office confirmed her
worst fears. Paper out of numerous client files littered
the floor. Meg was trying to clean up. There was a gaping hole in the wooden door that looked as if it had been
made with an ax. The door would have to be replaced
without delay.

A police officer took her statement, and a carpenter
was called to install another door. The job of restoring
the file cabinets to some kind of order wasn't completed until a little after three in the afternoon. It was a
laborious job. Corinne and Meg worked together six
hours, silently, going without lunch, checking a master
list to determine if any files were missing. None were.

At 3:10 Corinne slumped in the chair behind her
desk, fatigued and hungry, her nerves strung taut. Meg
was strangely subdued and quiet as she went into the
kitchenette to make more coffee.

Corinne tensed when her secretary walked into her
private office. Dressed in an expensive, tailored navy-
blue suit, high-necked ruffled blouse and navy-blue
Italian pumps, Meg was the picture of efficient elegance. Corinne had been able to tell that she had impressed the police officer. Meg stopped in front of
Corinne's desk, a heavy shoulder bag slung over her
shoulder. The office was cleared of workmen at last; the
new door to the hallway, in place and closed. The two
women were alone.

"He's left you, hasn't he?" Meg's voice was devoid
of expression, her face blank.

"I don't know. Maybe," said Corinne, holding back
tears borne of fatigue. Would Derek's experience with

his mother be a favorable one or bring him further hurt? Was something wrong?

"That's the way men are. You can't count on them. Willy left yesterday. I never told you about Willy. He lived with me for over two years. He just took off. He even took my 280 ZX. The SOB. Who needs him, anyway?"

"I'm sorry, Meg. Some men are reliable."

Meg's laugh was brittle, almost frightening. "Like who?"

"Stan, for one—"

A cynical laughter began to roll from Meg. She threw her head back, and her eyes gleamed like a malevolent banshee's. Terror struck in Corinne's heart. She rose from the leather desk chair, ready to flee the office.

"Get yourself under control!" Corinne ordered stiffly.

The laughter ceased abruptly. "I don't take orders from you anymore, boss lady!" Meg hissed. "Moar walked out on you. Stan would have walked out on you, too, eventually. Ms Mackerel."

"You're crazy," whispered Corinne. The woman standing before her had let all her defenses drop. She was naked in her hostility, honest in her hatred for the first time. *How does she know the name Gaterow spread around?* Corinne asked herself, her pulse pounding. *Through Gaterow, of course.*

"Stan was my lover. Didn't you know that, doll?" Meg's voice was silky-soft, caressingly sensuous.

A paralysis hit Corinne. Her body sank into the chair. Meg was the one? No, it was not possible. "I don't believe you. You're making it up."

Again Meg's brittle laugh assaulted the quiet room. She seemed to relish her employer's discomfort. "Stan came to my apartment to be with me regularly before—" Meg's face suddenly crumpled "—that ass Perlman talked him into flying to Boston with him. I hate Perlman!" Meg referred to the dead surgeon as if he were still alive. "Stan would have married me. You always stood in the way. Now you've driven Willy away, too. You bitch."

Corinne's pulse pounded in her ears. She struggled to maintain her objectivity. If she became emotional now, what might Meg do? "How did I make Willy leave you? I never even met him," Corinne said gently.

"He watched the videotape. It was his idea to mount the camera at the shop so that intruders could be identified. When we saw the footage of you and Tim Greer in that visit you paid ten days ago, he panicked. Then he took off. Took my car, the rat! My beautiful 280 ZX," she moaned. "I had to take a cab to the office. He knows I can't report the theft to the police because he'll spill everything if I do. It's all your fault, bitch. You stole the keys to the shop out of my purse, didn't you?"

"You stole the keys out of mine."

"That's different," hissed Meg. "I had a reason."

"Was it Willy who used the ax on the office door and stole the cash box? Why did he go through all the file drawers and dump everything on the floor?" lamented Corinne. It had been an act of willful vandalism.

"He didn't. I did," Meg answered calmly, her hand dipping into her handbag. The hand emerged with a loaded .38. Meg was aiming the revolver straight at Corinne's head. A graceful finger crept to the sensitive trigger.

DEREK JERKED his worn suitcase off the airline baggage conveyor on the lower level of the Circle City airport terminal. Worried about Corinne, he had cut short his visit with his parents. It had been a difficult thing to do. They'd begged him to stay.

Brent had responded to a new antibiotic, and the physician had given Derek much of the credit. "His will to live has returned," he'd told Brent's wife and son. Derek had been freed to return to Circle City to finish the job he had begun.

He glanced at the large clock on the terminal wall. It was 3:20 p.m. He went up the escalator, suitcase in hand, to a pay telephone and called the Alberts' number. No answer. Then he called Corinne's house. No answer there, either. He frowned, remembering Corinne had promised him she would remain at home. He resolved to try again as soon as he reached the nearest motel. First he had to rent a car.

CORINNE WAS STUNNED by Meg's confession. "But why? All this damage..."

"To force you to come down here. Believe me, calling the police was against my better judgment. I hate cops! But this time I can use the system to my advantage. When the cleaning crew finds you, the police will assume the thieves came back while you were working at night."

Corinne's temper failed her now. All she felt was a cold fear in the pit of her stomach. The pitiless expression in Meg's eyes, the calm manner in which she described how she would take her boss's life shocked Corinne. Taking one desperate chance to entrap Meg,

Corinne leaned forward to remove a handkerchief from her handbag on the floor beside the desk.

As she bent over, momentarily hidden from Meg's line of vision by the desk top, she dipped her hand quickly into the bottom desk drawer, which was partially open. She flipped on the switch of a tape recorder and turned up the volume to the highest position on the dial. Then she slowly straightened in her chair, a lace-bordered handkerchief conspicuous in hand. "Yes, Tim and I paid your place on Grant Road a visit. Sorry, Meg." She strove to keep her voice's pitch normal.

"Willy was really pissed when he watched the video taken by the surveillance camera at the shop and saw you and Greer. I'm sorry we weren't there to greet you at the time. If we had been..." The ominous tone of voice left little to Corinne's imagination. "The four people in the crew were taken by surprise when they reported to work."

"You 'borrowed' the keys from my purse when I was out of the office and had duplicates made of the keys to my Buick and my house, didn't you?" The question was for the benefit of the tape recorder. Corinne already knew the answer.

"I thought it was a good idea," answered Meg, smiling a faint smile that failed to reach her eyes. An energy was building in her that Corinne could feel. She recognized it as another one of Meg's inexplicable highs.

"So you wanted me dead?" Corinne spoke calmly, trying to appear detached, trying to keep control of the interrogation.

"Not so much after Stan's death. Fixing the Buick was James Gaterow's idea."

"You're in this counterfeit videotape racket with James Gaterow? How?" asked Corinne in a puzzled tone.

"I went to California after the memorial service for Stan, when you closed up the office for two weeks, remember?" Meg's emerald eyes narrowed to guarded slits, but she did seem eager to brag about her accomplishments. Corinne remembered how the distraught Meg had asked for time off, but in her own distress, Corinne had not connected Meg's distress with Stan's death. "I met Willy at a singles' bar. He was a technician who worked at a video production place. He had just gotten a termination notice for getting stoned on the job. He was madder than hell.

"You had taken that collection case for Tim Greer four months before, remember? Tim is a funny guy. He got here early for that first appointment, and he talked about his business a lot, trying to impress me about what a big shot he is. He told me about his latest job, duplicating training tapes to be shown in every franchise of the Douggal's fast-food chain.

"I mentioned this to Willy over a couple of drinks. Willy told me he knew all about that kind of business. He was a qualified technician and knew how he could make a lot of bucks with the right equipment. Right away I thought of James Gaterow, how he might like to strike a deal if I kept my mouth shut about what you kept locked up here in the cabinet. Who would suspect anybody in a town like this, in the cornbelt, for God's sake, of being behind an operation this sharp?"

Meg leaned back against the wall, the hand holding the gun on Corinne steady and calm. She seemed eager to talk, eager to gloat about how smart she was.

"When Willy told me he had a friend who made videotape masters for Metro Mega Studio and had con-
tacts who could smuggle masters out of other
Hollywood studios, too, I knew we were in business for
ourselves. So I asked Willy to come back to Indiana
with me." She gestured with the gun, waving it to one
side. "James was willing to invest in an enterprise with
a sure future. He put up the money for the equipment
on the condition that his name would be kept out of it."

"So it was you who sent someone to steal the papers
out of my safe at home." It was all Corinne could do to
keep her eyes away from the drawer in which the tape
was revolving on the small recorder. She prayed the
volume was turned high enough.

"Sure. It was part of the deal. James wanted those
papers back," answered Meg. "Since he supplied the
money—" She was interrupted by a timid knock on the
door to the reception room. Someone was in the hall.

Meg froze and stared at Corinne with a coldness that
was frightening. Not until that moment did Corinne
realize Meg had locked the door from the inside. The
knock sounded again, impatiently this time.

"Help me! Please! Call the police!" Corinne shouted
at the top of her lungs.

Meg raised the gun and aimed it right at the middle
of Corinne's forehead. "Shut up!" she hissed, a look
of such hardness in her eyes that it struck terror into
Corinne. A scream froze in Corinne's throat.

The knocking ceased and footsteps faded down the
hall.

DEREK THREW OPEN the door to his motel room. Without removing his classic navy worsted wool blazer, a

present from his newfound father, Derek went to the telephone on the dresser and dialed Corinne's home number again. Still no answer.

"So JAMES GATEROW put up the money—gave you cash, I presume," Corinne prompted. "That was really smart. How did my name get on the order for the equipment and the cashier's checks?" asked Corinne.

"You know about that? How?" Meg was astonished.

"Derek found out. A private investigator has ways. What bank did you go to, to have the cashier's checks made out?" Corinne asked this for the tape recorder's benefit.

"Avisco Trust. No one there knew either you or me. They were really impressed when I took all that cash out of a manila envelope," Meg answered.

A glow of satisfaction came over Corinne. Meg was tying the noose around her own neck and Gaterow's.

"Tim knows what's going on in your building on Grant Road. Getting rid of me isn't going to save you, Meg."

"He'll have an accident at work tomorrow. I remember hearing him tell you once that he works alone on Saturday. I've got two boys who know how to do a good job."

"The same two boys who kidnapped Matt Briggs and beat him up so he wouldn't testify against your salesman, Tony?"

Meg only smiled, frustrating Corinne. She had to get a verbal answer on tape.

"Well, yes or no? Answer me."

"Yes, bitch," Meg said coolly. She seemed amused. She was enjoying this cat-and-mouse game.

"Who was responsible for sabotaging my car? You or Gaterow?" Corinne persisted. She wanted as much of Meg's testimony on tape as she could get, gambling on Derek's thoroughness as an investigator. Seeing the tape recorder in her drawer, he would check it, she felt certain, even if she was dead. Her mind recoiled, and she concentrated on survival instead.

"James thought of that."

"James Gaterow?" Corinne repeated.

Meg looked at her with irritation all over her face. "Are we discussing any other James?"

"Why? Why did he want me out of the way? Because of the papers proving he kept a double set of ledgers while working for Mr. Bingham?"

"Of course. He couldn't figure out why you were waiting to turn him in. He thought you wanted to blackmail him at first. But you never mentioned it. I told him the papers were here in the office, so as long as I could keep an eye on them, he didn't worry. It was when you decided to take them home that he got nervous. Also, there was the Hawkins trial."

"What about the Hawkins trial?" Corinne prayed there was enough room left on the tape—enough room for Meg to hang Gaterow and herself.

"James had a lot at stake in the Hawkins case. His client was ready to give him a choice piece of land free of charge, plus his usual fee, if James got you and Debra Hawkins's parents off his back. Developers are eyeing that piece of land for a shopping center. James's client, the amusement park owner, doesn't know that, of course. James wanted you out of the way so the trial victory would go to him by default. Or, if you were badly hurt, you might have been willing to settle out of court for a reasonable sum. His client would have gone along with that. That way, James would still have gained the deed to the land.''

Meg leaned against the wall, obviously tired of standing in her fashionable pumps. ''But no, the jury had to decide in your client's favor. Not only did James fail to receive the deed to the land, now the amusement park owner is suing James for failing to represent him properly. James's reputation as an attorney has been slandered.''

''Slandered?'' Corinne gave a brittle laugh as she stared at the open end of the gun barrel.

The telephone rang, startling both Corinne and Meg. Corinne started to reach for the telephone on her desk, but Meg's warning stopped her. ''Do that and you won't live to say hello!'' Corinne's hand paused in midair. The phone rang a second time, a third time, then stopped. Corinne realized then that Meg had activated the answering machine.

DEREK HEARD Meg's recorded voice after three rings. ''I'm sorry. No one is available to help you now. At the tone, please leave your name and telephone number, and Mrs. Daye will return your call. Thank you.'' A bell-like tone sounded.

Derek hung up, leaving no message. He glanced at his watch. The time was 3:45. Ordinarily Meg did not leave the office until five. Why was the answering machine in use?

He left his motel room and hurried to his rented car.

"GATEROW HAS a reputation all right!" Corinne muttered. "I suppose he's your lover, too."

Meg's snort of derision surprised Corinne. "Mixing business with pleasure is what trips people up. Not me! He provided the money for the land and the construction of the building, as well as the electronic equipment. He got no fringe benefits," Meg declared.

"Why did you drag my name into the deal?" Corinne was finding it hard to stay objective. She wanted to scream at Meg.

"As a sort of insurance, in case the Feds started to nose around. James didn't want to be implicated, so the plan was I would say you bought the land and told me to front for you as part of my job. The Feds would believe it. I'd play the part of your gullible secretary who signed a deed and contracted for a building on the instruction of my overbearing employer who threatened to fire me if I didn't play along. No one would have put me in jail for that. It would have been your word against mine." Meg seemed pleased with herself.

The telephone rang again, shrill and demanding. As before, it rang three times before the answering machine responded. People were out there, trying to reach her, but were unable to get through. It made the situation seem even more hopeless to Corinne.

"It was you who left the roses at the nurse's station while I was in the hospital, wasn't it?" The sudden thought stunned Corinne.

Meg smiled slowly. "That was an artistic touch, don't you think? I wanted to remind you of Stan, keep your mind on him instead of the Hawkins trial. Almost worked, too, didn't it?" She preened. "Myself, I hate roses."

"So Willy is the brains behind the piracy operation," muttered Corinne, leaning back in her seat.

Meg gave a hoarse laugh. "Willy? That knucklehead? Oh, he was smart enough to tell me what equipment to order and how to maintain it. And he instructed our crew. But he was drunk half the time. Or stoned on grass. That's where most of his share of the money went, to him and his stoned buddies."

"When do you run the duplicate tapes, if I may ask?"

"At night when I'm supposed to be in night school." She gave Corinne a patronizing smile. "You didn't even check to see if I was really enrolled, did you?" The emerald eyes were too bright. She seemed almost euphoric, as if she were high on something herself.

DEREK TOOK the familiar steps leading up to the bank building entrance two at a time, trying to avoid the many people who were hurrying down the steps. The late-afternoon sun reflected coolly from the vertical expanse of blue-tinted glass. As Derek glanced upward toward Corinne's office, he felt a haunting apprehension.

"YOU'RE A REAL ENTREPRENEUR, Meg. Though I can't approve of what you and Gaterow are doing, I'm curious. Do you distribute your counterfeit tapes in other states beside Indiana?"

"We distribute nationally. We have a deal with a company in Hong Kong that packages the tapes so that our product resembles the legitimate stuff sold by the major videocassette suppliers. We have three small trucks on the road all the time, a salesman in each major city. There are always stores wanting a cheaper price than the major suppliers can give them.''

A knock sounded again on the door, raising Corinne's hopes that her cry for help had been heard. This time the knock was loud and strong, almost arrogant. Meg obeyed the summons immediately, leaving Corinne alone while she went into the reception room.

Corinne took advantage of Meg's momentary absence to flip the cassette in the small recorder to the second side.

"I came as quickly as I could." The voice of James Gaterow in the reception room dashed the last of Corinne's hopes. She felt the burden of despair. It was too late. It was two against one now.

DEREK LEFT the elevator on the twenty-fourth floor and hurried down the hallway. He was alarmed to see the new door, with no brass nameplate. Why had a new door been installed?

He turned the knob slowly and pushed. The door did not budge. Putting his ear against it, he heard voices.

I HOPE you kept your mouth shut in here with her,'' rumbled Gaterow in his deep voice. "Sometimes you talk too much!''

"So what if she knows? Who will she be able to tell? After we finish with her and wreck this place again, thieves will be blamed. A police report has already been filed about last night. We'll move everything out of the place on Grant Road and be over the state line before dawn.''

"What about the FBI agent parked across the road?''

"Tell the men to take care of him. There's only one guy, isn't there?" Meg said scoffingly.

"So you plan to do a disappearing act?"

"Want to see my tinted contact lenses? After a trip to a hair salon for a peroxide job, maybe I'll land a screen test and go to Hollywood. Then you can make duplicate tapes of movies in which *I* star," boasted Meg.

He laughed disparagingly. "Playing what part? Goofy in the Walt Disney cartoons?" He grunted suddenly as her foot came forward swiftly to land hard on his shin.

"Someday you'll find out how smart you *aren't*," Meg threatened in a loud voice. "I was smart enough to get Her Highness out of hiding and down here, wasn't I?"

THERE WERE TWO VOICES. Derek recognized one as Meg's. They seemed to be arguing. *Where's Corinne?* he wondered, agitated. He missed the reassuring pressure of the gun under his arm, the gun he had left with Corinne at her house. He sensed that knocking and announcing his presence would be foolish, especially since he was unarmed. The element of surprise, on the other hand, might be in his favor. An idea struck him.

He rushed back to the elevator, jabbing the down button repeatedly. Once downstairs, he hurried to the pay telephone and made a call, then to the drugstore on the first floor for a necessary purchase.

"YES, THAT WAS A SMART maneuver," Gaterow admitted, rubbing a shin that screamed with pain. "I brought a gun with a silencer. You can have the honor of using it, of course." He spoke as though such an act were beneath him. "I'll observe." He slipped the weapon with the silencer attached into the handbag hanging from Meg's shoulder.

Gaterow's powerful body moved into the opened doorway between Corinne's office and the reception room. There was a vengeful look on his face. "You've been a thorn in my flesh for years. Too many wins against me. And now you're the reason for a malpractice suit brought against me. I'll be glad to be rid of you," he hissed to a silent Corinne sitting behind the desk.

"We wait until five-thirty. Everyone should be out of the building by then since it's Friday. Then we tear up the office just like we did last night," Meg ordered.

"That's why I brought the silencer, woman! So the shots won't be heard," exploded Gaterow. "And do we have to go through all that kid stuff again? Knocking holes in doors and spilling the guts out of the file cabinets? Come on!"

"We do this thing *my* way. Or you can go right along with her, James, if you'd rather. That means I don't have to split the take with anyone."

Gaterow's stubborn jaw relaxed in astonishment. Meg had gotten her point across to the arrogant James Gaterow. She was in command, not he.

"Really, Krens, it's beneath me," Gaterow complained.

"Shut up!" Meg ordered.

For the first time the bile taste of fear rose up in Corinne's throat. She wished fervently that she had brought Derek's gun.

"Where does she keep the Scotch?" Gaterow opened the doors of the credenza. His burly form hunched over and he peered inside.

"There's no liquor in the place," answered Meg.

He rose slowly, the look on his face incredulous. "You've got to be kidding! No Scotch? What does the woman do for relaxation when five o'clock comes?"

"Nothing. No cigarettes, either. There's half of a pot of coffee in the kitchen. It's hot. Drink that. You'll keep a clear head."

"I've been drinking coffee all day. I want something real," Gaterow complained. He mumbled something unintelligible under his breath and left the room. He headed toward the kitchen. "How long do we have to wait?" he called.

"Another fifteen minutes, anyway," said Meg, pulling out the gun he'd put into her shoulder bag. Deftly, she slipped the one she'd been holding into her bag. She raised the revolver in both hands and pointed the barrel straight at Corinne.

"Come on, Cory. Where is that eloquence that can move a jury to tears?" mocked Meg. "Has the cat got your tongue?"

"Do what you have to do and get it over with," pleaded Corinne. The waiting was torment. She was slowly cracking under the pressure. Her glance strayed to the open drawer but so quickly that Meg didn't notice. "Everyone is allowed one last request—"

"No, you cannot go to the ladies' room," snapped Meg.

"That was not what I was going to ask," Corinne said wearily. "I still don't understand one thing. How are the master tapes coming to you from L.A. now? Not through the airline priority parcel service. I can't believe how smart you've been in all this." The praise was intended to inflate Meg's vanity. She liked to boast.

"Special delivery, U.S. Mail. Sent to this office." She looked smug when Corinne gasped. "Of course, the packages are addressed to me," said Meg.

Corinne closed her eyes and stilled the panic brewing inside her. A strange peace began to settle over her. She visualized Derek finding the tape in her desk drawer and playing it. Somehow Derek seemed nearby. Corinne wanted to leave a farewell message for him on the tape but to yield to that temptation would be too big a risk.

"Why did you continue to work for me if the counterfeiting business is so lucrative?" Corinne's eyes were closed as she addressed Meg. The sight of the open barrel of the revolver was too unnerving.

"Being your secretary was an excellent cover. Who would suspect a legal secretary of running a successful video piracy operation?"

"No one," commented Gaterow as he came into Corinne's office, carrying a ceramic mug filled with coffee. "Frankly, Krens, I'm surprised you even know how to type. Are you sure you can handle a firearm?" he asked Meg.

"My husband—the one I divorced—was a policeman. He taught me how to shoot his handgun. Hitting the bull's-eye on a target was the only thing that ever won me any recognition in that marriage," said Meg bitterly.

Revulsion was on the face of James Gaterow as he nodded. Without a word, he walked to the window, standing as far away from the desk as possible. He looked down to the street twenty-four floors below.

Corinne tensed, hoping he would not look toward her and notice what the opened drawer contained. She leaned forward and placed her elbows on the blotter and her head in her hands to block his view of the tape recorder that was taking every word down....

DEREK HURRIED from the drugstore and returned to the elevators. He darted into one whose doors had opened immediately. On the deserted twenty-fourth floor he ran to the men's room.

"Did you hear the elevator doors open?" Gaterow turned away from the window. "I thought I heard someone running."

"Probably the last worker up here trying to catch the elevator. The floor is probably cleared now. I'll go out and check. You keep her here," said Meg, slipping the handgun into the deep pocket of her suit.

Gaterow's big frame blocked the doorway after Meg left. His gaze challenged Corinne to rush him. She dreaded to think what he might do if he grabbed her, remembering his unwelcome advances the night of the party that had earned her the nickname Ms Mackerel. She shrank back into her chair.

The silence loomed heavy as they awaited Meg's return. A click sounded as the record button snapped back to its normal position. The tape had stopped, having come to its end.

"What's that?" asked Gaterow, looking around the room intently.

"The caster on my chair. It's loose. I moved the chair slightly when I crossed my legs," answered Corinne, breathless.

The scowl on the man's face revealed that he did not believe her. He moved toward the desk, his hard eyes boring through Corinne to discover what she was hiding.

Meg entered. "The offices are all dark. Everyone's gone. We don't need to wait any longer. When we're through here, James, you can leave and get that drink of Scotch. I think you need it. Just be sure to be at the Grant Road building at ten tonight to help with the move. We'll take care of that one FBI man and by morning, the Feds won't know what hit the place. We'll have it all cleaned out."

Gaterow turned to face Meg, a protest against such a plebeian task rising to his lips. His attention had been diverted from investigating Corinne's desk, however. She felt all the warmth drain from her body. In her lap she tightly clasped her hands, which were trembling, and bowed her head, trying to pray.

"In less than sixty seconds all your worries will be over, Cory. Say hello to Stan for me when you see him." Jealousy glittered brightly in the emerald eyes fixed upon Corinne. Both of Meg's arms were rising. The open end of the barrel pointed straight at Corinne's bowed head.

Goodbye, darling. I love you. There was no doubt about her true feelings for Derek now. Corinne only wished she had had the chance to let him know. Behind her closed eyelids, Corinne was seeing Derek once more—the angular face with the mustache that seemed so right for it, the magnetic smile. She grasped both arms of the desk chair with hands damp with cold perspiration, awaiting the gun's deadly whisper.

A bold, confident knock sounded on the door. Gaterow swore under his breath. Meg let the gun drop to her side. Fine beads of perspiration dotted her forehead and chin.

"Open the door and find out what the idiot wants, then get rid of him," she ordered.

Gaterow went into the reception room. Corinne heard him open the door and then she heard a startled gasp.

"Help me, please! They're planning to kill me!" Corinne shouted. Meg turned, her face filled with fury.

"Shut up!" Her whisper was menacing and carried into the reception room. "What's keeping you, James?" she called out loudly.

Gaterow stepped into the doorway, his mouth opened to speak, but no words came out. He appeared to be in a state of shock, pointing to the reception room.

"What is it?" Meg asked irritably. She turned away from Corinne and joined Gaterow in the doorway. She stifled a cry and stared, too, as if an apparition had manifested before her eyes.

"What's the matter? I was expecting a more joyful welcome after two years," said a resonant voice in cultured tones. "Why are you here, Gaterow? Is it you and my wife now?"

"Stan..." whispered Corinne, her mind whirling in disbelief. The aristocratic quality of the voice meant it had to be Stan, not Derek. She ached with disappointment.

Meg and Gaterow backed into the room toward Corinne's desk, and Stan appeared in the doorway, wearing an expensive navy blazer Corinne knew was not a part of Derek's wardrobe. He was Stan. There was no doubt of it. He was smooth-shaven; the familiar wave rippled his sandy hair.

"What is going on here?" Stan frowned, glancing at Meg's hand holding the revolver with the silencer.

Meg was mesmerized by the sight of him. The arm holding the gun sank down to her side. A yearning was in her face as she looked up into his. "Where have you been all this time, honey? You could have gotten word to me. I nearly went crazy with grief," said Meg. A tenderness softened her hard features.

"I love you, Meg. I tried not to come back. I needed out. I couldn't take the pressure of playing God with people's lives any longer. But I missed you too much. I had to come back. I want you to go away with me."

Meg's eyes became soft, limpid pools. Her arms went around his neck, one hand still holding the gun. Stan was taking Meg into his arms. Corinne felt a total blankness as she sat in the chair, seeing Meg in her husband's arms. She realized just how much her feelings for Stan had changed. She felt nothing.

It was Derek Moar she loved.

Stan's and Meg's lips met in a scorching kiss. Corinne saw Meg's body suddenly stiffen. Stan wrestled the gun from Meg's relaxed hand with one swift, hard motion. She pulled away from him.

"You're not Stan!" she cried, hysterical, rage on her face.

"Derek?" asked Corinne, not daring to hope. She, too, was shaken.

Stan—or Derek—was lowering the gun and aiming it at Meg and Gaterow. "Over there," he ordered. "Don't give me any trouble or I won't hesitate to use this. The police are on their way." He had called them from the lobby after he'd heard the two loud voices through the door and realized what was taking place inside the locked office.

"You can't be Derek—the mustache..." Corinne protested weakly, so joyful she wanted to shout aloud.

"I shaved it off in the men's room. I figured if I had an identical twin brother, I might as well make good use of him. The element of surprise, you might say."

"I'll tell the police you're threatening us. You're Stan and you're insane. They'll believe me. They'll let us go and lock you up." Fury gleamed in Meg's emerald eyes.

Corinne glanced at the half-opened drawer and smiled. "Say anything you like, Meg. We'll see who the police—and Arnold Zinser—believe. The tape recorder I normally use for preliminary interviews with experts whose testimony I need has been recording our conversation. Your full confession is on tape."

James Gaterow swore loudly, glaring at Meg. Meg, however, did not react with the expected alarm. She became suddenly docile. She appeared beaten. Corinne was alerted. The woman was planning something. As Meg's hand suddenly dipped into her shoulder bag, Corinne remembered the .38.

"Derek, watch out!" she shouted. He ducked just as Meg fired. The bullet narrowly missed him, leaving a hole in the wooden paneling.

Corinne's fear was swept aside in sudden anger. The woman had tried to kill the man Corinne loved. She leaped up from her seat behind the desk. Before either man could react she lunged at Margaret Krens and the collision was so forceful that they both fell to the floor. The gun flew out of Meg's hand, and Derek quickly snatched it up before Gaterow could move.

"I knew I could count on you!" he said to Corinne, grinning.

She straddled Meg's legs and sat hard on them while gripping her wrists. The fury pouring through Corinne endowed her with the strength of a man.

A knock sounded on the locked door. "Police. Open up!" came the muffled voice. Corinne released Meg and ran into the reception room to unlock the door. Two men in uniform, guns drawn, stood in the hall. They followed Corinne into the reception room and into the inner office. "What's going on? We got a call. We heard a gunshot as we got out of the elevator," said one.

"Arrest this man, officer!" Meg shouted hysterically, pointing to Derek. "He threatened to kill Mr. Gaterow and me."

"I'm Derek Moar, officer. I'm the one who called you."

"He's crazy! He's Stanford Daye. They're both crazy!" Meg babbled. "This man is James Gaterow, an important attorney in town. He'll back up everything I say."

Before Gaterow could bring his eloquence into force, Corinne pulled the recording machine out of her desk drawer and took out the tape. "Here's this woman's full confession of a felony and a murder attempt, which implicates Mr. Gaterow also."

Derek gave Corinne a look of such admiration and approval that it warmed her heart, and she forgave him the kiss he had given Meg a few minutes before. Margaret Krens and James Gaterow were handcuffed and led away after Derek promised he and Corinne would come to the police headquarters to press charges.

"I'm sorry I'm not really Stan," he said in a sad voice as they followed the rest of the group.

"I'm not one bit sorry," answered Corinne, lost in the sapphire depths of his eyes. "I love you, darling," she said. "I'll never be confused again." As she looked up at him, she whispered, "Please grow the mustache again, will you? You look naked without it."

A slow smile crept over Derek's face before he kissed her, leaving no doubt in Corinne's mind. He loved her.

EPILOGUE

THE SKY WAS CLOUDLESS; the golden sun, blinding and warm. Corinne and Derek stood on a hill overlooking Granada. Surrounding them was the brick-and-stone wall that contained the ancient Moorish fortress, the Alhambra, a group of fortified towers that rose to an impressive peak. They walked hand in hand. The breeze was fragrant with the odor of lush tropical flowers.

"You look like a bride," Derek said to Corinne, love glowing from his angular face, which sported a pinkish-red sunburn.

"I am. Two whole weeks now. And tomorrow we fly home to the States." Corinne's voice bore a trace of sadness at the thought of leaving Helen and Brent, their hosts in Spain. Brent had leased a condominium near Marbella. Soaking up the Mediterranean sun had proved good for his health.

"We'll have a week in Brookfield with Mom and Dad Moar before we open up the new office."

She took his hand as they strolled toward the gate through which lay the enchantment of the Alhambra. Derek looked relaxed in beige cotton chinos and a white cotton sports shirt. A thick and well-trimmed mustache graced his upper lip, and Corinne loved it.

"It was a beautiful wedding, wasn't it, darling?" murmured Corinne, remembering how Kate had helped

with the arrangements, dealing with the florist and the
caterer in order to help Corinne, who'd been busy
packing things up, preparing to move to a larger office
on the sixteenth floor of the Marotte Bank Tower.

Folding chairs had been set up in the woods for the
select audience of guests that included David and Erna
Moar and Helen and Brent. A minister in a black robe
had said the words that united Corinne and Derek before the assembled friends. Kate Albert had wept and
smiled, as beautiful as a bride herself in a long, pale
blue gown as she'd stood beside Corinne. Arnold Zinser, minus gun and holster, had served as Derek's best
man in a light gray tuxedo that had matched Derek's.

They had reminisced over the turn of events. More
than a year had passed since the cassette tape had
cleared Corinne of all suspicion in the video piracy case.
FBI agents had tracked down the missing Datsun 280
ZX in Georgia and found Willy, who'd wanted nothing
to do with a charge of attempted murder. He'd talked.

The court trials of Margaret Krens and James Gaterow were over. Meg's defense attorney had success-
fully gotten his client off on an insanity plea. The
testimony of three psychiatrists had validated the plea.
All had concurred that Margaret Krens was a psycho-
path. Stan's untimely death was the trigger that had set
her off from bad to worse.

Corinne thought of Meg, locked away in an institu-
tion for the criminally insane. "She'll never get out,"
one of the psychiatrists had assured Corinne.

For Gaterow, she felt less pity. He'd gotten twenty
years on the one charge and, in a separate trial, another five for video piracy, as well as a punitive fine that

took all the money he had. Disbarment proceedings had taken away his privilege to practice law.

The past was behind them, and the landscape of Granada spread below them, snow-white in the sun. Derek and Corinne were free to build a new life together as partners in marriage and partners in their own law firm. Their new office on the sixteenth floor was twice as big, with a new nameplate—Corinne Daye Moar and Derek Moar, Attorneys at law—on the door.

Corinne would take care of the civil cases while Derek would specialize in criminal law. His work experience had prepared him for it.

"The bar exam wasn't so bad now, was it?" she teased as they strolled hand in hand.

A sound that was half whistle, half sigh escaped Derek's lips. He had been hard at work for an entire year.

"You're some tough law coach, lady, better than any professor I ever had in law school!" said Derek.

Sunlight shone on Corinne's face, and happiness gleamed in her velvet-brown eyes. Derek had retired his gun and put down roots at last.

"Do you think Mrs. Harley will work out?" asked Derek, referring to the middle-aged woman they had hired to be their secretary before they'd left for Spain. She was learning how to operate a word processor in their absence and hadn't seemed dismayed by the prospect of working for two high-pressure attorneys. Polite and efficient and completely normal—Corinne had insisted a psychologist test the woman before she hired her—Mrs. Harley was the ideal secretarial candidate after the frightening experience with Meg. She did need a little direction, to be told what should be done next.

But that was fine with Corinne. She'd learned her lesson. She would never relinquish control to any paid assistant again.

"You know, I almost feel sorry for Meg," said Corinne as the sun shone warmly on her arms and legs. The festive cotton skirt, sleeveless blouse and sandals she wore had been gifts from Helen. As a mother-in-law, Helen was totally accepting, very different from Eileen Daye. And Brent was as considerate a man as Helen made him out to be.

Derek only grunted. As far as he was concerned, they could lock the door on Meg and throw away the key. Corinne glanced up at the face of her beloved, who walked tall beside her. How lucky he was. Blessed with not one, but two, sets of loving parents. That love was spilling all over Corinne as well.

"Maybe we should start a family right away," Corinne suggested. She had missed a period. She suspected she would soon have news for Derek. Better prepare him now.

"You know, I was thinking the same thing. We're not getting any younger. How do you feel about twins? Think you can handle a two-for-one deal?" He was grinning wickedly.

She smacked his arm good-naturedly, laughing, and hand in hand they entered the Alhambra through the graceful brick-and-stone arched entrance known as the Judiciaria.

The Justice Door.

COMING NEXT MONTH

#246 LOVE SONGS • Georgia Bockoven
Jo Williams's relationship with some of the senior
citizens who frequent her yogurt shop brings Brad Tyler
to her door one night, and once there, he never wants to
leave. But Jo soon realizes she'll have to help Brad over
the pain of a lost love for them to have their chance at
happiness. She'll have to risk losing him to gain his
heart forever.

#247 MASKS • Irma Walker
Despite appearances, Tracy Morrison is not a lonely
heiress. She's a reporter for the *Cincinnati Herald*,
working undercover to trap a couple of con artists—and
write the hottest story of the year. When Chris Collins
falls into her trap, she knows she's struck pay dirt. He is
manipulative, dangerous ...and absolutely irresistible.
But, as Tracy will discover, he's not what he seems....

#248 CHERISHED HARBOR • Kelly Walsh
U.S. Marshal Daniel Elliott and his latest assignment,
Marcy Keaton, are like night and day. Yet, as they fight
for their lives, they find themselves sharing passion-
filled nights and dreaming of a future they can't
possibly share....

#249 BELONGING • Sandra James
Mayor Angie Hall believes the small city of Westridge
is hardly the place for a tough ex-cop from Chicago like
Matt Richardson. But her new chief of police proves
her wrong. He fits in perfectly...*too* perfectly for
Angie's liking.

Janet Dailey

Americana

A romantic tour of America with
Janet Dailey!

Enjoy two releases each month from this
collection of your favorite previously
published Janet Dailey titles, presented
alphabetically state by state.

Available NOW wherever paperback books
are sold.

HARLEQUIN HISTORICAL

Explore love with Harlequin in the Middle Ages, the Renaissance, in the Regency, the Victorian and other eras.

Relive within these books the endless ages of romance, set against authentic historical backgrounds. Two new historical love stories published each month.

HIST-B-1

PATRICIA MATTHEWS

America's First Lady of Romance upholds her long standing reputation as a bestselling romance novelist with . . .

Caught in the steamy heat of America's New South, Rebecca Trenton finds herself torn between two brothers—she yearns for one but a dark secret binds her to the other.

ATTRACTIVE, SPACE SAVING BOOK RACK

Display your most prized novels on this handsome and sturdy book rack. The hand-rubbed walnut finish will blend into your library decor with quiet elegance, providing a practical organizer for your favorite hard-or soft-covered books.

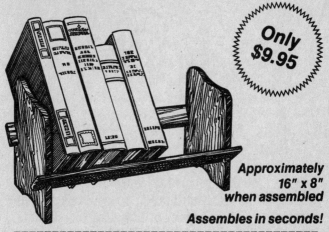

Only $9.95

Approximately 16" x 8" when assembled

Assembles in seconds!

To order, rush your name, address and zip code, along with a check or money order for $10.70* ($9.95 plus 75¢ postage and handling) payable to *Harlequin Reader Service*:

Harlequin Reader Service
Book Rack Offer
901 Fuhrmann Blvd.
P.O. Box 1325
Buffalo, NY 14269-1325

Offer not available in Canada.

*New York residents add appropriate sales tax.

BKR-1R